A Devilish Dilemma

What was Georgiana doing traveling unchaperoned and under a false name on the highways of England?

What was she doing with a woman of many charms but little virtue as her mentor in dealing with men?

What was she doing snowbound in an inn with a trio of rakes in need of diversion and in search of sport?

What was she doing attracting the avid eye of Sir Oliver Townsend, an ungentlemanly gentleman as unprincipled as he was irresistible?

And above all, so far from home and so close to ruin, what was Georgiana going to do now . . . ?

Galatea's Revenge

by

Elizabeth Jackson

A SIGNET BOOK

SIGNET
Published by the Penguin Group
Penguin Books USA Inc., 375 Hudson Street,
New York, New York 10014, U.S.A.
Penguin Books Ltd, 27 Wrights Lane,
London W8 5TZ, England
Penguin Books Australia Ltd, Ringwood,
Victoria, Australia
Penguin Books Canada Ltd, 10 Alcorn Avenue,
Toronto, Ontario, Canada M4V 3B2
Penguin Books (N.Z.) Ltd, 182–190 Wairau Road,
Auckland 10, New Zealand

Penguin Books Ltd, Registered Offices:
Harmondsworth, Middlesex, England

First published by Signet, an imprint of New American Library,
a division of Penguin Books USA Inc.

First Printing, August, 1993
10 9 8 7 6 5 4 3 2 1

 REGISTERED TRADEMARK—MARCA REGISTRADA

Printed in the United States of America

BOOKS ARE AVAILABLE AT QUANTITY DISCOUNTS WHEN USED TO PROMOTE PRODUCTS OR
SERVICES. FOR INFORMATION PLEASE WRITE TO PREMIUM MARKETING DIVISION, PENGUIN BOOKS
USA INC., 375 HUDSON STREET, NEW YORK, NEW YORK 10014.

Pygmalion, a sculptor and king of Cyprus in Greek legend, thought he hated all women but fell in love with his own ivory statue, Galatea. At his earnest prayer, the goddess Aphrodite gave life to the statue, and he married it.

Chapter 1

THE GROUP OF people making a stately progress down the wide, classically proportioned steps of Holcombe Hall resembled nothing so much as the bearers of a particularly fragile egg, in all probability one whose contents hovered precariously on the brink of extinction, and which must be delivered to its resting place with all the fuss and solicitude of members of the Royal Geographic Society whose reputations might be supposed to hang on the fate of the hatchling. The hatchling, however, was not per se a rare species but a girl of three and twenty, with no more fragility than was desirable in a young, unmarried lady. She had a vaguely mutinous look in her eye, tempered by sweetness of character and the conviction, based on long experience, that no protestation would avail against her entourage's assumption that she was a being to be cosseted and protected against the most trifling discomfort.

The butler, an old and valued retainer of awe-inspiring gentility and, upon provocation, an air of freezing hauteur, unbent sufficiently to cast an assessing eye over Miss's traveling costume. He reassured himself that her heavy pelisse and fur-trimmed Witchoura mantle, in addition to setting off her dusky curls to best advantage, could be reliably expected to provide warmth on a journey which must, he feared, be undertaken in inclement weather. He glanced worriedly at the gathering clouds to the north and imagined he felt an ominous drop in the temperature, but he confined his remarks to expressing the hope that Miss Oversham would have everything she needed for her comfort and safety. He also reminded her that if she found herself in want of anything whatsoever after she arrived

at Pemberton she had only to advise him, and he would see
that the item was sent down by carrier at once.

"Thank you, Ribble," replied Miss Oversham with a warm
smile that made her pretty face, even to eyes less biased, quite
beautiful. "As it is, we must hope that Grandmama is not posi-
tively *insulted* by the amount I'm bringing with me, when she
most particularly wished to outfit me herself." She eyed the
mountain of bandboxes and baggage attached to a traveling
coach of luxurious appointments and dimensions. Suppressing
the temptation to suggest the vehicle might be overbalanced
by such prodigious weight, she said with a twinkle, "I expect
she fears I'm a dowd."

Before Ribble could express suitable scorn for any such misapprehension, a small woman with a drawn face and the rather
frantic manner of a sparrow caught indoors laid her hand on
Miss Oversham's arm and said piteously, "Nonsense, Georgiana! You musn't talk so. Of course you must appear in the
first stare of fashion. That woman shall not think that
you . . . that we . . . ." She drew in a sharp, agitated breath.
"When I *think* of the things they said about your poor mama, so
that your poor papa had to cut himself off from them altogether
rather than see her suffer such slights, just because your
grandpa owned a mill . . . When he was the kindest, most respectable . . . Well, my dear, I say you must and shall outshine
them all! Mustn't she, Henry?"

Her spouse, of a more reserved and taciturn nature than his
wife, nevertheless took his niece's hands between his own and
said softly, "And so you will, Georgie. Hold your head up, my
dear, and remember your Sparlow blood is nothing to be
ashamed of!"

Miss Oversham, to whom this exhortation was nothing new,
was still moved to say quickly, "Oh, Uncle, how can you think
I need reminding of *that*? As if I could forget who I *am*!" She
gave him a swift, appraising look. "If my visit to Grandmama
will distress you and Aunt Eliza, I could always write and cry
off. Since she has taken no notice of my existence from my
birth until last month, she is hardly likely to be put out of
countenance by a postponement."

Her uncle shook his head. "Nay, my dear, it's time and past

for you to be reconciled to your father's family. He wanted it so when he was dying, but he was too proud to write them *then*."

Georgiana felt her eyes sting at the memory of her father's last, wasted year. "Did he want that?" she asked. "He never told me. I would have written her myself, if I had known."

Her uncle patted her small hand. "You're a good girl, Georgie. You've lived a quiet life here since poor Geoffrey took ill, and while it suits me and your aunt well enough, it's time you tried your wings a little." He hesitated and coughed. "I've not met your Grandmother Oversham, but your father would have it that she was very toplofty. That's as may be, and for all I know an earl's daughter may have a different way of looking at things. But if she isn't good to you, or if—" He broke off in confusion, unsure of how to proceed.

"If it is my fortune that is welcomed, and not myself," Georgiana finished for him. "It would not be the first time, Uncle Henry. Papa's illness protected me from 'basket scramblers' for a while, but since he has been gone even Holcombe Hall is no longer a refuge." She gave him a rueful smile. "It would be neither becoming nor sincere to complain about being left such a staggering fortune by Papa and Grandpapa, but just once it would be nice to know that one is valued for oneself alone and not for one's money."

Her uncle smiled and gave her a peck on the cheek. "You are, my dear, and you will be. I have the greatest faith in your ability to sort out the 'basket scramblers,' as you call them, or your aunt and I would be a great deal more loath to let you go. Just remember that you can always come home if anyone is unkind to you, or if you are unhappy."

"Thank you, Uncle Henry," replied Georgiana with a smile, "but I do not mean to be unhappy, you know!"

"No, of course you do not!" said her aunt, reinserting herself into the conversation. "And I am sure I do not know anyone who has a better disposition, unless it was your poor mama. Why even as a girl she—"

"That will do, my dear," said Uncle Henry to Poor Mama's loving sister. "If we stand out here too long Georgie will very likely take a chill." He handed his niece into the coach, and watched with approval as a footman tucked a rug snugly about her knees. "Now don't worry about anything, my dear; Timothy coachman has precise instructions and will take care to make all the necessary arrangements for your comfort. You shall meet Miss Bucklebury at the rectory, so you shan't be alone for long."

Georgiana, for whom the prospect of several days' travel with the garrulous Miss Bucklebury as chaperon and companion could only be viewed, however optimistic and dutiful one's better nature, as something in the way of an ordeal, smiled a trifle wanly and said nothing. The vigilant Ribble, subsequently inquired whether she was sure she was *quite* warm enough, or whether, after all, he should dispatch the footman indoors for another carriage rug. Several minutes were spent in debating the wisdom of this action, in which Miss Oversham's well-being, if not her wishes, was most scrupulously considered by the three most nearly concerned with it, while the object of their solicitude tried simultaneously to look grateful and to conceal an increasing desperation to get away.

At length the moment came when the farewells could no longer be drawn out, and the coach drew away from the front door, which was described in the guide book as "inordinately handsome," and one of the "finest to be found in all of Yorkshire." Visitors to Holcombe Hall were also called upon to admire its Corinthian columns and exquisite Italianate gardens. They were invariably surprised to discover that the mansion had been the residence of a man who had made his fortune in India rather than the principal seat of, for example, a duke or an earl. "For all the world as if they expected brass elephants in the drawing room," muttered Uncle Henry darkly, sometimes more solicitous of his wife's late brother-in-law's reputation than the gentleman himself had been. In fact, the estate had been purchased in very bad heart from a profligate and impoverished member of the nobility. The considerable investment required to bring it back to its former magnificence had achieved a near-legendary status throughout the neighborhood. The restoration of Holcombe Hall did much to reconcile his neighbors to the presence among them of a man who, while indisputably of impeccable lineage, was widely regarded as the black sheep of the family. Chief among Sir Geoffrey's transgressions was the fact that in addition to making his own fortune in India, he had married against his family's wishes the beautiful daughter of a Yorkshire millowner and in partnership with his new father-in-law had set about increasing an already indecent amount of money manyfold.

Aside from the unfortunate vulgarity of his connections and his Midas touch, however, Mr. Geoffrey Oversham had shown himself to be a model landlord and a good neighbor, and as his wife had died so soon after giving birth to a daughter that no one was obliged to receive her into Society, all obstacles to his own and his child's acceptance were removed. It was generally expected that a reconciliation with his family might have followed close upon his wife's removal from the scene, but those who believed so had underestimated his ire at his family's repudiation of her, as well as his quixotic refusal to relinquish his relations (and his partnership) with his in-laws. When Mr. Oversham died after a long and painful illness they were sorry; when it became apparent that his daughter had inherited not only the nabob's fortune but the better part of her grandfather's as well, they sent their sons to Holcombe Hall to console the poor orphaned girl.

In fairness to Georgiana, if her suitors were initially attracted by the Oversham fortune, they persisted because of other reasons. In addition to inheriting her mother's dark beauty, she had the liveliest of wits, and while the only child of doting relatives might be expected to have enlarged notions of self-consequence, her father's experience had taught him to view Society with a certain skepticism and to pass along such an attitude to his daughter. Though she had been sheltered from many of life's disagreeable encounters, she was not inclined to overrate her own charms or undervalue the appeal of her financial assets in attracting a husband, with the result that, through humor and a disarmingly frank tongue, she held her would-be suitors quite successfully at arm's length.

So far, none of the proper boys who came calling had touched her heart or inspired the sort of devotion which had caused her papa to abandon his family and position in favor of a life with Mama. While not precisely a Romantic, she yearned for a wider world than Holcombe Hall, with its assiduous luxuries and the sometimes' oppressive benevolence of her aunt and uncle. When her grandmother's summons—it could hardly be called less than that—had arrived the month before she had had to school her countenance into placidity to keep from wounding her guardians with her joy over her escape. Whatever her grandmother's motives and intentions, the visit would afford her the opportunity to move beyond the confines of her immediate neighborhood, to meet new people, and perhaps to travel up to London during the Season.

Meanwhile, there was still the adventure of the journey, tempered by the tedium of Miss Bucklebury's companionship. Amelia Bucklebury was the rector's younger sister, who had left a post as governess in one noble household and was traveling to Sussex to take up another. Her education was undoubtedly superior, and her birth and breeding must render her very acceptable in any gentleman's house, but it might be remarked that her charges seemed to outgrow her rather more quickly than was usual, and that no one, out of sentimental attachment, had ever asked her to stay on beyond her appointed time. Her heart was kind, but her tongue ran on like a fiddlestick, and she laughed with an irritating little titter that grated on the nerves of even such a saintly and patient soul as her brother.

By the time the Oversham coach had left the rectory bearing Miss Bucklebury and her rather more modest array of luggage, a light rain was falling, and a chill wind blew out of the north. Their pace was necessarily slower because of the inclement weather, and by the time they reached the coaching inn at night Georgiana was already quite tired and hungry. Miss Bucklebury had regaled her with a story, which had lasted well into Lincolnshire, of the lamentable antics of her much-beloved charges, ending with a particularly regrettable incident involving frogs in her reticule, and in this fashion they had bowled their way along the turnpikes at a stately pace. The appearance of the Mail-coaches, which breezed by them at lightning speed, never failed to inspire Georgiana with envy, and even the knowledge that the passengers were only allotted twenty minutes for mealtimes did not lessen her conviction that a speedier arrival might compensate for all manner of sacrifices.

The next morning Miss Bucklebury awoke with a case of the sniffles and a rather gloomy view of governessing in general and of her new post in particular. "I don't mind telling *you*, my dear, though of course you can have no idea of what one suffers—no one can, who has not experienced it, and of course *you* shall never have to work for your bread, though I have no doubt you could earn your way as a governess, so carefully did your dear papa educate you—well, be that as it may, if it were not that Lord and Lady Whetstone were expecting me, I would not scruple to give myself a very long rest. Perhaps I might even retire, which my brother has urged me to do often enough—so kind, but one doesn't want to be a burden. . . . Not but what my dear Anthea could not use my help in running the household, because there is so much to be done in the parish, you know, and while I shouldn't like to preen myself, because it is not at all becoming, it is the life for which I was raised." She fetched up a melancholy sigh and sniffed. "You mustn't mind my low spirits this morning, my dear. I'm feeling not quite the thing today, and when one is out of sorts one is tempted, you know, to overset all one's arrangements." She smiled grimly. "Not that I should ever desert *you*, Miss Oversham. I hope I know my duty better than that."

Georgiana, not wishing to be the unwitting cause of Miss Bucklebury's assuming a position for which, it was rapidly becoming obvious, she harbored very little enthusiasm, was unsure how to proceed. Any suggestion that she might return to the rectory in a post chaise hired at Miss Oversham's expense was rejected as an abrogation of responsibilities so shocking as to render her almost speechless ("How generous! How kind! Dear Miss Oversham! But I could not possibly! How could you continue without a chaperon? How could I serve your aunt and uncle such a turn, when they have entrusted me with your care? I must beg, dear Miss Oversham, that you will not venture to mention such a thing again!"). As Miss Bucklebury continued to remonstrate and protest the impossibility of even considering Georgiana's suggestion on the average of once every three or four miles, her hapless companion began to believe that, however much she might be expected to rejoice in her escape to the wider world, whatever might break up the exasperating tedium of the journey, be it the most ruthless highwayman alive, could not be anything but welcome.

In the end, her deliverance, if it might be called that, arrived in a much less dramatic fashion. The rain had stopped, and the temperature had fallen sharply, and gray clouds began to gather to the north. The ways were rutted and slick, and after a particularly jarring encounter with a large hole, the carriage began to rattle ominously. As they limped into the yard of the coaching inn, the perch broke, and the body fell forward with a thud. The pleasing circumstance of being so favorably placed in terms of the wheelwright and adequate shelter while they awaited repairs was somewhat mitigated by the intelligence that the repairs could not be effected in less than two days. Moreover, the ostler was convinced a snowstorm was brewing, and snow could delay them even further.

Miss Bucklebury, scenting a reprieve, displayed a reanimation of spirits and began at once to talk of a holiday and the probability of a week's passage before their departure. Georgiana could not face the prospect of so long a confinement with equal equanimity and began to cast about desperately for some alternative. The arrival of a Mail-coach inspired her with an idea, breathtaking in its simplicity, but of such an impulsive and unusual nature as to require all her courage to seize the situation. When she had ascertained that the coach would be traveling on to London within the half hour, and that since there were no other passengers aboard, she would certainly be able to secure a ticket, she still faced the far from trifling obstacle of putting her case to Miss Bucklebury.

The governess's indisposition threatened to lapse into a full-fledged case of the vapors, and even the vigorous application of her restoratives was insufficient to soothe her agitation of spirits. "You *cannot* mean it, my dear! You have no notion— no idea! It is out of the question for you to take the Mail into London unaccompanied. *Miss Oversham* may not do certain things which might be permitted, for example, to me. Whatever would your aunt and uncle say! If you must go, then I shall accompany you!" she concluded nobly.

Miss Oversham, who had been watching the coach's preparations for departure with a nervous eye, found her attention caught by one part of this impassioned speech. "Do you mean to say that it would be proper for *you*, dear ma'am, if you were alone?"

"Well, I own it would be a trifle unusual, and I cannot think why I would ever *wish* to do such a thing, but it would not be improper, precisely. But my dear Miss Oversham—"

"Why then, it is very simple," interrupted Georgiana. "I shall travel as Miss Bucklebury, the governess! And you will stay here until the carriage is repaired and then go home to the rectory. I shall do very well, I promise you! It will be a splendid adventure, and if I do not go now I will miss it."

Miss Bucklebury, whose experience of the less luxurious modes of transportation was rather wider than Georgiana's, said plaintively, "You cannot realize what you are about, Miss Oversham. It will not be *comfortable*. And you will only be permitted one portmanteau. Pray let us stay here and send one of the servants to your uncle. He will send another carriage for us, and perhaps you may resume your journey in a month or two, when the danger of bad weather is passed. I cannot think he would wish you to risk yourself in even the most trifling way, and what he would say to such a scheme as you suggest quite stands my hair on end to contemplate! Come, be sensible, and let us order our tea."

Georgiana, with a resolution born of desperation, made her way instead to the Mail-coach, gave her name as Miss Bucklebury, and directed that her portmanteau, which had been unloaded from the carriage, be loaded onto it. The driver, observing her dress and manner, ventured to inquire, when she had gone into the inn to make a hasty toilette, whether Miss Bucklebury was a very fine lady. Timothy coachman, still in blissful ignorance of his mistress's scheme, replied civilly but with surprise that he believed she was quite respectable, but merely a governess, and upon being applied to to point out her luggage, obligingly indicated Miss Bucklebury's rather travel-worn bag instead of the handsome portmanteau Miss Oversham had selected. Accordingly, it was that piece that was loaded onto the coach, and by the time Georgiana rather guiltily crept aboard, leaving the real Miss Bucklebury awaiting her tea with every confidence that her superior arguments and common sense had prevailed over Miss Oversham's impetuous plan, the damage was done, and no one the wiser for many miles.

A number of hours later Georgiana was forced to admit that some of Miss Bucklebury's most dire predictions might not have been quite so fanciful as she had assumed. The battering and tossing she endured as the coach sped along at a breakneck pace she discounted; if she arrived at her destination exhausted and travelworn, it hardly mattered, and though there had been no time to swallow anything but a mouthful or two of scalding coffee, hunger was a discomfort easily brushed aside. But the snow had begun to fall in earnest, and a storm came upon them with a ferocity that soon made it impossible to see more than a few yards ahead.

Georgiana, though in general of a decidedly optimistic turn of mind, could not but think that even the dauntless Mails must be impeded by such a circumstance, and she began to wonder, with some alarm, what would happen next. While engaged in these unpromising speculations, her eye chanced upon a figure, shrouded by falling snow but unmistakably human, beckoning frantically from the side of the road. In a moment the specter had disappeared into the storm, but Georgiana was sure someone must be signaling his or her distress, and called out to the driver to stop. This proved to be a somewhat difficult undertaking, and by the time she had managed to secure the guard's attention and make known her wishes, they had rolled some little distance along.

The guard, who had climbed down to see what the matter was, was not pleased by the interruption. "Begging your pardon, miss," he said through teeth clenched as much to stop their chattering as out of ire, "but we dare not stop. We have our duty, and our duty is to go on. His Majesty's Mail must go through." He looked around doubtfully and brushed the snow off his scarlet coat. "Very likely it was just a tree, miss, blowing in the wind."

"Oh no!" replied Georgiana. "It was a person, I'm quite sure of it. And I do see that we must go on, but what if someone does need help? A person could die in this storm, and surely the mail is not more important than that."

"No, miss," said the guard, somewhat less patiently, "if we were sure there *was* a person at all, that would be true. But Jack and I were on top of the coach, and we saw naught. So, miss, I'm afraid I must insist—"

"Oh look!" exclaimed Georgiana with a start. "I *knew* I could not be mistaken!"

The guard turned toward where she was pointing to a figure newly emerged from the snowy mists. He ran forward as the figure, staggering in the drifts, pitched forward onto the ground. In a moment he had scooped the person up, cloak and all, into his massive arms, and as Georgiana ran up to him he said breathlessly, "Will you be so good, miss, as to ask Jack driver for some blankets and for the brandy flask, please." While Georgiana set about these tasks he laid his burden down on the inside seat of the coach, and when she returned he was chafing a pale, delicate wrist, and the coach was redolent of the scent of lilacs. Eyeing the brandy doubtfully, she said, "Do you still want . . . ?"

The guard looked over at his shoulder, grinned, and said "Oh aye. Thank you, miss."

Georgiana found herself looking into a pair of intense blue eyes set in a pretty face framed by a profusion of curls of the palest gold, with just a hint of brass to bring them down to earth. Previously innocent of such things, she nevertheless recognized immediately that they did not owe their color entirely to nature, though the tinting had been very skillful. The girl was no longer in the first blush of youth, but she had contrived to hide it very well. Georgiana tucked the blankets about her shoulders and wondered silently how such an exquisite creature had come to be wandering the turnpikes in a snowstorm. "Oh, I am so glad you are all right!" she said aloud. "I—we thought we saw you beside the road, but there was so much snow—"

"Begging your pardon, miss, but we dare not stop longer," the guard interrupted. "The drifts are getting deeper by the minute, and the horses should not stand. If you have no objection, we'll take the lady up, and if need be, mayhap they'll be a doctor in the next town we come to."

"Oh no! Of course I have no objection, only—do you think we *shall* be able to continue?"

"The Mail must go through," he repeated grimly. "But if we must stop, we'll see you safely bestowed before we go on."

Leaving Georgiana to derive what comfort she could from this cryptic statement, he climbed back atop the coach and the horses resumed their lumbering progress through the snow. It was bitterly cold, and she was almost as wet as her companion from her time out in the storm. She huddled under her blanket, casting an anxious eye now and then at the girl opposite her, who seemed to have collapsed against the seat, her eyes closed in exhaustion. She would have thought she was sleeping, except that from time to time her companion took a delicate sip from the brandy flask. Once she opened her eyes and regarded Georgiana with a dazed, puzzled stare.

Georgiana smiled kindly. "Do you feel better? There is no need to worry now; you are quite safe."

Her companion seemed to rouse herself from her stupor. "I'm sorry; you must think me so ungrateful!" she exclaimed in a voice of schooled gentility. "I got so very cold, it seems to have scrambled my wits." She took another swallow of the brandy. "This will help to bring me round, I think. I am Cecilia Leroux—well, Nafferton, really. Leroux's my stage name."

"Oh, are you an actress?" inquired Georgiana with interest. "I've never met one, but I've always thought it would be so very difficult. And quite exciting, I should think. I beg your pardon! I am Georgiana"—she paused, remembering the governess's strictures—"Bucklebury."

"It *is* difficult," said Cecilia with conviction, fortifying herself with the brandy once again. She offered the flask to Georgiana, who refused it. "And then the gentlemen, you know, do not always treat you as if you were perfectly respectable."

"How—how dreadful," said Georgiana with a little choke. She was barely able to suppress a fit of the giggles when she thought of what her Uncle Henry or Ribble would make of this conversation.

"I daresay," began Cecilia a trifle muzzily, "that you are wondering how I came to be abandoned on the turnpike in a snowstorm."

"I assumed there was some accident. Perhaps to your carriage?" suggested Georgiana.

The other shook her head resolutely. "No accident. Pushed me out, he did. Said I was a 'prime bit of game' and if I wouldn't come the pretty for him I could get out and walk."

"Do you mean to say that some gentleman pushed you out of his carriage in a storm because you would not submit to his advances? That's monstrous!" cried Georgiana, shocked.

Cecilia shuddered. "Oh, he was a rum 'un, all right. A regular rabshackle. I never liked him above half, but he was full of juice, and he bled pretty freely." She frowned. "I mean to say that he was often generous to me. But he should not have told me he was taking me to meet his mother when he w-wasn't!" she concluded between a sob and a hiccup.

Georgiana, to whom half of this speech was incomprehensible, nevertheless perceived that there might be more to the story than she had first realized. She was now perfectly sure that her companion did not travel in the first circles of respectability, but she failed to see why that should induce her to treat the poor girl with hostility or contempt. "No, that was very wrong of him," she said soothingly. "What will you do now? Do you intend to return to the stage?"

Cecilia fetched up a deep sigh. "If I can talk Len into taking me back into the company. I told him I wouldn't be coming back because—" she caught herself up a little and looked at Georgiana with speculation. "Here! Why are you asking all these questions? What's your lay?"

"My l-lay?" inquired Georgiana innocently. "I'm a governess. I'm so sorry if I—"

"A *governess*!" exclaimed her companion with undisguised horror.

"Yes, I'm going to take up a post near London," offered Georgiana, amused.

"Lovely," muttered Cecilia and closed her eyes again.

They had traveled a few more minutes in this silent state when the struggling coach stopped again, and this time it was the driver who opened the door. "We must take shelter for a bit, ladies. The storm's too bad to go on. There are some lights over yonder, so there must be a house. Happen they'll take us in for a bit."

The snow was swirling in such quantities that it was difficult to see more than a few yards in front of her, but when she had gone a few feet she could make out the lights plainly shining through the window of a residence set back from the road. She stumbled a little, stepping on the hem of her dress, and she heard a tiny rip. The driver's hand came under her arm to steady her. Her teeth were chattering, and rivulets of slush ran down her face. She looked again at the lighted panes and thought that even if it were the Devil himself who awaited within, she would still seek his hospitality with the utmost gratitude.

Chapter 2

WHILE MISS OVERSHAM was floundering in the snowdrifts and, perhaps, beginning to regret the impulse that had propelled her into what was rapidly becoming a rather uncomfortable adventure, Sir Oliver Townsend was the center of a spirited debate between his friend and host, Lord Litchfield, and their companion Mr. Utterby. The gentlemen had been deprived of their sport by the unseasonal severity of the storm, and a bottle or two of port consumed among friends had gone a long way toward fueling the heat and passion of their conversation.

"I tell you, it's closer to the mathematical," insisted Lord Litchfield, shaking his head in wonder at his friend's pitiful ignorance. "Really, Utterby, you quite astonish me."

"Perhaps I do, my boy," retorted Mr. Utterby, relishing the challenge, "but if you think that is the mathematical you are sadly out, I fear. Brummell himself could not have tied a more perfect example of the Oriental. Moreover, I had it from my man, who had it from Rainsford, that Oliver tied it *on the first attempt*!"

"No!" cried his lordship, lowering his voice to an involuntary hush. "Impossible!"

"I assure you. Oliver?"

Sir Oliver, who had so far contributed little to the debate but his presence, leaned casually against the mantelpiece, his face set in a rather ironic smile. Thus appealed to directly, he shrugged.

"You see?" said Mr. Utterby triumphantly.

"However," Sir Oliver ventured languidly, "I feel I should just mention, in the interests of our continued harmony, that my cravat is tied in neither the mathematical nor the Oriental."

This intelligence appeared to please neither of his friends. "What then?" they asked in unison.

Sir Oliver coughed discreetly. "I fear it is a style of my own invention. And if my valet is spreading tales about my dressing habits I shall have him sacked on the spot."

"You'd do no such thing, Oliver, and you know it," said Mr. Utterby with a smile. "It would quite break his heart. It is Rainsford's chief pride in life that you allow him to dress you."

"Oh, he would soon come about. I should send him to Litchfield here, and he would forget me in a week."

Lord Litchfield grinned at him. "None of your gammon to me, Oliver! *I* don't set the fashion. Ten to one they'll be calling your newest arrangement 'The Townsend Fall' or some such thing within a fortnight of your return to town, and you shall have a horde of aspiring sprigs of fashion gathering at your door in the hopes of watching you dress."

"I do most sincerely hope not," replied Sir Oliver with a shudder of distaste.

"My dear boy," said Mr. Utterby, raising an eyebrow in surprise, "surely you don't *complain*?"

"Perhaps it does not precisely become me to do so, but one cannot rejoice in such absurd notoriety."

"*Absurd*?" protested his lordship. "How can you say so? Since Robert Neville married the Wentworth girl and retired to Wyndham Priory, you are the acknowledged leader of Society! Everyone follows your lead! Why, you have only to take a fancy to something and it is no time at all before everyone else does the same."

"How eloquently you put my case, Lionel," commented Sir Oliver with a sardonic smile. "Do you remember that fellow a few years back who wore ragweed in his buttonhole for three weeks until everyone else had taken it up? Half of the town sneezed through the Season, but no one wanted to be the first to abandon the style."

"No, r-really? But—"

"Oliver, you really must desist. You are shattering poor Litchfield's illusions," interrupted Mr. Utterby. "In any case you go too far. Would you really have us believe you do no

njoy lifting the latest heiress onto the pinnacle of fashion with
nly the minutest degree of notice on your part? Why else are
ou the most accomplished flirt in London?"

"Clearly I must be a trifle disguised, or I would scarcely
leign to respond to such flummery," said Sir Oliver with a
warmer smile. "But I feel obliged to point out that you have il-
ustrated to perfection the very reasons why I am under no il-
usions about the set I lead, if, as you so flatteringly suggest, I
lo in fact lead it. It is the purest absurdity that elevates anyone
o 'rage of the ton,' nothing more."

"Oliver, I must protest," replied his friend with a laugh. "Do
irth, breeding, beauty, and fortune count for nothing in the
ocial lists?"

"They count for a great deal less that you imagine," said Sir
Oliver grimly. "It takes only the slightest whim for Society to
iscover that a girl it has previously condemned as a dowd
vith neither wit nor style possesses an 'expressive counte-
ance,' that her stupidities are 'delightful utterances,' and her
lainness a 'charming simplicity,' merely because she has
een taken up by someone important."

"My friend, you really are foxed," said Mr. Utterby. "Not
ven you could make an accredited Toast out of a girl with no
tyle or background."

"Not out of a hag or a scullery maid, perhaps," acknowl-
dged Sir Oliver. "But given a modest degree of natural en-
owments and no extreme vulgarity of speech or manner, I
ould tutor any girl of gentle birth sufficiently in how to get
n, and plant her feet firmly on the social ladder. And what-
ver her background, I feel quite sure I could deceive even
igh sticklers like Princess Esterhazy and Maria Sefton."

"And I say you could not," said Mr. Utterby. "The ragweed
one thing, but what you suggest is quite impossible."

"Oh, a bet!" cried Lord Litchfield happily. "Let us make a
ager! I'll lay you a pony Oliver can do it!"

"Your confidence quite unmans me, Lionel, but I have not
id I *will* do it, merely that I could," Sir Oliver reminded him.
Besides, there would seem to be a dearth of suitable candi-
ates just at the moment."

"Really, Oliver, it would be most unsporting of you to back

out now," remonstrated Mr. Utterby. "I propose you put your hypothesis to the test with, shall we say, the first 'suitable' female we encounter, provided, of course, that you can convince such a person that becoming the 'rage of the ton' however briefly will be the fulfillment of her life's ambitions. And to make the wager more interesting, I suggest we risk something more valuable than Litchfield's paltry pony. Shall we say your grays against my chestnuts?"

"Devil!" cried Sir Oliver. "You know I've envied you those chestnuts these past six months or more!"

"Then you agree?" inquired his friend.

"Done! It might prove most amusing. But your team are safe for the moment, Utterby, because the snow does not appear to be letting up, and I fear we shall be trapped here for some time!"

Sir Oliver was still enduring his friends' good-natured animadversions on hardened cynics whose unwarranted self-confidence rendered them nearly intolerable when Lord Litchfield's butler entered the room to announce that a Mailcoach had been forced to stop outside the gates and the passengers, driver, and guard were seeking temporary shelter under his roof.

"Passengers?" inquired his lordship. "In this weather? I don't suppose there are any ladies among them!" he asked pessimistically.

The butler, who had been in service with the household since his lordship was in leading strings, replied with a certain primness that there were two females among those desiring admittance.

Something in his tone arrested his lordship's attention. "I say! What do they look like, Leighton?"

"They are both young, my lord, and, if I may venture to say so, quite pretty."

"Capital! The very thing. See that the men have everything they need, Leighton, and show the ladies in."

"As your lordship pleases," answered the butler, disapproval almost curling his lip.

"Paphians!" cried his lordship when the door had closed on the Leighton's back. "What splendid good fortune!"

"Surely not, Lionel," said Mr. Utterby with a twisted smile. "I should doubt very much that two high flyers should be abroad in a Mail-coach in this storm. No doubt they are servants, going down to take a place in London."

"Leighton would never be confused about anything of that nature," Lord Litchfield insisted. "I haven't heard such a chill in his voice since my cousin Sylvester set fire to the curtains in the library. Mark my words, they will be women of easy virtue! I wonder what sort of entertainment they would prefer? It is the hand of Providence, just when we were thinking we should be trapped here for days."

"I should not have thought it would be at all necessary to inquire as to what sort of entertainment they would prefer," said Mr. Utterby dryly.

"I know!" cried Lord Litchfield, undeterred. "Oliver shall make one of them the Toast of London!"

"Litchfield, you really are in your cups," said Sir Oliver fondly. "Whatever degree of contempt I may harbor for Society, I am not so lost to propriety that I would attempt to foist a fair *incognita* upon my acquaintance. I admit that some of the *chères-amies* who have lived under my protection have had excellent understanding, but one does not, as my great-aunt would say, dress mutton up as lamb."

"Noble, my dear Oliver," rejoined Mr. Utterby. "I am relieved to see that you possess some scruples. But I must remind you that under the terms of our wager, should we find one of these females suitable you are obliged to chance your arm."

"As you say," agreed Sir Oliver. "But it should be a matter of small difficulty to determine whether Lionel's speculations are indeed correct. I shall make the essay, and you shall confirm it. If they are Paphians, we must search elsewhere for our candidate."

Georgiana, upon entering the very comfortable hunting box of Lord Litchfield's, found herself subjected to the discomfiting appraisal of three pairs of eyes. The nature of this regard, rather too warm and direct for scrupulous politeness, led her to suspect that the gentlemen were, if not precisely very well to live, at least a trifle disguised, and on the whole she thought she would prefer the safer comforts of the kitchen with the guard and driver to the luxurious uncertainty of the salon. She was about to thank her hosts for their hospitality and effect a strategic withdrawal, when, beside her, Cecilia took off her cloak.

The atmosphere changed at once from speculation to frank admiration. Georgiana could not help uttering a little gasp herself. The actress really was magnificent, and her voluptuous body was draped with the most expensive possible means of showing it off. The wet weather had the effect of making the cloth cling all the more tenaciously to her form. In that room, there was no mistaking her for anything but a woman of experience, and Georgiana, standing there shivering in her sodden dress, could not help admiring her utter lack of self-consciousness.

"How do you do?" said Lord Litchfield, overcoming his moment of involuntary stasis. "Won't you come nearer to the fire? You must be dreadfully chilled. I've asked Leighton to bring up some champagne, and of course you will stay to dine with us," he said, bending over Miss Leroux's fingers. "Oh, your hand is quite cold. You must permit me to warm it."

A warning bell clanged in Georgiana's mind. She frowned. "I'm not sure we—"

"Oh, dinner would be lovely," said Cecilia, overriding her and making no attempt to withdraw her hand. "I am very hungry," she said confidingly, "and it was most *shockingly* cold in the snow. I should no doubt have perished if the coach had not stopped for me, for you know—"

"Yes, yes," said Mr. Utterby with a little cluck of sympathy not unmixed with amusement, "I am persuaded it must have been an ordeal for you both. Perhaps you would like to change into some drier clothing before we dine, as I feel sure that, however much your dresses become you, it cannot be comfortable to be quite so damply attired."

"I have asked Leighton to see to your luggage," volunteered his lordship happily.

"Oh, but—" Georgiana began to protest, for the second time.

" 'No beauty she doth miss, when all her robes are on, But beauty's self she is—' " said Sir Oliver, in an amused voice.

Cecilia giggled, but Georgiana, who knew the end of the quotation ("when all her clothes were gone") blushed furiously, which caused Sir Oliver to regard her with rather more interest. He raised his looking glass, and Georgiana, who was rapidly becoming rather dismayed with the way the situation was developing, put up her chin. "Perhaps you would be so good," she said in a cool voice, ignoring the disconcerting inspection of the extremely handsome gentleman by the fireplace and addressing her remarks to Lord Litchfield, "as to desire your housekeeper to conduct us to one of your guest chambers at once. I am very sorry to trespass upon your hospitality, but I fear Miss Leroux will take dreadful chill if she does not remove her wet clothing without further delay."

"Oh yes," agreed his lordship, somewhat taken aback. "I shall ring at once."

"Just a moment!" said Sir Oliver, advancing upon her. Georgiana was well acquainted with well-dressed gentlemen, but the elegance of the approaching personage far exceeded her previous experience. She was not acquainted with the names of Weston or Stulz, but the olive green coat of superfine looked as if it had been poured onto its wearer's body, so perfectly did it suit his form. The arrangement of the neckcloth she recognized at once as expert, and the powerful legs sheathed in tight pantaloons, ending in shining Hessian boots, would have created a most pleasing figure, were it not for the faint suggestion of arrogance in the way he bore himself and the expression of cynical boredom in his dark eyes. Georgiana was inclined to shrink back, but she stiffened her spine instead.

"We have made Miss Leroux's acquaintance, but I fear I did not catch your name," he said smoothly.

"I am Miss Bucklebury," she responded in what she hoped was a blighting tone.

"Perhaps she is an actress too," remarked Lord Litchfield, who had extracted the secret of her profession from the voluble Miss Leroux.

Sir Oliver took her hand from her side, though she had not

offered it, turned up her palm, and kissed her wrist with an expertise which, if she had not been so offended by the lack of propriety, she might have enjoyed very much.

"Please, sir, I wish you—" Before she could finish her protestation, he had his arm about her, and with his free hand had pushed away her bonnet. He then planted a light kiss on her lips and said maddeningly:

> Whom she refuses, she treats still
> With so much sweet behavior
> That her refusal, through her skill
> Looks almost like a favor.

She struggled strenuously to break free from his grip, but he only laughed and, releasing her, said lightly, "You need not regard it, you know. It is quite the fashion now, and poor Litchfield there must have some forfeit paid for his hospitality."

Struggling to control her anger, Georgiana said frigidly, "You appear to be laboring under the misapprehension that your advances, which no amount of quotations will render acceptable to me, must be welcome. If that is indeed the fashion, or Lord Litchfield's notion of how to treat his guests, I must tell you that so far from not regarding it, I must beg leave to quit this house at once!"

A stricken silence befell the denizens of the room, as if a potted plant had spoken.

"Not an actress," remarked Lord Litchfield gloomily.

"Oh, la!" tittered Cecilia, her gentility slipping again.

Sir Oliver, an arrested look in his eyes, drew a breath to speak, but the door opened to the housekeeper before she could learn what he might say. He did not look particularly contrite, and Georgiana thought it was just as well there would be no further opportunity for discourse between them. "Please conduct Miss Bucklebury and Miss Leroux to the guest room, Mrs. Rowbotham, and give them whatever they require," ordered Lord Litchfield in a strangled voice. "We shall dine in half an hour."

The housekeeper's rather grim tightening of the mouth revealed to Georgiana with devastating clarity exactly how she and her companion were regarded belowstairs. She had to admit the drama had its comic aspects, but she thought that the sooner she extricated herself from a situation so fraught with embarrassment for all concerned, the greater would be her peace of mind. She said to Mrs. Rowbotham, when the good lady had shown her with forced civility to the guest room, "Thank you so much. I am sorry to put you to the trouble, but would you convey a message to his lordship that I would like to remain in this room until the Mail-coach is ready to proceed?"

"Shall I bring up a tray then, miss?" inquired the housekeeper a bit more respectfully.

"No, that will not be necessary," said Georgiana firmly, nobly suppressing her ravenous hunger pangs.

"You can't mean it!" cried Cecilia, who was dragging a comb through her tangled locks. "Not have dinner? Whyever not!"

"Miss Leroux," began Georgiana patiently when Mrs. Rowbotham had left, "surely you've noticed that the gentlemen are foxed and that their manner towards us is, well, a trifle less than *gentlemanly*?"

"Oh, that does not signify," replied Miss Leroux airily. "I believe it is very well known that country manners are a great deal more informal, and besides, I am quite sure *I* should not mind if a gentleman as handsome as Sir Oliver were to wish to kiss *me*."

"Should you not?" asked Georgiana, fascinated. "Well, you must do as you think best, but I am sure I shall feel a great deal more comfortable remaining here until it is time to leave."

A half hour later, her empty stomach was less happily sustained by her principles, and she was just wishing she had compromised her dignity enough to ask Mrs. Rowbotham to send up a tray, when there came a knock at the door.

The housekeeper, already thawing, was moved to entertain much warmer thoughts of Miss Bucklebury when she was thanked so civilly and graciously for the dinner tray she had brought up. Now that she had cleaned herself up a little, it was easy to see that Miss was Quality, not a lightskirt like that brassy-haired hussy downstairs. All sorts of folks were obliged to travel Mail-coach, and it wouldn't do to hold it against such a charming young lady.

"You'll be wanting your night things, I expect," she told Georgiana kindly. "I'll send Jenny to help you unpack."

"Night things?" cried Georgiana in horror. "We mustn't stay, surely!"

Mrs. Rowbotham shook her head dolefully. "The coachmen say it's too foul a night to go on in, and they should know. You might be here two or three days, maybe more."

In the face of this discomfiting announcement, it did not do much to elevate Georgiana's spirits, when, an hour or so later, a servant brought up her portmanteau and she discovered, with chagrin, that the real Miss Bucklebury's luggage had been substituted for her own. A perusal of the clothing now at her disposal confirmed her worst suspicions, but at least, she thought ruefully, examining a severely cut merino wool morning dress in dove gray, no one who saw her in any of these outfits could have further doubts about her respectability.

She put on one of Miss Bucklebury's unadorned, scratchy nightdresses, blew out the candle, and fell into an exhausted sleep.

Chapter 3

GEORGIANA AWOKE the next morning in a state of unaccustomed confusion, her senses confounded by the unfamiliar furnishings, and her thoughts in disorder. Recollection of the previous evening's events brought her a certain agitation; besides renewed indignation at the impropriety of Sir Oliver Townsend's behavior to her, she harbored the quite lowering suspicion that he had mistaken her for a woman of easy virtue, and that perhaps she should have done more to convince him that she was, after all, a delicately nurtured female. A girl of more acute sensibility might have swooned or at the very least been cast into a state of extreme affliction by such ungentlemanly advances. She could not but feel that another meeting with *any* of the gentlemen she had met in the saloon downstairs would be uncomfortable, and she hoped that the combined effects of the evening's overindulgences and the lateness of the hour of their retiring would contrive to keep them in their beds until long after the Mail-coach had departed.

In these hopeful speculations, however, she was destined to be disappointed. A serious examination of the night's snowfall from her bedchamber window had convinced her of the impossibility of the coach's setting out that day, so it was with surprise and horror that she learned from the maid bringing up the breakfast tray that it had in fact departed about three o'clock in the morning.

"There was a break in the storm, miss," said the girl apologetically, pouring out her chocolate, "but they were that desperate to be on their way that they couldn't wait."

"But why wasn't I told?" asked Georgiana with a little gasp.

"Someone should have sent for me! I have no wish to remain *here*!"

"That's as may be, miss, and we did wonder whether to send up to you, but Sir Oliver said you were not to be disturbed."

"Sir Oliver!" cried Georgiana, her anger kindling. "Is he the master here? I thought this was Lord Litchfield's house."

The maid pressed her lips together firmly. "Of course the house belongs to his lordship," she said finally. "Only Sir Oliver is a frequent guest here, and there's none of us who would like to contradict him, if you see what I mean."

Georgiana thought she saw very well. "Well, would you kindly convey a message to his lordship that I would like to see him as soon as may be convenient? I must discuss what is to be done!"

"Begging your pardon, miss, but his lordship won't be out of his bed for many hours yet. But Sir Oliver has sent up a note, and begs you will come down to the library as soon as you have breakfasted."

Georgiana recognized the implacable power of the inevitable and reached for Sir Oliver's envelope. She expected it to contain, at the very least, a handsome apology for the liberties he had taken the previous evening, but what she read on the cream-colored stationery made her choke on her bite of toast: "I have a proposition I think may interest you. Please meet me in the library at your earliest convenience. Oliver Townsend."

Georgiana was filled with a flaming wrath. Not only had this arrogant rake sent away the Mail-coach and left her stranded here in a house full of would-be debauchees, but, not content with insulting her the night before, he now apparently intended to approach her with an improper proposition. Georgiana could think of nothing else he could suggest that would be of the remotest interest to her, so she was forced to suspect the worst. She did not flatter herself that he had fallen violently in love with her at first sight and thought rather that the boredom of being trapped in a snowstorm had led him to look for a *convenient* close at hand. She could not entirely blame him, in light of Cecilia Leroux's more compliant attitude, for his initial assumption about her virtue, but surely her subsequent behavior would have convinced him she would not welcome *that* sort of arrangement. Self-doubt assailed her again, and if she could not quite wish that she had done so vulgar a thing as slap his face, at least she might have made her protestation in a more forceful manner.

She dressed herself rapidly in the merino gray and surveyed the results with some satisfaction. She was tempted to pull her hair back in the severe style much favored by an earlier governess of her own, but the curls *would* peek out, and they quite ruined the hoped-for effect. Nevertheless, she had to admit she looked the picture of rather dull respectability, and not at all likely to ignite any man's baser impulses. The thought gave her a momentary pang, so that she had to laugh at herself. She laughed again when she thought of how Sir Oliver would feel when he discovered he had made improper advances to a Miss Bucklebury, the rector's sister, and looked forward to vanquishing that arrogant gleam in his eye with something like militant anticipation.

A cold sunshine was filling the room by the time Georgiana descended the staircase to the library. A fire was burning in the grate, and the impassive gentility with which the butler opened the door for her reassured her that her rather formidable attire was having the hoped-for effect. She had little imagined that she would ever be compelled to wear such clothing, much less find herself grateful for the mischance that had bestowed Miss Bucklebury's portmanteau upon her; her only regret was that nature had not seen fit to endow the governess as amply in the bosom as herself, with the result that the confining fit restricted her movements a bit uncomfortably.

"Miss Bucklebury, sir," announced the butler, and Georgiana was afforded her second look at the man she was rapidly coming to think of as her adversary.

The night before, darkness and the evening's events had conspired to give him a Byronic look, and the daylight did not alter this impression. There were no signs of weariness or dissipation on his handsome face, but his eyes looked as cynically bored as ever and probed her mercilessly. If he felt any surprise at seeing her attired in clothing not inappropriate for one who has taken vows of eternal chastity, he did not show it.

"Sit down, please, Miss—uh," he said, waving her grandly to a chair when the butler had closed the door on them. "I have a proposition which I hope may interest you and prove to your advantage as well."

Though he scarcely had the air of a man besotted with passion, Georgiana, her spine stiffening under his steady gaze, felt it was time to assume control of the conversation. "I do not know what liberties Lord Litchfield permits you in his home, nor do I care, but I should very much like to know by what right you sent away the Mail-coach without informing me, thereby trapping me in his lordship's house!"

Sir Oliver, who was seated on a comfortable-looking sofa next to the fireplace, crossed one leg over the other and raised an eyebrow. "Did you wish to go on in the snow, then? I should have thought it would be devilishly uncomfortable," he said languidly.

"Well, of course I wished to go on! Whatever could have suggested to you that I might have the slightest wish to remain *here*?" she sputtered. "Besides—"

"You refer, of course, to last night's regrettable, ah, misunderstanding," he said, not sounding regretful in the least. "We were all, as I am sure you realize, a trifle well to pass. And if you will insist on traveling unattended, and in rather dubious company, you can scarcely wonder at it if disinterested onlookers fail to perceive your respectability!"

"I did not set out unattended!" cried Georgiana, goaded into a retort. "My companion fell ill, and I was obliged by circumstances to travel on. And am I to take it that if you had known of my *respectability* you would not have molested me? How very gentlemanly!"

He sketched her a mocking bow which annoyed her even further. "There is no point in dwelling on an incident which reflects but little to the credit of either of us," he said imperturbably. "Let us talk instead of the 'circumstances' you mentioned which oblige you to travel on to London."

"I do not wish to talk to you about my circumstances or about any subject whatsoever, unless it may be how I am to leave this place with the utmost haste," said Georgiana, rising to her feet.

"But you have not allowed me to put to you my most obliging proposition," he said calmly, "and it would be quite foolish of you not to at least hear me out."

"I had hoped," said Georgiana icily, "that I had made it sufficiently clear that nothing of *that* nature would be of interest to me."

His dark eyes glinted with amusement. "My dear Miss . . . confound it, what *is* your name?"

"Miss Bucklebury."

"Miss Bucklebury, I must own that you are a most attractive girl, but I fear you are laboring under a misapprehension. I have no designs on your virtue. Please hear me out. In that attire, it is quite obvious that you are no actress. If I were to hazard a guess, I would say you are traveling down to London to secure employment. You are in, shall we say, straitened circumstances, are you not? What are you, a governess?"

Georgiana, who was finding it less easy to lie in the face of these direct questions than she had imagined, blushed and lowered her eyes. "How did you guess?" she asked, letting just a trace of Yorkshire accent creep into her voice.

"I should not have thought of it, because there is too much height in your manner, but your dress gives it away. It will be your first position, will it not? Miss Bucklebury, I have seen more of the world than you, and I promise you that you will not like it."

"Very likely not," agreed Georgiana.

"Then will you please be seated and listen to what I have to propose? I promise that, beyond a mild deception in which no one will be hurt, there is no harm in my suggestion."

Georgiana, who was itching to give this imperious, high-handed aristocrat the set-down of his life, thought that the opportunity for doing so might best present itself through seeming to entertain his proposal. "Very well," she said, resuming her chair.

"That's better," he said with a smugness that made her long to slap him. "Now, how would you like to become the rage of London?"

Whatever she had been expecting, it certainly was not that. "I—I beg your pardon?"

"I have the honor of holding a position in Society which would make my sponsorship quite beneficial to anyone I introduced," he said matter-of-factly.

"Yes, but why should you wish to?"

"That need not concern you," he began. "But—"

"Of course it concerns me," she interrupted him. "If you wish to sponsor me into the ton on the basis of less than twenty-four hours' acquaintance, naturally I should like to know why. Besides, though I may not know much of the world, I am not so naive as to suppose a governess may become the 'rage of London,' whoever introduces her into Society."

He regarded her speculatively for a few moments, seemed to come to a decision, and sighed. "Very well. I suppose you must know the whole story. I have told you that I occupy a certain social position, but I have not said that I find myself worthy of such deference as I receive. In fact, it is my contention that virtually anyone can be elevated to the first stare given the proper launching and a few judicious hints as to how to proceed."

"And I, I take it, am 'virtually anyone'?"

"You are quick," he admitted with a grim smile. "I made a bet with Leighton and Utterby, you see."

"Odious," she muttered.

"Perhaps," he conceded. "I was foxed at the time, and Utterby bet me his chestnuts against my grays. But since you have dropped, as it were, like the veriest honey fall into my lap, I am honorbound to proceed. Moreover, I have thought of a way in which you can do me the profoundest personal service, quite independent of winning this preposterous bet. In return, you shall have position, clothes, and excitement for a few weeks at my expense, and if you are very clever perhaps you will form an eligible connection by the end of the Season. Or if you wish, I will help you secure another position as a governess. Someone among my friends and acquaintance would be bound to know of something."

Georgiana dug her nails into the palms of her hand, wonderng how she could have gotten herself into such a ridiculous position. To tell the truth about her true identity now would be nothing short of scandalous, however much she would have enjoyed the discomfort such a revelation must have caused him. She sighed. For the foreseeable future at least, she must continue as Miss Bucklebury. "Is that the harmless deception you spoke of?" she asked blightingly. "I am to set my cap for a brilliant match? Represent myself as a woman of rank and fortune under your aegis? What a present for the wedding morning, to find oneself so materially deceived! Thank you, no, Sir Oliver; I may be poor, but I am not unprincipled."

"Well, whether you pursue a match is your affair," he said affably. "Naturally you could not expect to persist in representing yourself as something you are not once affairs reached a certain pass, but I assure you there are men to whom a lack of rank and fortune would not be an insurmountable obstacle, once their affections are engaged. Not men of the first consequence, perhaps, because a brilliant alliance generally requires a fortune to match. In any case I would be prepared to make a generous settlement on you as well, should we succeed in winning the bet. Do not be too hasty in refusing; in your position you cannot imagine how advantageous it might be to be presented to the world as my cousin."

"Your cousin!" she cried in surprise. "How could you hope to carry it off, when everyone must know all of your relations already?"

"That is where we come to the personal service I mentioned," he admitted. "I have, I fear, a somewhat vulgar connection, whom my great-aunt has determined I should marry."

"How very distressing for you," commented Georgiana tartly.

Sir Oliver grinned appreciatively. "I do not expect you to be sympathetic. I've nothing against the girl personally; actually I've never met her. Her father was Great-aunt Louisa's son, but he threw over the family to marry some weaver's daughter from Yorkshire. The man was a nabob and rich as Croesus before he died. The daughter's his heiress, and—have I said something to upset you?"

"N-no," said Georgiana, coughing into her handkerchief, "pray continue."

"Well, it's of no great importance, but my great-aunt has determined to bring the girl's fortune back into the family, and since *I* am Aunt Louisa's heir, she has determined that I shall be the chosen instrument of implementing her scheme. I must say that I do not care for the idea in the least."

"Because of the vulgarity of this girl's connections?" asked Georgiana in a stifled voice.

"You could scarcely expect me to rejoice in them," suggested Sir Oliver equably.

"Then, pardon me, why do you not merely say so to your great-aunt?"

"I have a particular reason for not wishing to disoblige her."

"I see."

"I am quite sure you believe you do, but I assure you you are mistaken. My great-aunt is rather elderly, and although her general health is sound, her heart is weak. The doctor has warned her against emotional scenes of any kind."

"I am sorry to hear it," said Georgiana with rather more sincerity than he realized, "but I still don't quite see how my appearing in the guise of your cousin—the unfortunate heiress, I assume—will serve to extricate you from what you apparently regard as an undesirable entanglement."

"It's really very simple," he said, removing an enameled snuff box from his pocket, flicking open the lid, and taking a delicate pinch between his finger and thumb, "you shall travel down to my great-aunt's estate as the rich Miss Oversham, where I shall introduce you into Society. I will make you an offer, and *you* will tell Aunt Louisa that we do not suit. It will ruffle her feathers a great deal less that way, I assure you. She would expect the girl to be a bit of an eccentric, naturally."

"Naturally," agreed Georgiana in a voice of dangerous calm. "But if, as you suggest, it is the connection to her fortune your great-aunt desires rather than to herself, she is still very likely to experience the emotional scene you are so eager to prevent. Why not leave well enough alone, and hope the heiress never comes within her ambit?" She watched him carefully from underneath her eyelids, because she thought she had already guessed the answer to her question.

"Well, the devil of it is, the girl's already been invited down to Pemberton. Aunt Louisa was forced to write and put her off because Great-uncle Hubert has the gout, and she felt it her duty to post up to London to visit him. But I fear she can't be fobbed off for long!"

"Do you mean to say that this girl—Miss Oversham, I believe you said it was—was about to pay your great-aunt a visit, but that it's been *canceled*?"

"Why yes. I told you so. You might have met her on the road otherwise."

"Then why not wait until she does make her visit? Surely there is always the possibility that *she* will not wish to marry *you*."

"I acknowledge the hit, Miss Bucklebury. I am not such a coxcomb that I cannot conceive of the possibility. But the girl is three-and-twenty, and likely to remain on the shelf. Who knows what ambitions she may harbor, or how she might contrive to upset my great-aunt? She is an unknown quantity, and I would rather not take the risk. Besides, you are forgetting the bet."

"And am I less likely to upset your great-aunt, then?" inquired Georgiana with a touch of acid.

"Most certainly, because you will do exactly as I say. If you do not, I will disclose your identity at once, and turn you out of the house without a penny."

Georgiana had to bite her lip to keep control of her temper. "Well, that's clear enough. But I still do not quite understand how you propose to insinuate me into the household."

"I have thought of that," he said, taking another pinch of snuff. "I suggest that we say you never received my aunt's letter, and that your arrival was delayed by the storm. That would give me time to outfit you suitably, and to arrange for a carriage to convey you to Pemberton. And for lessons, naturally."

"Lessons?"

He smiled. "Have you forgotten you are to be the rage of the ton?"

Georgiana frowned, thinking. "It seems a shabby trick to

play on your relations, not to mention poor Miss Oversham. Perhaps she would like to know her father's family?"

"I will be answerable for my relations' response, and I promise you I will concoct a suitable explanation when you disappear in a few weeks' time. They will think she . . . you . . . have returned to Yorkshire, and they will breathe a sigh of relief, I assure you. As for the girl, she would thank me if she knew I was delivering her from the clutches of Clarice, and her schemes to—well, you don't know the half of it. There will be time enough to make you acquainted with the family's distressing history at a later point. But now, what do you say? May I count on you?"

Georgiana, faced with an intolerable dilemma, could scarcely think what to reply. There seemed to be only two choices: go along with this preposterous deception, which would not really be a deception at all, except of Sir Oliver, or confess all and demand to be conveyed to her grandmother's as soon as might be arranged. Her family's reception of her must be forever tainted by the knowledge she had received, and she did not see how she could face them with equanimity after what she had heard. Her overmastering desire was to snub the arrogant Sir Oliver, with his cold, quelling eye and his superior manner, beyond any hope of recovery. How dare he say such things about the "inferiority" of her connections, or make such assumptions about her character and desires? For all his protestations about how much he disdained his social position, he was the most unrepentant snob she had ever met. If she had been a man, she would have called him out. As it was, she seethed with a desire to revenge herself upon him in some fashion.

Suddenly, and with great clarity, she saw how she might gratify her most pressing wish. She almost laughed. "I'll do it," she said firmly.

Sir Oliver, all unsuspecting, gave her a complacent smile. "I knew you would," he said serenely and closed his snuffbox with a snap.

Chapter 4

GEORGIANA, WHOSE CONSCIENCE had been troubling her ever since her impetuosity had led her to accept Sir Oliver's astonishing proposal, was both dismayed and relieved to learn that Cecilia had taken to her bed with a sick headache and would not be downstairs for dinner. She did not relish the prospect of dining alone with Sir Oliver, Lord Litchfield, and Mr. Utterby, but neither was she eager to make Miss Leroux acquainted with the particulars of her new circumstances, as she felt quite certain that discretion was not a major component of the actress's character. Her own besetting sin, she thought ruefully, was a willingness to plunge headlong into rather reckless adventures, particularly when her wrath was provoked. The sheltered life of the last few years, along with the solicitude of her guardians, had not succeeded in quelling a little rebellious streak in her nature, but this time she had far exceeded minor mutiny. If only that odious Sir Oliver had not behaved with such condescension and snobbery, she might have confessed the truth! As it was, she could hardly extricate herself without the greatest embarrassment, and, when she considered the opportunity she hoped she would have to snub him beyond redemption, she was not perfectly sure she *wanted* to extricate herself from the situation. She recalled what he had told her about his family's feelings toward her, assuaged her wounded feelings with the common-sense reflection that it was no more than might be expected under the circumstances—and indeed was what she had halfway suspected herself—and consoled herself with the realization that in going to visit them as the Yorkshire heiress Miss Georgiana Oversham she would pre-

sent them with nothing less than the absolute truth. If Sir
Oliver chose to believe she was a penniless governess whom
he could blackmail into following his commands, he would
soon discover otherwise, but at a time when *she* chose to reveal it and in a fashion which, it was to be hoped, might cause
him the acutest possible discomfort. She armed herself with a
dress of navy blue silk, cut, like all of Miss Bucklebury's
wardrobe, to reveal as little of the human form as possible and
to reflect a severe disapproval of fashion's frivolities besides,
and descended to the drawing room to meet the gentlemen for
dinner.

Nothing could be further from the previous evening's liberties than the civility with which they now received her. Georgiana, with a more practiced eye than they might have
supposed, detected the amusement beneath their manner toward her, but she was grateful to be treated with respect when
a poor governess might very well expect to be snubbed and
slighted. Lord Litchfield, apologizing for his poor hospitality
on the earlier occasion, led her into dinner, while Sir Oliver
bent over her hand with a sardonic smile, and Mr. Utterby kept
up an entertaining flow of lively banter while the butler and
footmen served a sumptuous array of filets of turbot, spinach,
mushrooms, partridges, and a mutton pie. Georgiana remembered in time that such fare was supposed to be quite beyond
her normal experience and tried to appear suitably impressed
and to hover indecisively a moment or two before picking up
her utensil. The unblinking scrutiny of the other three at the
table, as well as a general feeling of nervousness, went a fair
way toward putting her off her food, and if they chose to believe she was bedazzled by such luxury and variety it was not
to be wondered at.

"You need not go through with the bet, if you do not wish
to," said Lord Litchfield kindly, when the servants had removed the last of the pastry baskets and Rhenish cream, and
left them alone. "We were all a trifle disguised, and I am quite
sure Oliver cannot *really* mean to pass you off as his cousin,
and I do not know what else!"

"You are far out there, Lionel," said Sir Oliver, "for that is
precisely what I mean to do. Furthermore, Miss Bucklebury

has agreed to take part in our little plan, so there is no more to be said."

"My dear Oliver," said Mr. Utterby with one of his dark smiles, "I concede you have found a most suitable subject to launch upon the ton, but are you quite sure Miss Bucklebury is aware of what she is getting into in terms of your family? It may not be quite fair to her, you know."

"It is not a question of fairness, Robert," replied Sir Oliver. "I have explained to Miss Bucklebury upon what terms she will stand in the family, and she has accepted them. She will be amply rewarded for any pains she may suffer, I promise you."

"But can it be worth it, I wonder?" murmured Mr. Utterby darkly. "A few weeks of attention and popularity, some new clothing"—he eyed Georgiana's dress with ill-concealed loathing—"some new clothing, surely, Oliver? Good!—and a lifetime of memories, against—"

"It is nowhere near so bad as that," said Sir Oliver decisively. "Are you trying to back out, Robert?"

Mr. Utterby shook his head. "Merely prompted by my better angel. I'll say no more."

Georgiana, who was feeling both alarmed and annoyed by this conversation, said firmly, "I can't help believing that there is a great deal more to be said."

They all turned to her as if a chair had spoken. "Miss Bucklebury," began Sir Oliver.

"For example," she went on relentlessly, "it will be quite impossible for me to stay here once the snows have thawed enough to travel. It would be most improper, and of course Miss Leroux must be conveyed to London as well."

"Well, you will *not* be traveling with Miss Leroux again," said Sir Oliver. "The rich Miss Oversham would never countenance such an arrangement, and you must strive to behave as she would in all particulars."

"Are you quite sure she would not?" inquired Georgiana, ruffled.

"Oh there is no one more toplofty than a nabob," inserted Mr. Utterby with a slight sneer. "They think it adds to their consequence to seem unbending. You can be sure of it."

"I have undertaken to send Ceci—Miss Leroux to London in my carriage as soon as the roads are clear," said Lord Leighton, blushing slightly.

"Admirable," said Mr. Utterby dryly. "But what is to be done with Miss Bucklebury?"

"I thought, if I may further trespass upon your goodwill, Lionel," said Sir Oliver with the air of one who knows very well he will not be denied, "that I might send her to your sister for a day or two. Hartfield is on the way to Pemberton, and Jeannette is much of a size with Miss Bucklebury. I hope she might contribute some clothing until Great-aunt Louisa can outfit her, because if Miss Bucklebury appears at Pemberton in such a costume as she is wearing now no one will ever believe our Banbury tale."

"Fascinating," said Mr. Utterby with a smile. "And just how do you propose to explain Miss Bucklebury to Lord Litchfield's sister? I've no doubt you'll come up with something, but I find myself most curious to know how you will contrive."

"We could say that my chaperon took ill, and there was an accident to my traveling carriage, and my luggage was lost," said Georgiana promptly.

"Excellent," said Mr. Utterby. "The story is so preposterous it might even be believed. I confess that I am enjoying this extremely. It might even be worth parting with my chestnuts just to see Oliver carry it off."

"Do you think he has a chance then?" inquired Lord Litchfield with much of the enthusiasm he managed to muster for an engagement at Tattersall's or Gentleman Jackson's salon.

Georgiana, who thought that her own rather significant part in this scheme was being shockingly underrated, gave a little cough. Lord Litchfield absentmindedly offered to secure her a little more wine, but Sir Oliver regarded her with a gleam of amusement in his eye which made her feel perfectly sure he knew exactly what she was thinking and served to infuriate her all the more. "I have every confidence of success," he said equably, "and I feel sure Miss Bucklebury will prove an apt pupil. It really is a matter of almost ridiculous simplicity." He fixed Georgiana with an inquiring look. "Bye the bye, Miss Bucklebury, do governesses have first names?"

She had already considered this hazard and answered him with what she hoped was stiff dignity. "My name is Amelia Georgiana."

"Excellent!" cried Sir Oliver. "My cousin's first name is Georgiana as well. I shall call you Cousin Georgiana, and when we have returned the lovely Miss Leroux to her proper place in London, I think we should begin referring to you as Miss Oversham, even among ourselves. You must begin to answer to it at once, for we've very little time."

"Do you not think it would be wise to supply me with some of the details of Miss Oversham's past, since I am to impersonate her?" asked Georgiana, wondering what he would say. "What should I tell my—your great-aunt, when she inquires about the family?"

Sir Oliver gave a short laugh. "She will not make any such inquiry, I promise you. Great-aunt Louisa would like to forget altogether the entire inconvenient fact of her son's marriage to an unsuitable girl. As for supplying you with facts, I have very few, but I should doubt there is any need. Whatever Banbury tale you choose to concoct will be believed—"

"I dislike lying," interrupted Georgiana before she considered how ironic this statement might seem to her listeners.

"Really? How very odd," replied Sir Oliver, fixing her for a moment with a look of intense scrutiny. "Well, it seems most probable that the real Miss Oversham would take a rather romantic view of her father's throwing off his family for a weaver's daughter, however full of juice, and since my great-aunt is unlikely to partake of her sentiments in this regard, it would not be wondered at if she—you—were to maintain a tactful silence on the subject. I feel certain that is the best way to proceed."

"Bravo, Oliver!" cried his lordship. "You are awake on every suit."

He acknowledged the compliment with a slight bow and a sardonic lift of the eyebrow, and Georgiana, rejecting the first idea which came into her head—namely, of hurling the contents of the wineglass squarely into his arrogant face—dug her nails into her palms and said nothing.

Mr. Utterby sat back in his chair and smiled slightly. "I wonder," he said enigmatically.

Chapter 5

"Now LET ME SEE you enter the room," said her tutor, his arms folded across his chest and one exquisitely clad shoulder resting against the door frame. "I am the footman, and I shall open the door for you."

"Is that really necessary, Sir Oliver?" asked Georgiana.

"Cousin Oliver," he prompted her.

"Cousin Oliver," Georgiana conceded reluctantly. "I feel quite sure I am up to entering a room without giving occasion to negative comment."

"*While I*, on the other hand, am possessed of no such certainty," he told her. "My great-aunt is a very high stickler, and in your station in life you cannot have been accustomed to dealing with so many servants. It does no good to say that if you set the servants' tongues to wagging by showing that sort of familiarity which my great-aunt is sure to deprecate it will not be everywhere known. There is no topic on which a servant loves to gossip more, I assure you."

"Well, if you expect me to treat the servants with incivility or comport myself as if they are beneath my notice, simply because Lady Louisa does not deign to recognize them if they perform a service, you are quite out, I can tell you. That does not fit my notion of Quality whatsoever!"

"Really?" he asked curiously, a flicker of amusement in his dark eyes. "And just what *is* your notion of Quality, Cousin Georgiana?"

"I am not perfectly sure that I can define it," replied Georgiana, mustering her dignity. "But I am quite sure I can identify that which it is not."

"And so can every servant in my great-aunt's establishment," he persisted, "so I am persuaded you must see the importance of setting off on the right foot. I am certain you are too well brought up to *gossip* with any of them, but perhaps, at the rectory, there was an atmosphere of—shall we say?—informality which might have led you to confide more of your feelings than would be appropriate in a grander establishment. And one does not wish to disclose one's thoughts or feelings to a servant, ever."

Georgiana thought that that stricture applied more to him than to anyone else she had ever met, and an apt quotation leapt into her mind. "With such true breeding of a gentleman, You never could divine his real thought," she murmured.

Sir Oliver burst out laughing. "Bravo! But if you are a fan of Byron's you will surely know that the 'gentleman' he is referring to was a pirate—'the mildest-mannered man that ever scuttled ship or cut a throat,' if I do not misremember."

Georgiana smiled. "The context will not do, I grant you."

"Nor, if you will not eat me for saying so, will the source. Byron is no longer quite the thing, you know."

News of Lord Byron's disgrace had not penetrated as far as Yorkshire, apparently. "Why not?" she asked him curiously.

"If you do not know, I do not intend to tell you," he said firmly. "And in any case, you will not wish to appear too bookish. One should be able to talk of the latest poems, should they become the rage, but to seem *blue* may prejudice your chances."

Georgiana, who had had the best education her fortune and situation could buy, almost sneered at this. "I suppose it is preferable to speak of nothing but fashions and frivolities."

"Yes it is," he said with brutal frankness. "Or at least, it has been my experience that young ladies who succeed on the ton and the Marriage Mart seem to talk of little else."

"Is that what you profess to admire?" she asked him incredulously.

"Cousin Georgiana," he said with a twisted smile, "it has been some time since I have become inutterably bored with what is commonly referred to as Polite Society, which is why I have so often found female companionship outside of it. Nevertheless, I believe you will find it worthwhile to heed my advice, as you have neither the fortune nor the background to carry off being known as an Eccentric. My good opinion, or lack of it, need not concern you in the least."

"But surely, when you marry, it must be to a girl of birth and breeding. Are those the qualities you would want in your wife?"

"Do you know, Miss Bucklebury," he said, dropping the "Cousin Georgiana" for the moment, "I am quite curious as to why you agreed to take part in my little wager. You do not appear at all eager to play the part into which Fate has so obligingly cast you."

"My reasons, or lack of them, need not concern you in the least," she said, deliberately echoing him.

"In that case," he said with provoking mildness, "we shall rub along tolerably well together if each of us refrains from impertinent inquiries into the other's motives and philosophy. For my own part, I intend to remain quite indifferent to your *reasons* for entering into our pact, so long as I have your full cooperation."

Georgiana, digging her fingernails into her palm, was forcibly reminded of another of Byron's lines: "There was a laughing devil in his sneer." This time she did not utter it aloud.

"And let me give you one more piece of advice," he added, watching her closely, "when you are annoyed, you really should take more pains not to show it. Your cheeks flush quite unbecomingly, and your eyes flash in a manner that is not at all the thing, and rather alarming besides. Remember, I speak in your best interest, and not out of personal pique."

This was the beginning of many pieces of worldly wisdom he conferred on her between the time of Miss Leroux's departure and her own removal to Lord Leighton's sister. Georgiana was glad when the snow melted enough for Cecilia to be sent on to London in his lordship's carriage, because it became quite evident that the actress had formed an altogether unflattering notion of what was afoot and of Georgiana's part in it. She seemed to reassess her evaluation of the governess's character, and treated her with the envious certainty that Georgiana had somehow stumbled onto a Very Good Thing and snatched it right out from under Cecilia's nose. Her leavetaking, while expressing affectionate gratitude for Georgiana's part in rescuing her from Dire Peril, seemed to suggest that they were sisters under the skin and was accompanied by more than one knowing wink.

"And I hope you will all come to see me in my new play in London," she said grandly as she was about to sweep away in Lord Litchfield's traveling carriage. "His lordship has offered to invest in it, providing *I* am given a leading role. I think it will answer very well, and I shall be very pleased to receive you all backstage in my private dressing room. Miss Bucklebury," she added with just a trace of a smirk, and extending a gloved hand to her with what she imagined was the air of a duchess conferring favors on the less fortunate, "naturally you must apply to *me* if ever I can be of service to you. I hope I may see you all in town as soon as may be. Good-bye!"

"Do you know," said Georgiana warmly when the carriage had rolled out of the drive, "it is very kind of you to sponsor her in a play, Lord Leighton. I fear she was not on the best of terms with her company, and your intervention might be the very thing to boost her career."

"Kindness has very little to do with it," muttered Mr. Utterby darkly.

"I would like very much to see her play," she continued, ignoring him. "I wonder if I ever shall?"

"If you clear the first hurdle at Pemberton, my great-aunt will take you up to London for the Season. We will have our work cut out for us there, but perhaps I could arrange for someone to escort you to the theater," commented Sir Oliver.

"And perhaps I will arrange my own escort," retorted Georgiana tartly.

"Perhaps, Cousin Georgiana, but I should not lay money on it if I were you. Now let me hear your catechism: who are the Patronesses of Almack's and what are their rules?"

Georgiana sighed. "Lady Sefton, Lady Jersey, Mrs. Drummond-Burrell, Lady Castlereigh, Lady Cowper, Countess Lieven, and Princess Esterhazy. Balls on Wednesdays, no admissions without vouchers, gentlemen must wear knee breeches and chateau-bras, and one must never never dance the waltz without first securing the permission of one of the Patronesses. Have I got that right?"

"Admirable," said Sir Oliver dryly. "Take care you remember as well that some of these ladies, in particular Mrs. Drummond-Burrell, are quite awesomely correct, and that should you offend their notions of propriety, for example by appearing at the theater without a proper escort, even my intervention could not save you from social ruin."

Georgiana, who had every intention of unmasking herself and returning to Yorkshire before any such eventuality could take place, nonetheless shivered a little at the prospect. "Point taken," she conceded.

"Good. A great deal is riding on your success, remember."

"Yes, your grays," she said bitterly.

"Among other things. Above all, I do not like to be disappointed."

Only the thought that her revenge would be certain to wound him where he was most vulnerable, in his insufferable pride, led her to bite her tongue on a most unladylike retort.

To Georgiana's considerable surprise, Lord Litchfield's sister Jeannette, Lady Lonsdale, seemed to accept the appearance on her doorstep of Sir Oliver Townsend and his most unfashionably clad cousin, Miss Oversham, without benefit of a chaperon, with unruffled equanimity. She entered with enthusiasm into the project of attiring Georgiana suitably before she ventured south to meet her family and seemed to find the tale of sick companions, lost luggage, and blinding snowstorms entirely probable.

Like her brother, Lady Lonsdale was angelically fair and not possessed of a powerful intellect, but she had an unerring eye for fashion, and she realized at once that Georgiana's severely cut dresses had been molded for a figure other than her own.

"My dear, it must have been perfectly *dreadful* to attire yourself so," she said with real feeling. "Were it not for the fact that the clothing is undoubtedly female, I should say they had switched your luggage with a *boy's*. I hope it did not bind you too much! And such a style! Even my governess did not dress so forbiddingly."

Georgiana was glad that the gentlemen's eyes had been less acute and mumbled something to the effect that it had not been so very uncomfortable, begging her ladyship not to mention it to her cousin, who should in no event be further troubled on her account.

"You must call me Jeannette," said Lady Lonsdale with a lovely smile. "Our two families have been close since Lionel and Oliver were in leading strings. As for not troubling Oliver, he particularly wishes me to array you becomingly before you meet your grandmama. Heaven only knows what a taking she would be in if she were to find her granddaughter looking like a—an evangelical tractist!" She giggled. "I'm sorry, Georgiana, but it's quite true. And Lady Louisa's stiff as bark, you know." She looked at Georgiana assessingly and sighed. "We are much of a size, but you are a dark beauty, and the clothes that set off *my* fairness will not do you justice." She tilted her head, thinking. "Perhaps the green silk. Yes, that might do. I could not quite like it with my blue eyes, but it will go most enchantingly with your gray ones. And you must have my lace shawl. Oh, it is such fun! Almost like having a sister! I am *so* glad Oliver brought you."

In the face of such friendly acceptance, Georgiana felt a pang of guilt until she remembered that she was not deceiving this kind woman in any material fashion, and that she really was who she represented herself to be. In the five days since the Mail had set her down on Lord Litchfield's doorstep, she had almost convinced herself that she *was* Miss Bucklebury, the spinster governess, and that her impersonation of Georgiana Oversham was a duplicitous scheme hatched for frivolous and rather mercenary reasons with a man she had every reason to believe was a hardened cynic without a conscience. She comforted her own troubled conscience by reminding herself that Sir Oliver was the only person who would be materially deceived, and that he richly deserved any embarrassment which might result when at length he came into full possession of the truth.

Lady Lonsdale, or Jeannette, as she continued to insist that

eorgiana call her, had not erred in her selection of the green
lk. It fell in graceful folds over Georgiana's slim body, and
et off her coloring to perfection. Jeannette pressed it on her as
 gift so firmly that she felt it would be uncivil to refuse, but
he could not accept the beautiful lace shawl except as a loan,
hough she admired the way it complemented her costume's
oft elegance. Her new friend sent her own dresser to arrange
er hair, and when all was done she escorted her, arm in arm,
own to dinner.

Georgiana had been unbecomingly attired and rather
edraggled for such a long time that the pleasure of dressing
p again acted as a tonic to her spirits. She harbored a some-
hat irrational but truly feminine desire to stun the odious Sir
liver with her transformation into a woman of looks and
ashion, so she was disappointed when her arrogant cousin
fted his quizzing glass with a languid air and said merely:
My compliments, Jeannette."

"Oh, Oliver, you are past bearing!" exclaimed Lady Lons-
ale with a little laugh. "You must own that your cousin is the
veliest creature imaginable and would be so in a sheet!
nathan, dear," she addressed her esteemed spouse, "do you
ot think Oliver's cousin is quite taking? She tells me she has
ever been up to London, and may be introduced into the ton
is year. If she goes up to town I predict she will be the Rage
ithin three weeks. Oh, Oliver, you *must* persuade Lady
ouisa to go up for the Season."

Her husband replied obediently that he had seldom seen a
ettier girl, which caused Georgiana to blush like a school-
om miss, and Sir Oliver said diffidently that his great-aunt
o doubt had plans for her granddaughter, but he did not yet
ow what they were.

Jeannette persisted. "But you must insist, Oliver. You really
ust. You know that Clarice and Amabel will not like it, as
on as they see her. And they will try to persuade Lady
ouisa—"

Her husband lifted her hand gently to his lips and kissed it.
That is quite enough, my dear," he said softly. "I think you
ay safely leave it to Oliver to decide what is best."

Jeannette gave her a chagrined smile. "Of course, my hus-

band is right. I do go on too much. Jonathan, won't you lea⟨
Georgiana into dinner? Alphonse has prepared dressed duck ⟨
la Normande and is quite enraptured over the sauce. He wil⟨
never forgive us if we are late to the table. Such a tyrant, but ⟨
genius, I do assure you."

Thus diverted, Georgiana never got to learn what it was tha⟨
Clarice and Amabel, whoever they were, would not like a⟨
soon as they saw her.

While Georgiana and Jeannette were engaged in the delec⟨
table pursuit of selecting the ensemble which would most ef⟨
fectively complement dusky curls and fine gray eyes, the⟨
ladies at Pemberton were less agreeably occupied. Mrs. Over⟨
sham, a faded blond woman with a rather anxious air, wa⟨
turning over the missive clutched tightly in her hand as if i⟨
contained imminent warning of an outbreak of plague, while⟨
her sister Amabel, Miss Ponsonby, regarded her with a forth⟨
right frown. "I cannot like it, Clarice," said Miss Ponsonby⟨
with what her older sister felt was gross understatement⟨
"What can Oliver mean by it?"

"I do not know, because I most *particularly* wrote to put he⟨
off when Lady Louisa left to visit Sir Hugh. And now Olive⟨
says he is bringing her here tomorrow, and I do not know wha⟨
Lady Louisa will say," cried Mrs. Oversham. "Especially⟨
since she is sure to be cross when she returns this evening. Si⟨
Hugh always has that effect on her."

Miss Ponsonby, in general a rigidly correct girl, forbore to⟨
remark that in that regard Sir Hugh was scarcely alone. Instea⟨
she commented dolefully, "I fear dear Lady Louisa will be⟨
sadly put out of frame. Perhaps this will put an end to he⟨
plans." She sighed. "I wonder what she looks like."

"Oh, my dear, we need not worry on *that* score I am sure,⟨
said Mrs. Oversham consolingly. "Lady Louisa sent someone⟨
to Yorkshire years ago, quite privately, you know, and he re⟨
ported that she was spotty and rather fat. And you know, tha⟨
countryside is so bleak I should not be at all surprised if he⟨
complexion was rather coarse as well. It is quite likely, with⟨
such a background, that she is a trifle vulgar. I am sure," she⟨

id, arriving at the heart of the matter, "that Sir Oliver could
ot but find her not at all in his style."

"I do not doubt that you may be right, Clarice, but I cannot
elp wondering if you really want such a creature as you de-
cribe to become a wife to your Freddy."

"Well, there is no reason to suppose that she is not an ami-
ble and quite biddable girl," suggested Mrs. Oversham rea-
onably. "And she is quite staggeringly rich, and you know
reddy must marry money. Lady Louisa will do nothing for
m, though I am sure Gayford always regarded him as almost
s own son. Oh, if only he *had* been Gayford's child instead
my first husband's! I must say it seems *most* unfair that she
ould make Sir Oliver her heir when he is full of juice al-
ady. Not that I should not like to see it come to *you,* my
ear, when the time comes. But Lady Louisa plans—"

"I know," said Miss Ponsonby with a touch of asperity,
vhat her ladyship plans. But surely Sir Oliver is not the sort
gentleman who would allow even so beloved a relative as
dy Louisa to dictate whom he must marry."

"Well, no," admitted Mrs. Oversham a trifle worriedly, "but
e does not like to disoblige her when her heart may give way
any moment. I am sure my poor Gayford was much the
me, and she was not even ill then! None of her relatives
es to cross her in the least, I do assure you."

"But if Sir Oliver's heart were engaged elsewhere . . ." sug-
sted Miss Ponsonby with a little smile.

Mrs. Oversham smiled at her sister in return. "In that case,
y dear, I'm sure Lady Louisa will not insist. But I own I can-
t think it *quite* convenient that Miss Georgiana Oversham is
riving just at this moment, because Freddy has been a little
ll lately, and I do not believe we can depend on him to make
push to engage her affections. And if Lady Louisa takes it
to her head to go up to town for the Season, there are sure to
gazetted fortune hunters who will not care a whit if an
iress's face and breeding do not match her fortune."

"Good God!" cried Miss Ponsonby, forgetting herself for a
oment. "Is that what she is planning?"

"Well, you know, Amabel, she does not confide in me,"
id Mrs. Oversham candidly, smoothing down the lilac silk of

her gown a shade regretfully. "You know how she is when sh
takes an idea into her head about something." Mrs. Oversham
who had few ideas of any sort, shook her head wonderingly
"Something she said about the London house put it in m
mind that she might wish to go there this year."

"Perhaps she will dislike Miss Oversham and will not wis
to introduce her to the ton," suggested Miss Ponsonby hope
fully.

"Oh, that is quite possible," agreed Mrs. Oversham, "be
cause there are very few people she *does* like. When I think o
the way she treats poor Freddy . . . And in any case she has no
allowed Geoffrey Oversham's name to be spoken in the hous
this many years, so there is every hope she will continue t
mislike the connection excessively. But," she added with
worried frown, "if she intends for the girl to marry Oliver, sh
will have to introduce her into Society."

"Then we must move quickly," interposed Miss Ponsonby
"I fear that dear Lady Louisa may be misled by her own gen
erous nature and, perhaps, just a trace of regret over the lon
estrangement with her son, into attempting to bring about
connection with her heir that may not be desirable, and indee
might be injurious, because what will happen to Sir Oliver'
social position should he ally himself with a nobody fror
Yorkshire, however great her fortune may be? I cannot bu
feel that it is your duty, dear Clarice, to spare your mother-ir
law the certain anguish she will suffer when Sir Oliver rebuff
her scheme by making plain the disadvantages of such a cor
nection before it ever has a chance to take place."

"Oh, but I could not . . . that is to say, I cannot *bear* to cros
swords with her, especially when she is in one of her fidgets
She shuddered. "You don't know the half of it. The third mai
has already left this year, because Lady Louisa gave her such
dressing down as even a servant could not bear. She quite pu
me in a quake, I swear to you."

Miss Ponsonby, who had long yearned to occupy that pos
tion in the household which would afford her some say in th
running of it, had renewed cause to regret her sister's lamenta
ble lack of firmness with her mother-in-law. She said pa
tiently, "There is little need to cross swords with anyone,

promise you. Indeed, I would not urge you to anything so improper. It only wants tact and careful handling to show Lady Louisa that Miss Oversham is not quite the bride she would wish for her heir."

"Oh yes!" cried Mrs. Oversham, enthusiastically welcoming her sister's implicit offer of help, "and Freddy must be made to exert himself as well!"

Chapter 6

PEMBERTON WAS AN Elizabethan house, considerably altered and expanded by successive generations of Overshams, but still retaining much of its original integrity and beauty. It was set among a variety of well-tended gardens at the end of a row of handsome trees. The grounds were still blanketed by snow, but a glimmer of sunlight reflected off the mullioned windows and cast a warm glow over the golden bricks.

Georgiana, her mind in turmoil, felt a lump rise in her throat at her first gaze upon her father's boyhood home. His own estate equaled or surpassed this one in size and style, but she knew he had cherished an attachment for Pemberton that had little to do with riches or status and had always lamented his estrangement from it. Sir Oliver, seated across from her in Lord Lonsdale's traveling carriage, raised an eyebrow in inquiry, but she could only shake her head at him and hope he could not see how affected she was. She was spared the necessity of conversation on the subject by the presence of Lady Lonsdale's maid, who had been lent to her for reasons of propriety as well as to attend to her comfort.

All this time, the prospect of Pemberton and its inhabitants had been like a dream to her, and it was not until the carriage turned into the lane that she was overcome by the liveliest sense of dread. She had no doubt of being civilly received, but the hints she had received from Sir Oliver as to the real motives and plans of the members of her family could not but make her doubt that she would be valued or welcomed for herself alone, and she could not help wondering whether, if Sir Oliver—she must remember the "cousin"—had not believed her to be someone else and confided the true story to her, she

might have been happily and innocently deceived. She could
not help thinking that this might not have been such a very bad
thing, and consoled herself with the certainty that complex re-
lationships were the rule in all families, and that anyone given
a candid glimpse into a loved one's heart and mind might well
expect to encounter there some discoveries of a surprising and
occasionally disappointing nature.

Traveling in Lady Lonsdale's carriage, in her ladyship's
clothing, and accompanied by her maid, and under the escort
of a man who believed her to be someone else, Georgiana felt
unlike herself, and restless, and not a little lonely. The intensity of this sensation did not lessen when the carriage drew up
to the imposing front of the house, and the door was opened
by a footman of stern mien and freezing gentility. Knowing
that from this moment on she would be under inspection by
every servant for the least evidence of Mushroom Manners,
she forbore to thank him, which she had reason to believe her
grandmother would deprecate as excessive familiarity, and instead favored him with a slight smile, which caused that impassive personage to later remark belowstairs that it was plain
as a pikestaff that Miss Georgiana Oversham was Quality,
whatever the stiff-rumped old lady upstairs might have to say
about it.

Her ladyship's butler, Raskins, was gaunt and imposing,
and many years in her service had worn away his youth and
strength, supplanting these attributes with dignity and self-
consequence. Thus did Lady Louisa's servants find compensa-
tion for her exacting demands and uncertain temper, and those
that survived their first year of service were bonded together
fiercely, rather like members of a religious cult whose initia-
tion rites were particularly rigorous and unpleasant.

Georgiana noted with approval that the wide hall was lofty
and well appointed, with none of those florid period-piece em-
bellishments owners so often employed to instill onlookers
with a sense of the house's history rather than its comforts.
The furnishings were neither too faddish nor too shabby; they
were, like the house itself, merely old, elegant, and graceful.
She was allowed only a momentary contemplation of these
discoveries, however, as Raskins crossed the hall with surpris-

ingly firm steps and led them to a large saloon, where, he told them, her ladyship and the other members of the household were waiting to greet them. Sir Oliver, coming up behind her, placed an admonitory hand on her arm and bent over her, breathing in her ear, "Remember that it will be much better if I make the explanations to the family. Say as little as possible."

Georgiana, who was feeling rather scared, did not find it difficult to nod her agreement.

A fire was lit in the saloon, casting long shadows before it in the gloom of the March afternoon and making it difficult, at first, to make out the figures who were seated in front of the hearth like a panel of angels at the Last Judgment. Her grandmother, Lady Louisa Oversham, the last surviving child of the Earl and Countess of Calvano, was seated in a straight-back chair, the blanket covering her legs and lap the only apparent concession to the demands of age and infirmity. She had been a great belle in her day, and traces of the beauty that had driven more than one duke, and, reputedly, a king to his knees, were still visible in the perfect bones of her face. She had never, even as a girl, been known to indulge in useless tact or anything less than blunt speaking, and the habits of a lifetime had hardened into an air of imperiousness that made her the terror of her surviving relatives and servants. She fixed Georgiana with a piercing stare from beneath still-dark eyebrows, but said nothing until Sir Oliver stepped forward, bowed deeply over her hand, and said calmly, "I've brought your granddaughter, Aunt Louisa."

"So it's you, is it?" inquired Lady Louisa in a surprisingly deep voice. "Come here and let me look at you."

Georgiana obligingly moved forward and curtsied to her grandmother, aware of the scrutiny of the others in the room but unwilling to take her eyes off of Lady Louisa's face.

"Hmmph," remarked her ladyship in a tone which Georgiana feared did not signify approval. "You do not have the look of your father."

Georgiana took a deep breath. "I am said to favor my mother, Lady Louisa."

"Nonsense!" cried her ladyship with obvious displeasure.

"There are dark hair and eyes on the Calvano side as well. My great-great grandfather was a Spanish nobleman. No doubt that is where it comes from. And you may call me Grandmama. Hmmph!" she said again, casting her eyes over Sir Oliver's handsome person. "You look well enough, I suppose, if you did not rig yourself out like some London bow-window piece. I can't abide dandies, and in my day no gentleman would have come calling without his powder and lace, I can tell you! And how came you to bring the girl here after all?"

Sir Oliver, smiling, said merely, "A long story, ma'am. But may I not make Miss Oversham known to the rest of her family before I recount it?"

Lady Louisa waved a hand dismissively, which Sir Oliver correctly interpreted as permission to introduce Georgiana to the other three in the room, who were regarding her with varying degrees of curiosity, surprise, and (at least in one case) displeasure. "Mrs. Oversham, Miss Ponsonby, you'll allow me to present Miss Oversham to you."

"Oh, you must call me Clarice," said a soft-voiced blond woman, taking Georgiana's hand with a smile. "I am your Uncle Gayford's widow, you know. And my sister is Amabel. May we not call you Cousin Georgiana, as Oliver does?"

"Of course," murmured Georgiana, finding herself on the receiving end of a rather cool bow from Miss Ponsonby—Amabel—whose aristocratic face bore a smile but whose eyes held no warmth whatsoever.

Miss Ponsonby was a tall, rather elegant girl with neat brown hair, a thin bosom (quite discreetly covered up by her somber gown), and a manner which, though it could not be criticized as proud, showed that she was very well aware of her own worth. At the moment she was highly displeased, although she took some pains not to show it. The Ponsonbys were a very old family which had fallen on rather impecunious times through the successive idiocies of several generations of Ponsonby men, who had frittered away the family fortune on preposterous schemes upon the 'Change, on gambling, or in lavish expenditures upon the muslin company. The current members hoped to rectify this lamentable state of affairs through advantageous marriages, though Clarice had had two chances, and in each case early widowhood and an imperfect understanding of how the fortune was tied up had had much less than satisfactory results. Her first union had been a love match, the second, more carefully considered, might have brought better results if Mr. Gayford Oversham had not stuck his spoon in the wall before his wife could provide him with an heir. Miss Amabel Ponsonby was considerably wiser than her sister and fully intended to profit from a knowledge of her mistakes; she regarded it as the epitome of good fortune when Fate, in the form of Clarice's invitation to come and share the tedium of life under Lady Louisa's roof, had thrown her into the path of Sir Oliver Townsend. Sir Oliver, in addition to his own rather magnificent fortune, stood to inherit her ladyship's as well. He was also a man of fashion, address, and breeding, and if Miss Ponsonby did not quite have a heart to lose to him, she could not remain unmoved by the desirability of such qualities in a husband.

Under the circumstances, she could not welcome the arrival of the house of Miss Oversham, however much Clarice schemed to match her to Frederick, and however unlikely it was that a man of Sir Oliver's impeccable ton would overlook the vulgarity of her Yorkshire connections. Like all persons of high birth and low income, Miss Ponsonby sneered at newly made money, and she could have borne with only a few pangs Georgiana's immense fortune, if only she had been, as expected, a dowd, or squabbish and spotty. But Miss Oversham, decked out in a rose-colored traveling dress of the first stare of elegance, with fine gray eyes and lustrous dark hair must be acknowledged a Beauty, and Miss Ponsonby found herself gripped by an overwhelming sense of antipathy and a determination to rid the house of her presence, in one fashion or another, as soon as may be.

Georgiana, privy to none of these reflections, saw only the momentary flicker of hostility in Miss Ponsonby's—"do please call me Amabel"—eyes. "How do you do?" she inquired uncertainly.

"And here is my son Frederick, Lord Nugent," said Clarice with the air of one producing a delightful surprise at the very last moment. "Freddy, come and greet your cousin Georgiana."

This gentleman, who had been staring absently into the fire for some moments, appeared startled at the interruption. "Yes, Mama," he said dutifully, reaching for Georgiana's extended hand. He looked into her face with an expression of amiable vacuity, which marred an otherwise startlingly handsome countenance. "Are you my cousin? Didn't know I had any more!"

"Now, Frederick," said his mama with a strained smile, "you are quizzing us most shockingly. I made sure to tell you all about Cousin Georgiana when dear Lady Louisa invited her to visit."

Dear Lady Louisa muttered something which sounded to Georgiana very like "Block!" but she couldn't be sure.

Freddy gave no sign of having heard this remark and said placidly, "So sorry. Always forgetting things. Habit of mine. Mama will tell you."

"Dear Freddy is always teasing, aren't you, my dear? Now whatever will Cousin Georgiana think of us? We've left you to stand about, when you must be tired and in want of refreshment. Do sit down here next to Frederick and warm yourself by the fire, while Raskins procures some sherry for us. Oliver, my dear, you must tell us how you came to escort Cousin Georgiana to Pemberton."

Georgiana, listening to his improbable tale of carriage accidents, lost luggage, sick chaperons, and chance meetings, could not but wonder how all of this would strike his listeners, but in fact, she need not have worried. Sir Oliver was not a man to brook contradiction, and the tone of his recitation carried more weight than its content.

She felt compelled to add, when he had finished, "I am so sorry if my coming now has been inconvenient, Grandmama. We never received your letter putting off my visit and when Sir—Cousin Oliver rescued me from the snowstorm, we thought—oh!"

A sharp stab at her ankle caused her to look down quickly, in time to see a gray paw disappear behind the legs of the settee. Freddy, who was seated beside her, made an involuntary choking sound, and threw her a glance of what she interpreted as entreaty, as if he were a schoolboy rather than a grown man.

"What is it?" asked Lady Louisa crossly.

"I beg pardon, ma'am," said Georgiana, smoothing her skirts down to cover as wide an area beneath her as possible. "I have just remembered a letter I should have written before now, and it quite distracted me for a moment."

"What letter is that?" inquired her grandmother with what Georgiana felt was somewhat impertinent curiosity.

"To—to my guardian, ma'am," she answered with perfect truth. "I must let them know I have arrived safely."

"You may do so," snapped Lady Louisa, "but after that I wish you to understand that all intercourse between you and your mother's family must be at an end while you are under my roof. I wish never to hear her name spoken, or to be reminded of a connection about which too little cannot be said."

"I am sorry to disoblige you so early in our acquaintance, Lady Louisa," replied Georgiana, her temper flaring at this, "but I could not behave in so uncivil a fashion to persons who have treated me with nothing but kindness *all my life,* even to please you." A warning look from Sir Oliver caused her to plunge recklessly forward. "I am sure you would not wish me to act in such an ungrateful or contemptible a fashion."

"I daresay not," replied her grandmother to nearly everyone's amazement. "Hoity-toity! No need to cut up stiff with me! 'Lady Louisa,' indeed! But you cannot expect me to welcome your confidences about the woman who stole my son from me, so don't be forever prosing on about her or her other relatives."

"Very well, Grandmama," replied Georgiana with determined amiability in the face of her ladyship's unexpected concession. A prick at her ankle, more insistent than the first, caused her to lower her hand, ever so slowly, to the floor, with a bite of the excellent ham Raskins had provided concealed stealthily within her fist.

This offer apparently proved acceptable, because the claws were sheathed, and a slight rumbling noise issued from beneath her skirts.

"Frederick," said Miss Ponsonby with a virtuous smile, "I fear your cat has strayed into the saloon again."

"Dash it all, Aunt Amabel—" began Lord Nugent.

"Vermin!" expostulated her ladyship decisively. "I will not have it my house! Raskins!"

"Oh, Frederick, you know Lady Louisa does not like cats in the house," interjected Clarice worriedly, torn between her fear of displeasing her mother-in-law and her indulgence of her only son.

"Drown it!" commanded her ladyship imperiously.

"No!" cried Freddy, stricken. He was making rather ineffectual efforts to drag the offender out from beneath the settee, but was not meeting with any degree of success.

"My son is foolishly tender-hearted," Clarice told Georgiana with a rather thin-lipped, apologetic smile. "He has such compassion, even for a cat."

"She shall not drown it," said Freddy obstinately, his hand closing around a long gray tail which switched angrily at such undignified treatment.

"Raskins!" called her ladyship again.

"Cook will not thank you if you do," said Sir Oliver in a languid tone, unexpectedly entering the lists on the side of feline accomplishment. "There were mice in the kitchen the last time I was down."

"Very well, then," said Lady Louisa irritably, "but get it out of my sight!"

Georgiana offered Freddy another slice of her ham. "Try the effect of this," she suggested.

The culprit, a very large gray tabby whose insouciant air must be ascribed to his remaining in ignorance of how close he had come to the end of what appeared to have been a long and rather interesting life, responded to this enticement with marked enthusiasm, and Frederick was able to restrict his movements with some difficulty and gather him, squirming, into his arms.

"His name is Burdick," he said, to no one in particular.

Burdick, apparently in full possession of his wits, now began to look hopefully around the room from this new vantage point, apparently in search of further refreshment. When none was forthcoming, he tried the effect of a rather hideous wail and, doubtless pleased with the results, repeated the exercise almost immediately.

Sir Oliver, whose hand was frozen in the act of reaching into his pocket for his snuffbox, said in his most bored voice, "I really should remove him at once, if I were you, Frederick."

"Shall I take the animal?" inquired Raskins, who had arrived in obedience to her ladyship's summons, in frigid tones.

"You'll drown him," accused Lord Nugent with a fearful glance at Lady Louisa.

"Indeed I will not, sir," replied the redoubtable butler, his voice thawing a little. "I shall see that he is made comfortable in the kitchen. Cook no doubt has some scraps to spare."

Burdick, who would tolerate being constrained against his will for only the briefest of intervals, began to sharpen his claws against Mr. Nugent's coat.

"Oh, Freddy," began his mama hopelessly.

"Take him myself," Mr. Nugent told the butler with resolution. "Might rip you to shreds."

Raskins, with only a momentary shudder causing a ripple in his impassive countenance, condescended to open the door for him.

"Looby!" ejaculated Lady Louisa loudly when the door had closed on them.

Mrs. Oversham cast a worried look at Georgiana, who pretended not to have heard.

"My son follows the fashion for exotic pets, you know," she said in a confiding tone. "I fear it may seem a trifle eccentric, but I'm told it is quite the thing in London to carry one's animal everywhere. There are stories about Robert Neville transporting a pig in his sporting curricle, and he was the height of à la modality, I'm told!"

Sir Oliver, arrested in the act of taking a pinch of his mixture, coughed violently and was forced to cover his face with his hand.

"What a droll creature," remarked Miss Ponsonby to Georgiana, leaving some doubt as to her meaning. "I am not, in general, fond of pets in the house, though I believe a pug or some small, well-trained dog of that nature to be unexceptionable."

Georgiana could think of nothing suitable to reply to this, and the remainder of the interval before the ladies retired to dress for dinner was passed in such commonplaces as might be appropriate to one whose every gesture and utterance would be observed and analyzed by every other occupant of the room. Indeed, when she at length rose gratefully to follow the housekeeper to her room to change out of her traveling dress, Sir Oliver detained her with a restraining hand on her arm, saying in a low voice, "Coming it much too strong, *Cousin* Georgiana! How came you to rise to the defense of a guardian you have never met? You might have offended Aunt Louisa, you know, when there was no need whatsoever to cross swords with her."

Georgiana, finding herself unable to explain to him precisely why she had taken offense at her grandmother's strictures against communicating with her uncle and aunt, had to content herself with saying: "I cannot believe that your real cousin would have conducted herself in any other fashion. Even Lady Louisa could hardly expect her to disown her mother's family, and to forbid contact with them for the duration of the visit was outrageous."

"Cousin Georgiana," said Sir Oliver with a look in his dark eyes which had blighted the pretensions of upstarts and social aspirants for every Season since he had made his own come-out some years before, "you are not here to reform my family, however much it may seem to you that they stand in need of it. You need only avoid offending my great-aunt and fob off Clarice's rather clumsy attempts to attach you to her son. In a few weeks the Season will begin, I shall make you the toast of London, and then you may retire into whatever future you find meets your exasperating standards. But till then you are to do as I say, and avoid calling attention to yourself by such foolish displays of temper as I saw today. You are too intelligent not to be sensible of the dangers of exciting suspicion, and you will not wish to give me cause to unmask your charade."

Georgiana almost succumbed to the overmastering desire to give him the finest trimming he had ever had in his life. "Un-

mask me, then," she said icily, "and see whether you can explain to Lady Louisa how you came to bring such an impostor
as I am under her roof!" She turned on her heel before he
could reply and ran to follow the housekeeper up the stairs to
her room.

Chapter 7

LADY LOUISA WAS insensibly gratified by the discovery that her nephew and heir was planning to make a stay of indeterminate length at Pemberton—possibly even until the family removed to the London town house for the opening of the Season. While Sir Oliver might be said to be punctilious in fulfilling his duties to his great-aunt, he had shown no previous inclination to pass several weeks at a time in her company. Her ladyship was quick to attribute this noteworthy change of habit to an interest in furthering his acquaintance with her granddaughter, and she lost no time in attempting to set in motion the machinery for fulfilling her dearest dream. Her worst fears about her granddaughter had not been realized: her accent was excellent, her manners—except for a lamentable tendency to cross the will of her elders, and an overfrank tongue—were pretty, and, despite the unpromising report she had had a number of years before, she was undeniably a Beauty. Lady Louisa was determined to detach her favorite son's only child from the pernicious influence of her Yorkshire relatives, and return her person and her immense fortune to Oversham control. She could wish that it was in her power to exert more control over Sir Oliver as well, though she would have liked him less if he had conciliated her more, because she could not be perfectly sure of his cooperation in her scheme, whether it might be in his best interest or no. He had an independent fortune and a reputation for avoiding the parson's mousetrap with determined skill. He was the most hardened flirt in London, but he had never yet, to his great-aunt's knowledge, lost his heart, despite all the snares that had been laid for him by several Seasons of the loveliest Beauties on the

Marriage Mart and their matchmaking mamas. Lady Louisa placed no dependence whatsoever upon his falling in love with a green girl from Yorkshire, however taking, and relied instead on the probability of finding her granddaughter more malleable and enthusiastic than he. She would try the effects of proximity, the pressure of affection, and the undoubted advantages of such a match to work their influence on her great-nephew. Of Georgiana's complicity there could be little doubt.

Georgiana received her grandmother's summons to attend her in the library with some trepidation. It was oddly reminiscent of her meeting with Sir Oliver at Lord Litchfield's hunting box, an encounter which, Georgiana felt, was the beginning of some huge Celestial Joke forthrightly aimed at upsetting the hitherto unappreciated tranquillity of her life. Already it seemed as if that life and the frank, straightforward character who had inhabited it belonged to the past, and Georgiana could not but believe that the person who had left Holcombe Hall would not be the same one who returned to it.

The library had been the province of Lady Louisa's late, not much lamented husband, Mr. Oversham, but the combination of the very pleasant prospect from the windows and her ladyship's determination to manage all his business affairs herself until her sons came of age soon accustomed her to its use. The untimely death and estrangement of her two male children had left her in firm possession of both the room and what it represented. She received her granddaughter sitting behind her husband's overlarge, rather formidable desk rather than in one of the more comfortable armchairs provided for reading, and Georgiana, upon being ushered into the room, saw at once that her grandmother was bent on intimidation. She was suddenly very glad she was *not* the penniless impostor Sir Oliver believed her to be, because however outrageous Lady Louisa's demands on her, Georgiana would always have her home and fortune to fall back on. Besides, she very much doubted that the scheme she and Sir Oliver had concocted could ever deceive such a formidable and astute observer as her grandmother appeared to be.

Lady Louisa was not in an affable mood. She appeared to be staring out the window in thought, but when Georgiana entered she said irritably, "So here you are at last! Of all things, I most detest unpunctuality! You may take that chair."

Georgiana, who knew that the interval between her receipt of the summons and her acting upon it had been of the briefest possible duration, closed her lips firmly and seated herself with every outward appearance of docility.

For several moments her ladyship said nothing more, apparently waiting for some response, but when none was forthcoming, she said more tartly, "I suppose I shall have to buy you some clothes. You can hardly go about all Season in what you borrowed from the Lonsdale chit."

Since her grandmother had insisted, in the letter she had written to Holcombe Hall, upon outfitting Georgiana in the first stare of fashion upon her arrival at Pemberton, Georgiana could not help feeling that the indignation she now expressed was not genuine. In fact, she was inclined to believe that her grandmother was one of those persons who derive stimulation and entertainment from discomfiting others, and who take perverse pride in their inconsistencies. In any case, the problem of her wardrobe was something she had devoted some thought to. She could hardly send up to Holcombe to retrieve her misplaced clothing; it would be too difficult to explain how a governess and rector's sister had come into possession of such expensive articles. A hastily (and secretly) dispatched letter to her aunt and uncle had explained, in the briefest of terms, her confused arrival at Pemberton without mentioning the intervention or existence of the irksome Sir Oliver, and begged them to retrieve her luggage from the coaching inn, saying that her grandmother had kindly offered to supply all she needed. She knew that Miss Bucklebury would have regaled them with the tale of her scandalous behavior, but since neither her aunt nor her uncle was a comfortable correspondent, she had no real fear of their taxing her with it until she returned. Besides, when she had dispatched the governess's clothing to the rectory, she had included, by way of apology, a sum which might go some considerable way toward alleviating that good lady's indignation.

"I thank you, ma'am," she said smoothly, "but there is not the slightest need for you to trouble yourself. If you could merely direct me to a suitable dressmaker, I shall have a few things made up. I shan't require very much, you know!"

Lady Louisa, whose relatives, with the exception of Sir Oliver, were not in the habit of rejecting her largesse, however grudgingly proffered, experienced the novelty of a rebuff. She had been planning on quashing any attempt on her grand-daughter's part to turn her up sweet with an acid rejoinder about maw worms and unctuous gentility, but she was sur-prised into a reluctant civility. "Nonsense! Of course I'll stand the huff. I've brought you down to Pemberton to bring you into the family, and Oliver means to introduce you to the ton. You have no notion of the endless fripperies you'll require, and I've said I'll provide them for you and I will. So let me hear no more about it!"

"Very well, Grandmama," Georgiana replied meekly.

"Can't say I hold much with the ton myself," commented Lady Louisa reminiscently. "A lot of foolish nonsense about nothing. Bowing and scraping to the likes of Sally Jersey! Hmmph! I knew her when she was nothing but a scrubby schoolgirl. I don't like London much either. It's full of cits and mushrooms, and it's too noisy to sleep at night."

"But I thought you enjoyed going there for the Season?" in-quired Georgiana, interested in this disclosure.

"I detest it," said her ladyship frankly. "But I like to see cer-tain of my acquaintance there, and Clarice would give me no peace if we didn't open the house every spring. She brought out Amabel there last year under my sponsorship, but she didn't take. No wonder! Has a face like a poker. Clarice wants Frederick to settle eligibly as well, so if I don't want the pack of 'em on my hands till I'm in my shroud I let her have her way."

Georgiana, who had not formed an extremely favorable im-pression of either Mrs. Oversham or her sister, nevertheless felt that much might be forgiven those who were forced to live on Lady Louisa's unwilling charity.

Lady Louisa eyed her shrewdly. "No doubt it will fret you to be under obligation to me."

Georgiana smiled. "I would not allow it, Grandmama, if I did not think it was what you particularly wished."

Her ladyship glared at her. "When you know me better, my girl, you will realize that it is very dangerous to cross swords with me. I'll brook no opposition, not from the likes of you."

"You will forgive me, ma'am, but barring the fact of your existence and your opposition to my parents' marriage, I have had little opportunity to discover anything about you whatsoever!"

"And you blame me for that, don't you?" the old lady snapped. "I don't scruple to tell you that when your father married your mother, however estimable her character might have been, he cut himself off from his family forever. It's no use saying the match wasn't beneath him, and so I told him. When he wouldn't listen, he quite ruined himself with me. No doubt he lived to regret it."

"I never heard that he did so, and as you know he stayed close to Mama's family," replied Georgiana, seething. "We must agree to disagree, ma'am, and perhaps it would be best to avoid the subject altogether. I fear that if we do not, I should feel a great deal of discomfort trespassing on your hospitality any further."

Lady Louisa's face became alarmingly suffused with color, and her hand went involuntarily to her heart.

Conscience-stricken, Georgiana remembered Sir Oliver's warning about the apparent fragility of her grandmother's health. "I beg you will be comfortable, ma'am; I really am delighted to be here and would not willingly distress you. But perhaps it would be better to avoid a subject likely to throw both of us into a passion," she said apologetically.

Georgiana thought she saw, for just a moment, a flash of humor in the old lady's eyes. "You don't want for spirit, I'll say that much for you," said Lady Louisa rather grumpily. "Your father was just the same." She gave her a searching glance from under still-dark brows. "You haven't lost your heart to some red-faced squire in Yorkshire, have you? I can't believe with your face and fortune the basket-scramblers haven't been buzzing round you like flies to the honey pot."

Georgiana made haste to reassure her that her affections were still unengaged, an action she came to regret a moment later.

"I thought as much. You look like a girl with too much sense to throw away her chances before she's had a chance at a really eligible match. It's a pity you aren't a year or two younger. What do you think of your cousin Oliver?"

Miss Oversham, unable to respond to this question with perfect candor, confined her answer to the briefest possible acknowledgement of his kindness in escorting her to Pemberton.

"Yes, yes," agreed her grandmother impatiently, "but you must realize he's been the biggest prize on the Matrimonial Mart these many years. I can't tell you how many handkerchiefs have been tossed at him!"

Georgiana murmured that she was sure her cousin must be very well thought of.

"Well thought of!" exclaimed her grandmother with a note of scorn. "Milk and water! I recommend that you get on terms with your cousin. He means to try and make you the toast of London, you know, for so he told me, and I am sure I have never before seen him so exert himself for anyone."

Georgiana said a trifle mulishly that she was very obliged to him, but she was not sure she wished to be the toast of London, and she was quite certain her cousin could have no personal motive for attempting to confer such a favor on her.

"No need to turn missish!" cautioned Lady Louisa. "You'll be thinking of your vulgar connections, but I assure you there is no need to scruple about that. The Oversham name is enough to carry you into the very highest circles—even the Prince visits us from time to time. If Oliver vouches for you, the town will be at your feet in a week. You could do far worse than make a push to engage your cousin's affections, for I assure you, you could not set your cap for anyone higher."

Georgiana gritted her teeth. "I hope I will not 'set my cap' for anyone at all, ma'am. And as for entertaining any idea of a warmer relationship with my cousin than a civil friendship, I fear it is quite impossible. I beg you will not distress yourself by wishing for something that is most unlikely to occur."

"Nonsense," said her ladyship dismissively. "You cannot have taken him in dislike, for you have scarcely known him but a few days, and his manners are everything that is amiable.

I shall say no more on that head at present, however. No use cramming the fences!"

Georgiana could not but feel that no amount of handling, however adroit, would ever serve to make her receive Sir Oliver's assurances with anything but a shiver of displeasure, but she was finding herself strangely unequal to the task of convincing her grandmother of this fact. She concluded that it was too soon to appear to set her face mulishly against the fondest wish of the old lady's heart, though she more than half suspected that her grandmother's affection for her fortune far exceeded her attachment to her person. She had underestimated, however, the extent to which her ladyship's determination to see her wishes carried through would outweigh the contradictory inclinations of the parties involved. She began to understand better why Sir Oliver had enlisted her to reject his suit in addition to her role in his ridiculous bet. It was early days yet, and for now she must place her reliance in the certain knowledge that *he* had no more wish for a match with *her* than she with him.

Despite the less than satisfactory nature of their last conversation, Sir Oliver lost no time in beginning his "cousin's" instruction into the finer points of succeeding on the ton. Accordingly, on the evening before they were to journey up to London for the shopping expedition which would complete her transformation from Cinderella into a certified belle, he leaned close to her at the dinner table and said in her ear: "Can you dance?"

Georgiana, who had had the finest dancing masters her fortune and situation could provide, saw little reason to make things easier for him. "I am afraid the rector frowned on dancing," she whispered shamelessly, though it was perfectly true.

"Good God," he said, as though much struck. "I should have thought of it sooner. All the best caper merchants will be engaged. We'd be obliged to wait a month before one of them could find the time to come to the London house, much less to Pemberton."

Miss Ponsonby, who had been eavesdropping on this conversation with unrestrained delight, set down her glass delicately and offered: "It is indeed unfortunate that Miss Oversham has not thought to engage a dancing master before now, because, as dear Lady Louisa always says, one can always tell a true gentlewoman by the way she conducts herself on the ballroom floor. And while I do not, in general, approve of the waltz as an appropriate dance for unmarried girls, there cannot be the least objection to a quadrille. Miss Oversham, I know you will not object if I venture to give you a hint. The veriest breath of impropriety might reach the ears of one of the Patronesses of Almack's, and then it would be quite difficult for you to obtain vouchers, you know, so you must be careful even here!"

"Oh, I doubt that the strictures are anywhere near so dire as that," said Sir Oliver, sounding amused.

"Well *you* of course need not concern yourself with the rules that govern the rest of us," suggested Miss Ponsonby archly. "Whatever you do must always be acceptable to the ton."

Georgiana, who was more annoyed by the slight, sardonic bow that responded to this fulsome remark than by the comment itself, gratified Clarice's fondest maternal hopes by suggesting brightly, "Perhaps Lord Nugent would be so kind as to teach me to dance."

Frederick, whose wits had been wandering during the course of this riveting conversation, did not appear to immediately perceive that his cooperation had been solicited. He gazed in confusion at Miss Oversham's expectant face until a sudden activity beneath the tablecloth commanded his attention. "What the . . . ?" He appeared to satisfy himself on one point at least and lifted his head. "Not Burdick," he said with assurance. "Left him in the kitchen, and anyway, no claws. Oh! It's you, Mama! Why are you pinching my knee? Dashed odd thing to do, now that I think of it."

"Frederick, my dear," said his mama in dulcet tones, "you are quite mistaken. I never *pinched* you. And now I fear you are quite distracted, when you were just about to tell Cousin Georgiana how delighted you will be to teach her to dance."

Freddy appeared to be somewhat startled by this intelligence. "I was?"

Georgiana, taking pity on him, said warmly, "There is no need, if you had rather not."

Freddy ran his finger under the rim of his cravat and looked uncomfortable. "Thing is, not much of a dancer. Daresay you wouldn't like to, Miss—Cousin Georgiana—that is, don't wish to be disobliging, but—" He looked helplessly at his mother, who said with angelic sweetness, between closed teeth: "My son has always been too modest, Cousin Georgiana; I am sure there are few young men his age who are so graceful on the dance floor."

"Looby!" croaked Lady Louisa from the head of the table, like some demented raven.

"Sorry!" said his lordship with a red face.

"There is no need to distress yourself, Frederick," said Sir Oliver in what, for him, was a surprisingly kind tone. "I will teach Cousin Georgiana to dance myself."

The magnificence of this condescension appeared to strike awe into his listeners and drove Georgiana to say swiftly, "Oh, that is most kind of you, Cousin Oliver, but I am far beneath your skills, I am quite sure. Do let me try with Frederick first, if he is willing!"

"Of course you are willing, aren't you, Frederick?" prompted his delighted mother, unable to believe her good fortune. Against all reason and expectation, the heiress apparently favored the company of her son to that of Sir Oliver. Clarice could only conclude that the girl was dazzled by the title, mistakenly valuing any lord higher than a mere "sir," and she would take good care she did not disabuse her of this convenient notion.

"Naturally—delighted!" said Freddy with a worried look.

"Well, since you appear to have settled it so amiably between you, I would not for the world interfere," said Sir Oliver in a drawl which sounded dangerous to Georgiana's ears. "Perhaps, when the lesson commences, my cousin will allow me the pleasure of leading her onto the floor for just one dance, if you, Clarice, will be good enough to play for us."

Miss Ponsonby looked as if she had bitten into a sour fig, but Georgiana knew at once that he meant to show her up on

the floor. She was quite willing to indulge him. It fit rather
nicely into her plan to take him down a notch or two.

"What shall we start with?" inquired Clarice, settling herself
gracefully on the piano stool. Lady Louisa having retired with
a muttered admonition to "mind how they tore up the furni-
ture," Clarice, Amabel, and the luckless Frederick joined
Georgiana in the drawing room for her dancing lesson. Sir
Oliver, his arms folded across his chest, leaned carelessly
against the door frame and scrutinized his cousin in attentive
silence.

"Oh, the waltz, by all means," replied Sir Oliver, determined on punishing Georgiana's disobedience.

"Thing is," said Frederick in a slightly strangled voice,
"know how to do the thing, but not explain it!"

"There will not be the slightest need for you to do so," said
Sir Oliver. "I shall demonstrate the steps with Cousin Georgiana, and then leave you to practice them with her. I am sure
that will make you both a great deal more comfortable," he
said, directing a sardonic lift of the eyebrow at Miss Oversham.

"Perhaps," suggested Clarice hopefully, "it might be best
for our cousin to learn by observation. If you were to partner
Amabel instead . . ."

Sir Oliver bestowed a charming smile on Miss Ponsonby.
"Your sister dances delightfully, Clarice. But if it will not dis-
compose you too much, Amabel, I think you might best employ your superior talents by watching Cousin Georgiana
carefully and instructing her as to how she should best go on.
A keen observer may often detect what a partner will miss,
you know!"

"Naturally I will do all that is within my power to be of assistance to—I hope you do not mind if I call you Cousin Georgiana?" said Miss Ponsonby, restored at once to high spirits.
"We are not, strickly speaking, related, but dear Clarice's relation to your grandmama will surely admit to a kinship something very like cousinhood. I trust there will be no impropriety
in my naming you so!"

Georgiana assured her of her grateful acceptance of the

pleasure of being admitted to such a near degree of kinship
with Miss Ponsonby and her nephew as well, and of her eager-
ness to encourage Cousin Amabel's scrutiny on the dance
floor in order to point out every flaw and graceless moment in
her performance.

Thus avenged, Sir Oliver led her onto the floor, while
Clarice coaxed the opening strains of a waltz from Lady
Louisa's perfectly tuned piano.

Under the practiced tutelage of her dancing master, Georgiana had learned to perform the waltz quite expertly, but now
she learned that the experience of twirling around the room in
the arms of Monsieur Lamont was quite different from the
novel and not entirely disagreeable sensation of doing so with
the arm of a handsome and undeniably powerful masculine
presence like Sir Oliver encircling her waist. However odious
and condescending he might be and however much she might
dislike him, she could not deny that he was a very attractive
man, and his proximity was suddenly rather disturbing. She
had meant to make a great many missteps; now she had little
trouble in convincing him she had never waltzed in her life.

"You really must look up at your partner now and then,
Cousin Georgiana," said Sir Oliver, enjoying her discomfort.
"One hopes, of course, that one's shoes are always polished to
perfection, but one does not expect them to exert such fascina-
tion upon one's partner."

"You must not seem to be minding the steps quite so
much," offered Miss Ponsonby kindly, from the sidelines.

The effect of these helpful pronouncements was to make her
put up her chin and tread, quite firmly and deliberately, on one
of her partner's exquisitely shod feet. "Oh I do beg your pardon, Cousin Oliver," she said sweetly. Whatever wounds her
self-esteem might suffer by hoaxing him into thinking her so
clumsy on the dance floor were assuaged by the briefest of
winces that crossed his arrogant features. "I hope I have not
scuffed your shoes."

His eyes regarded her with a flash of amusement, so quickly
gone she wondered if she had imagined it. "Touché," he said
softly, and then more loudly: "It is of no consequence. I be-

lieve my valet to be unsurpassed in such matters." He let her go then, saying with a graceful bow, "I will relinquish our cousin to you then, Frederick. Perhaps, when you have rid her of the trick she has of treading on her partner from time to time, she will begin to move with more assurance." He leveled a serious, probing gaze at Georgiana. "It is of the utmost importance that you acquit yourself with grace in the ballroom, Cousin Georgiana. I am sure I can rely on you to spend the time necessary to acquire such skill as will bring credit to the Oversham name." He bowed slightly, turned on his heel, and left the drawing room.

"Well, I must say," said Clarice with a worried frown, "it was perhaps coming it a bit too strong to put it in those terms. He will have Cousin Georgiana in a quake if she does not learn to dance, and I am quite sure he could not have meant to be so very—*fierce* about it. It is not your fault if you have not learned to waltz, my dear, and I cannot but feel that you will come along quickly."

"Sir Oliver was perhaps a trifle harsh in saying that Cousin Georgiana would reflect ill on the Oversham name if she does not learn to dance," suggested Miss Ponsonby helpfully, "but it does not overstate the case to say that everyone will be watching a cousin of Sir Oliver Townsend with more than a casual degree of interest. He no doubt felt that it would be unfair not to warn his cousin that she will be the object of intense scrutiny and speculation."

Georgiana, who knew precisely what Sir Oliver's comments were meant to convey, said with a touch of weariness, "It is of no consequence. I am sure Cousin Frederick will be able to teach me the steps."

Cousin Frederick, hearing his cue with no very great degree of confidence, took his place beside Georgiana on the drawing room floor. "Hope I can pull off the trick," he said glumly.

"Of course you shall," said Georgiana, feeling a little guilty over causing him so much apparent misery. "I am sure you shall teach me very well, which Sir Oliver himself was not able to do!"

"Really?" asked Frederick, brightening.

"Yes," said Georgiana firmly, almost pulling him into position.

Frederick was not so accomplished a dancer as Sir Oliver,
but it was remarked with some surprise that he nonetheless
managed in a very short time to achieve what his more illustrious relation could not. Miss Oversham blossomed under his
tutelage into a dancer of remarkable grace and skill, and
Clarice, pride swelling her maternal bosom, could not forbear
boasting just a little to Lady Louisa. The news that her granddaughter would not after all disgrace the Oversham name with
clumsiness on the dance floor did not produce the hoped-for
congratulations; in fact, her ladyship went so far as to remark
that any skill which Frederick possessed in a greater degree
than Sir Oliver was manifestly not worth having, which
caused Clarice such an unusual spasm of irritation that she had
to flee her ladyship's presence rather than give vent to some
utterance for which she would afterward be sorry. Frederick's
triumph also caused conflicting emotions in Miss Ponsonby's
breast: while she could not be unhappy with anything which
drew Frederick and Georgiana together, she nevertheless
found it difficult to rejoice in the latter's acquisition of a skill
in which she knew herself to excel, and whose absence must
cause her to be an object of scorn to Sir Oliver.

To Georgiana's considerable disappointment, Sir Oliver
was not immediately privy to the discovery that he had been
bested by the unwilling Frederick. He left immediately for
some business on his own estates, which would coincide with
the timing of her shopping visit to London, so she had to content herself with imagining, with unbecoming relish, what
must be his ultimate chagrin.

Chapter 8

GEORGIANA'S FIRST VIEW of London, even in such company as that of Clarice and Amabel, who had graciously consented to accompany her on her shopping expedition, did not disappoint her. Sir Oliver, who had implicit charge of his cousin's transformation into a girl of undoubted à la modality, had directed Clarice to take Georgiana to Madame Lachatte's, one of the city's most renowned modistes. Once she had passed through its venerable portals into a showroom furnished in the French style with gilded chairs, deep carpeting, and a complex maze of mirrors not inappropriate to the Roi-Soleil himself, she had to admit to a moment of misgiving. Not all the wealth in Yorkshire could command such fashions, and Georgiana, while reasonably sure of her own taste at home, could not be so confident of her ability to select in such a milieu. Moreover, while her fortune was more than adequate to meet any staggering sum shopping in such surroundings would almost certainly require, she foresaw some difficulty with the bills. Her grandmother, on the one hand, and Sir Oliver, on the other, were determined to meet her expenses, each from a different motive, and she was equally determined that they should not. However, an immediate insistence upon meeting them herself would inevitably necessitate a confession of her true circumstances, and she was not willing to unmask herself yet.

She sighed and supposed she would have to reimburse Sir Oliver when she revealed that she had been hoaxing him all along. She had no doubt that he would wrest the bills from her grandmother, because he would not wish her ladyship to meet the expenses of an impostor in her house. It was clear that his conscience was at least partly functional, and if Georgiana still

wondered why he did not scruple to play such a trick as he had
suggested on his unwitting family, now that she had met them
her sympathies were not so readily engaged on their behalf.
She clearly perceived that each of them (with the exception of
Frederick, whose wits would not take him so far) was bent on
using her for his or her own purposes in an equation into
which affection was absent altogether. She wished them well,
particularly her grandmother, but when she returned to Yorkshire it would not be with any grief that the connection had
been so long severed, or that it would be so unlikely ever to be
renewed.

Meanwhile, there were still Madame's delectable fashions,
and the delights of selecting among such wonders as pearl
rosettes, spider gauze, silver fringes, or French bead edges.
There were dresses for every occasion—flounced, ruffled,
braided, adorned with lace—and in every material. Even Miss
Ponsonby, who had hitherto confined her remarks to commonplaces and unyielding strictures on what must not be done,
said, or worn in London if one is to maintain one's ton,
thawed a little and allowed herself to be talked into the purchase of an amber-colored Berlin silk, with the happy result
that the three ladies passed a reasonably agreeable afternoon
under Madame's expert guidance. Georgiana, surveying herself in a rose pink gauze ball dress, felt that she had shed her
old self entirely, and the completion of the expedition with the
purchase of a number of walking dresses, a round dress, a riding habit, a sea green robe of lace and satin, and a number of
scarves, reticules, bonnets, gloves, and other incidentals, made
her feel quite the equal of anything Sir Oliver should propose.

The Oversham mansion in Berkeley Square was handsome
and well furnished in a rather old-fashioned style which Lady
Louisa refused to alter by so much as a throw rug, partly because she begrudged the expense and upkeep of a house which
afforded her no pleasure, and partly because her notions of
style had been forever frozen some decades earlier, after
which she had ceased to notice or care. It was a house in
which the pernicious French Influence had never set an inva-
sive foot, nor any of the graceful styles of Sheraton and his
school. Indeed, His Majesty King Henry, the eighth of that

name, might not have felt unduly out of place amid Lady
Louisa's rather heavy and baronial couches and tables. Georgiana, who knew that Axminster carpets, guilded scroll ends,
and delicate blue wallpaper were the first style of elegance,
nevertheless had to admire her grandmother for clinging so
stubbornly to her own notion of the appropriate. When Sir
Oliver married, his wife would no doubt sweep away every
trace of her ladyship's massive furnishings, and Georgiana
was surprised to discover that she could not contemplate this
prospect without at least a mild pang of regret.

The future Lady Townsend, whoever she might be, might
look forward to the renovation of the mansion, but it was
Clarice who had the ordering of it now. The preparations for
the family's arrival in some two week's time and for the ball
that was to mark Georgiana's debut in London Society required numerous consultations with the butler, the housekeeper, and various other members of the household staff, as
well as the assorted tradesmen and shopkeepers who would
furnish what was necessary to the comfort of the family and
the elegance of the affair. Georgiana, who had been used to
thinking of Clarice as somewhat ineffectual and a victim of
Lady Louisa's whims and caprices, now saw her in her ele-
ment, a general officer of whom even the great Wellington
might have approved. It was, she reflected, a pity that Clarice
did not have a household of her own to manage, with an indul-
gent, and perhaps elderly, husband with a great deal of money
and no burdensome relatives to cavil at her exorbitant expenditures.

Since Clarice's unexpected competence in arranging domestic matters left her little to do, Georgiana was free to spend
an afternoon or two discovering the delights of London out of
season. These, Clarice assured her, did not exist, but the books
at Hatchard's, the elegant shops of the fashionable quarter, and
such touristic delights as the museums or the Tower kept her
highly entertained and in a state of sustained excitement for
the duration of her brief visit. This accomplishment was by no
means so effortless as it might be supposed, since she was accompanied on these excursions not only by a maid and footman, but by Miss Ponsonby as well. Cousin Amabel's

conversation was chiefly of a didactic nature, and she was pleased to impart to her less knowledgeable companion such pieces of information as she considered essential for survival on the London social scene. Georgiana must not, under any circumstances, be seen driving or walking down St. James Street, where all the men's clubs were; she must not fail to be seen in Hyde Park between the hours of five and six in the afternoon; she must show a proper humility should she chance to meet any one of the Patronesses of Almack's, but particularly Mrs. Drummond-Burrell; she must depress the pretensions of anyone not her own (or Miss Ponsonby's) social equal who attempted to address her with unwonted familiarity. Had Georgiana not been made of sterner stuff, she would have been in a quake over these strictures, lest she fall unknowingly into error, a state Miss Ponsonby let her know that she not only expected, but felt herself obliged to point out whenever it might occur. "For you know, Cousin Georgiana, whatever we say and do reflects on Sir Oliver and the family, and I hope I do not presume too much if I say that I am sure he would wish me to venture a tiny hint to you from time to time if you are at a loss as to how to conduct yourself. My sister, I know, will gladly do the same. I am sure our London ways are quite different from your Yorkshire ones. The rules are very strict, and must not be contravened by a hairsbreadth!"

"How terrifying," remarked Georgiana, whose attention had been wandering a bit during this discussion. It was suddenly arrested again by the sight of a familiar face coming toward them on the street. Mr. Utterby raised his hat and bowed to them, and favored Georgiana with a sardonic smile. "Miss Ponsonby, Miss Oversham," he said, giving Georgiana's name a slight stress she could not like, "what a delightful surprise to see you up in town so early. I had quite succumbed to a fit of the dismals, because London is so very thin of company. Won't you allow me to accompany you to your destination?"

"We have been shopping," said Miss Ponsonby with majestic calm. "You have made Miss Oversham's acquaintance, then? I was just about to present you."

"Oh, Miss Oversham and I are quite well known to each other," he replied without offering further explanation. Georgiana thought it was most unfair of him, because she knew Miss Ponsonby would question her when he had gone, and he might just as easily have pretended not to know her. She saw him watching her out of the corner of his eye, and realized that he had actually intended to put her out of countenance. The result was that she put up her chin and said blightingly, "Oh yes, of course, sir; I did not recognize you at first. Cousin Amabel, I made Mr. Utterby's acquaintance at Lady Lonsdale's when Cousin Oliver conducted me there. How do you do?"

Georgiana thought she had rather neatly conveyed that the intimacy he had suggested showed a slightly encroaching manner on his part and was not surprised when he bowed again, acknowledging the hit. "Very well, thank you," he said with a dry smile. "I have been attending the theater lately and have chanced to discover a remarkable new actress. Her name is Cecilia Leroux, and she is something quite out of the ordinary. Perhaps when Sir Oliver returns to town we can make up a theater party?"

Miss Ponsonby, who was not at all sure that the theater would be a proper excursion for a young lady of excellent ton but was unwilling to offend an acknowledged friend of Sir Oliver's, murmured something scarcely intelligible about her gratitude for his suggestion, combined with the rather plainer comment that she was not certain what dear Lady Louisa's plans would be during the family's sojourn in London.

Georgiana thought she must have imagined the slightly sinister note directed at herself in this invitation, for though he had impressed her as a cynical and rather sarcastic man, there had not been anything in his earlier manner to her that had given her pause. She decided he was merely teasing her by bringing up Cecilia's name, and was just about to make further inquiry about Cecilia's progress as an actress when he turned to her and said: "Miss Oversham, Miss Ponsonby, I had meant to accompany you, but I have just been put in mind of a prior appointment. Running into you has made me quite lose track of my obligations, but I fear in this case I dare not give in to my wishes. How long do you stay in London?"

"We return to Pemberton tomorrow afternoon and will remain there until we come back for the Season," said Miss Ponsonby.

"Then perhaps, with your permission, I shall call on you and Lady Oversham tomorrow morning before you leave."

"I shall be out," said Miss Ponsonby definitively. "No doubt my sister and Lady Louisa will be very happy to receive you when we come up to town again."

He bowed again and left them. "You do not like him?" asked Georgiana curiously.

Miss Ponsonby looked somewhat taken aback at this suggestion. "He is a friend of Sir Oliver's," she said.

"Forgive me. I thought you meant to discourage him from calling."

"I would certainly never presume to discourage any friend of your cousin's from calling on my sister and displaying those courtesies owing to one who is acting as the family's hostess. But I do not wish to encourage any closer relationship, because, although Mr. Utterby is very good ton, I do not think Lady Louisa would approve of admitting him onto terms of intimacy with the family. There have been unsavory stories about him from time to time, which of course I will not repeat, and I believe he is quite heavily in debt. In your position you cannot afford to be seen overmuch in such company."

"In *my position*?" inquired Georgiana in a tone which would have given pause to a person possessed of less self-confidence than Miss Ponsonby.

"You are a stranger to London society," explained Miss Ponsonby kindly. "Your . . . connections in Yorkshire and your large fortune will place your every action under such scrutiny as those whose characters are sufficiently well established will not have to endure."

"A character such as yours, for example?"

"Why yes, I hope I may say so," she replied with assurance. "My dear Cousin Georgiana, you will not take it amiss, I know, if I tell you that my family's name is a very old one, and sometimes that gives one advantages. It may be unfair, but I may sometimes do with impunity what others do not dare."

"Such as receive Mr. Utterby."

"If I chose," said Miss Ponsonby complacently, "but I do

not choose, for the reasons I have already indicated." She flashed white teeth at Georgiana. "You are still a bit at sea, naturally, but do not let it trouble you. Lady Louisa's name will afford you protection, and I will be happy to guide you whenever possible. Indeed, I feel it is my duty to your grandmother to do so. And Sir Oliver—" she broke off suddenly, as if she had repented of what she was about to say.

"And Sir Oliver?" prompted Georgiana, barely suppressing her anger.

"You are offended," remarked Miss Ponsonby with apparent surprise. "I have said too much."

"I should like to know whether my cousin has chosen to complain of my conduct to you."

"Oh no," replied Miss Ponsonby innocently, "it would be most improper of him to do so. You must not take offense at what must be a natural concern of his. He merely remarked to Clarice that he was not sure you would know how to conduct yourself in accordance with your station, and that she was to give you any assistance possible. And of course we are only too happy to oblige."

"Of course," replied Georgiana bitterly.

After his dismissal at the hands of her cousin Amabel, Georgiana had no expectation of seeing Mr. Utterby before their return to Pemberton, so it was with some surprise that she encountered him the next morning on her way home from the library. She had been unable to resist a book of Byron's poetry she had seen there two days before and had read it quickly enough to return it before her trip home. She almost ran into him coming out of the door, and she had the sudden, rather disturbing feeling that he was waiting for her. She was not too much concerned, as her maid was with her, but she did not like the intensity with which his eyes regarded her.

He took his hat off to her. "Miss Oversham! How delightful to run into you once more! May I be permitted to take advantage of my good fortune and walk a little way with you? It might be some time before we meet again."

Georgiana, scenting a perplexing and somewhat uncomfortable undertone beneath the banter, was just about to put him off when she recollected that a report of their meeting would be almost certain to annoy Miss Ponsonby. She halted and said graciously, "That would be most kind. Indeed, I myself did not expect to meet any of our friends again, as we journey back to Pemberton tomorrow."

"I waited for you to come out," he said quietly, leaning close to her ear. "In a moment or two you must send your maid on an errand, so I may have a few moments of speech with you. It concerns Sir Oliver!"

She could not fail to do as he asked, as his voice held a note of urgency she had not previously heard him use. She began to imagine that something evil had befallen her cousin, though she did not think he would wish to impart such news on the street. In a few minutes she said, "Betty, I fear I have left my shawl at the library. Perhaps it slipped from my shoulders while I was looking at the books."

"Oh no, miss," replied the diligent Betty, "I am quite sure you did not have it with you today."

"I am certain I remember having it over my arm," insisted Georgiana a trifle guiltily. "Do run back and check, please, while Mr. Utterby accompanies me home. I do not like to ask it, but there will be no time to retrieve it later, and it is my favorite."

"Yes, miss," agreed a dubious Betty. When she had gone, Georgiana turned to Mr. Utterby inquiringly. "Is there something wrong?"

"You look very fine, Miss Oversham," he said in a slightly mocking tone of voice. "I fear it is safe to say few would recognize the Yorkshire governess now."

"Lady Louisa has been very generous," she agreed a bit impatiently, "but what—?"

"Yes, with her *granddaughter*," he said, giving the word a sarcastic emphasis which made Georgiana wish she had not agreed to see him alone. "I wonder what she would say if she knew the truth about who you really are."

"Mr. Utterby, what is that to the purpose?" she asked him. "The bet has been entered into, and surely it is too late for second thoughts now!"

"That is where I find I must disagree with you," he said

smoothly, taking her arm to help her into the flagway. "I am prepared to pay you a very handsome sum if you will withdraw from this ridiculous charade altogether and return to Yorkshire, or wherever it was you came from."

She smiled at him, certain he must be joking. "You cannot be serious."

He did not smile in return. "I was never more so, I do assure you. I am prepared to give you a check drawn upon my bank this very day, if that is convenient."

She looked at him searchingly. "Are you so afraid you will lose the bet?"

"I must own that I thought it an impossible task, until I encountered you and Miss Ponsonby on the street. You seem quite the genuine article, Miss Bucklebury, and if I were to allow Sir Oliver to do so, it is not outside the range of possibility that he really could elevate you to the very highest ranks of the ton without detection."

"How very flattering," said Georgiana. "You do not, I collect, mean to allow him to make the attempt."

He shook his head. "No, I do not."

"May I ask how you intend to stop him?"

He gave her a steady, penetrating look. "I do not need to stop *him* at all. It is you I mean to stop. Will you accept my offer?"

"Of money in exchange for my disappearance? I think not."

"That is very unwise."

"Perhaps. Mr. Utterby, forgive me, but surely it is not merely the fear of losing your horses that has provoked you to make such an ungentlemanly suggestion?"

"How very astute you are," he said with a slight sneer. The skin on his neck tightened. "My chestnuts are pledged," he said quietly. "They are no longer mine to surrender if I lose. In fact, a great deal of what I used to have is no longer mine," he added bitterly.

"Then why do you not tell Sir Oliver so at once?" she suggested. "I am sure he has more than once regretted the impulse that prompted him to accept the challenge. Tell him, and we might all go back to being comfortable!"

"And make myself the laughingstock of London? Put myself in Oliver's debt for the rest of my days? You cannot be serious!"

"You prefer to bribe or perhaps blackmail me?" she inquired.

"You, my dear Miss Bucklebury-Oversham, are expendable. My good name is not." He looked at her strangely. "Would you really withdraw without a fuss if Oliver and I canceled the bet?"

"As soon as I could do so without hurting Lady Louisa—why yes, of course."

"What a very odd girl you are. Do you know, I have never quite believed you were merely a governess, and a rector's sister at that. There is an air about you of something more—or less—than the rectory and the country."

Georgiana started. "What are you suggesting, Mr. Utterby?" she asked him calmly.

He smiled at her in a way she could not like. "That you are hiding something, Miss Bucklebury. Your self-assurance is almost sinister under the circumstances, and I can't help feeling that somewhere in your past is a very dark secret."

"I think you will discover that I am exactly what I say," said Georgiana steadily.

"Perhaps. But I mean to discover the truth about you, and whatever it is, I will use it if I have to to prevent Oliver from winning the bet. So you see it will be very much more comfortable for you to accept my first offer."

They had, by this time, come up to the front door of the mansion in Berkeley Square.

"There is really no need for that, you know," she said in a quiet tone. "There is every possibility that you may win the bet without resorting to such tactics."

He bowed over her hand, which she almost snatched away from him till she remembered she could be seen by the footman. "Ah," he told her, "but you see, recent, bitter experience has taught me that it is not safe to leave anything to chance. Good day to you. My compliments to your grandmother and Mrs. Oversham," he called after her, and his mocking laugh rang out over the square.

* * *

The trip back to Pemberton was accomplished in an atmosphere of unnatural silence. Clarice had succumbed to a severe headache, an affliction which occasionally struck her down after a period of particular animation and gaiety, and could only manage to bathe her temples in vinegar water and moan delicately whenever the carriage hit a jolt in the road. Amabel, prevented by her sister's indisposition from delivering the lecture she had formulated on the inadvisability of being seen on the streets of London unattended by either a maid or a footman and in the company of someone she had only recently issued a warning against, likewise lapsed into sullen silence. Georgiana, her mind full of her meeting with Mr. Utterby, made only a polite attempt or two at conversation, and that was when, as they approached the neighborhood of Pemberton, she ventured to inquire into the ownership of some of the large and rather formidable mansions she could glimpse from the road.

Miss Ponsonby replied rather peevishly that those were Whig estates, and that therefore the Overshams did not stand on terms with their neighbors. Georgiana, to whom politics was a bit of a mystery, did not quite see the connection. Clarice roused herself from her cushions a bit to explain it to her. "They support Princess Caroline," she said thinly, "and dear Father Oversham was part of the Prince's set. It simply wouldn't *do*."

Georgiana was amused to think that the disastrous royal marriage could affect neighborhood relations to such an extent, however fractious and bitter the famous litigants. Clarice, apparently convinced that she had clarified matters to everyone's satisfaction, settled back against the pillows again with a sigh, and the carriage rolled on in the quiet afternoon to Pemberton.

Chapter 9

SPRING CAME AT LAST to Pemberton, and the household, restive after such late and heavy snowfalls, turned out-of-doors to welcome it. It would be some time before the leaves were out on the trees, but the weather turned unexpectedly mild, and Clarice proposed an expedition to Barton Abbey, which she promised would provide a suitably picturesque setting for a family picnic. Lady Louisa flatly refused to stir from the comfort of her hearth, saying she would soon enough be forced by her own generous nature to make the arduous journey up to town and needed to recruit all her strength for that undertaking; she would leave the hazardous trip to Barton to those whose less obliging natures left them the leisure for such an enterprise. Since the abbey was no more than three or four miles distant, it was not immediately apparent what the hazards of such a journey might be, although in this case her ladyship was undoubtedly, if accidentally, prescient.

As Sir Oliver had not yet returned from his own estates, Miss Ponsonby's enthusiasm for the project was also somewhat tepid, and she more than once suggested that it was no doubt a bit damp for picnics, and that one or the other of them was almost certain to take a chill. Clarice, however, was anxious to promote a scheme that would throw Frederick and Georgiana together in a setting that did not include Sir Oliver's distracting presence, and she delicately overrode such objections as immaterial, if not poor-spirited.

Frederick did not register any notable degree of either disapproval or delight until a happy thought occurred to him. "I know!" he declared with sudden inspiration. "Take Burdick!"

Miss Ponsonby shivered with distaste. "Clarice, I promise you I will not set one foot out the door if that cat is to accompany us. You know I particularly detest them—horrid, sly creatures!"

"Yes, you know, my love, that cats are not lapdogs, to go everywhere with one!" Clarice reminded her son. "I daresay he would be quite uncomfortable, and then he would start to wail, and there is no telling how it would end."

"Wouldn't wail," insisted Frederick stubbornly. "Likes to get about. Enjoys himself."

"But in any case," persisted his mama a trifle desperately, "you must be our guide and conduct us over the abbey grounds, so there will be no time to attend to a pet. Cousin Georgiana, who has not seen any of our local scenery, will need you to explain some of our local sights and customs. And I am quite sure you would not wish to fail in any little duty or attention to our cousin," she concluded archly.

Georgiana, who was saved from an agony of embarrassment over this suggestion by the fact that Frederick obviously had not attended to it in the least, murmured that she would be happy to fit in with everyone else's plans, whatever they were. It was decided that the young people should ride, a form of exercise in which Clarice knew her son would show to advantage, and that a carriage would follow with herself and the picnic implements and supplies. If the weather should suddenly turn foul, they would thus have a conveyance to conduct them home, and the day of the excursion was fixed for the next sunlit morning.

Georgiana, who was still used to country hours, was surprised to find herself the first down to breakfast by at least an hour. Returning downstairs sometime later after completing her toilet and fidgeting about her room for a considerable period of time, she found the family just getting up from the table and by no means ready to set out. So it was that, a full two hours later than the appointed time, the excursion finally got under way.

A competent rider who had been in the saddle since she was three years old, Georgiana was dismayed to see that she had been given what her uncle Henry might have called a "straight-shouldered cocktail" whose gait and pace made for a most uneven ride. Since Amabel and Frederick were both well mounted, she suspected that Miss Ponsonby had had a hand in choosing her hack. Frederick, who was as kind as he was distracted, would not have selected such a poor creature for her; his empathy with animals obviously extended to horses, and he rode with the natural style and grace of a born horseman. When Amabel asked her smoothly if she would be quite comfortable putting her horse at a hedge so that they could cut a corner, she felt certain she had guessed right.

Georgiana, perceiving her duty readily enough, made every effort to converse with Frederick as they rode along. This was conducted in a rather unnerving fashion, in which she put a question to Frederick about some aspect or other of the passing landscape, he responded in a pleasant but inarticulate manner, and Miss Ponsonby proceeded to correct whatever he said. Georgiana was grateful when a narrowing of the track made it impossible for them to continue to ride three abreast and she had leisure to enjoy an unedited version of a morning's ride in early spring.

The abbey ruins were extensive and just coming out with spring wildflowers. The whole now belonged to the estate of Lord Eddington, who graciously allowed his neighbors access to his park, only fencing off his wood and some of the more dilapidated areas, such as the crypt, where, he ventured, the unwary visitor might come to harm. The family party, though not a success in terms of the true compatibility of its members, nevertheless passed off with all the civility and amiability which might reasonably be expected of a group of persons determined, if not to enjoy themselves, at the very least to preserve an outward appearance of harmony and good spirits.

The very good lunch Pemberton's cook had prepared for them acted as a further tonic even to Miss Ponsonby's rather stifling presence, so that when Georgiana spied a large basket stowed next to the picnic supplies in the carriage apparently begin to move of its own accord she was careful to say nothing to spoil the day. If Frederick wanted to risk incurring the wrath of his mother and aunt by bringing along his cat on the outing, she would not be the one to cast a spoke in his wheel.

When the lunch had been consumed, Clarice announced that her ankle, which she had twisted some weeks before while descending the stairs, was paining her a little, and that she would rest on the blanket while the others explored on foot. Miss Ponsonby, in response to a sisterly nudge, said rather sourly that she herself would prefer a quiet hour with her book to a walk, but she did not feel there could be the slightest objection to Frederick's conducting Cousin Georgiana on a further tour of the grounds, although she was rather inclined to believe that before the afternoon was out it might rain again. The distant clouds having been banished as a present threat, it was agreed by all that Georgiana and Frederick should set out through the wood, while Clarice and Amabel remained behind with the carriage.

Georgiana, who had caught Frederick more than once casting anxious glances at the basket in the back of the carriage, said suddenly, "Do you bring that basket, Cousin Frederick, and let us see if we can find any berries."

Frederick's look turned to one of gratitude when she smiled reassuringly at him. Miss Ponsonby regarded her a trifle blankly and said, "I fear it will be a great deal too early for berries, so it will be quite useless for you to try."

"Then I shall collect . . . specimens!" replied Georgiana, undaunted. "I am very interested in nature, you know, and I should like to compare the woods here to those of Yorkshire. One can learn a great deal from samples of shrubs and trees."

"Really?" inquired Miss Ponsonby. "I am sure it must be very diverting for those who have that inclination."

"I assure you," replied Georgiana mendaciously.

"Knew you were a right 'un, Cousin Georgiana," commented Frederick when they had passed out of earshot. "Aunt Amabel would be in a terrible pucker if she knew. Can't abide cats," he added unnecessarily.

"Well, you were taking a terrible chance," said Georgiana. "The basket was *shaking*. Are you going to let him out?"

"Over near the crypt," said Frederick. "There's an opening in the gate. Likes to chase mice."

Georgiana, who thought that squeezing through her neighbor's gate in order to visit a rat-infested crypt was an experience she could not but regard with a certain distaste, nonetheless held her tongue when she saw the look of determined pleasure on her companion's face. She thought how much better it might have been for Freddy if he had been born into a family of either greater affluence or lower expectations, so that he might follow his own simple inclinations with fewer obstacles to his enjoyment.

Burdick did not greet his release from captivity with an excess of good temper. His response, though voluble, was indicative of a rather peevish reaction to his prolonged incarceration, and the somewhat militant posture of his tail and ears suggested an unforgiving character. Presently a butterfly appeared to distract his attention from the litany of his grievances, with the result that he soon disappeared into the wood in search of more agreeable pursuits.

"Oh dear," cried Georgiana. "Should we go after him?"

"Come back," commented Freddy with assurance. "Always does."

"Do you come here often, then?" she inquired.

He glanced up at the splendid, soaring skeleton of the abbey. "Often as I can," he said simply.

Something about his statement suggested a new possibility to her. "Freddy, do you—is it the church? Is that what you wish to do?"

He shook his head sadly. "Haven't the brains for it. No use saying otherwise, because haven't got 'em." He looked at her. "Everyone says so."

Georgiana could not refute this contention, but she said soothingly, "Well, but you would not wish to be Archbishop of Canterbury, would you? One need not be so very . . . scholarly if one had the living at a quiet country church." She thought that a country curate's position, always subordinate to and supervised by another clergyman, might be just the thing for him. In fact, he might prove a very valuable assistant to Rector Bucklebury, who would doubtless find his quiet amiability a welcome alternative to Amelia's rather more wearing presence. She was just beginning to scheme when Frederick brought her up short.

"Wouldn't do," he said glumly. "Break Mama's heart. She's set on my marrying some heiress." He looked up at her in surprise. "Think it was you, Cousin Georgiana."

Georgiana smiled at him kindly. "You need not let that weigh with you, you know."

"Don't know Mama. And Aunt Amabel's just as bad. Always going on about debts and the ton! Said you're very plump in the pocket, and that I must make an offer for you. No help for it."

"Then, if you wish, Freddy," said Georgiana gently, "you may tell your mama that you offered for me and I refused."

"But I haven't!"

Georgiana was forced to admit that Frederick's family's exasperation with him was not entirely unjustified. "Well if you *were* so obliging as to make me an offer, I should refuse, so that is almost the same."

"It is?" he asked hopefully.

"Yes," Georgiana assured him. "You do not wish to marry me, and I do not wish to marry you, so now we may be comfortable again as friends."

Frederick's momentary optimism faded. "No use," he muttered disconsolately. "Bound to say I made a muff of it. Wasn't supposed to cram the fences. Get to know you, Mama said. Point out the advantages of a title."

Georgiana could scarcely refrain from patting his hand consolingly. "Then perhaps it would be best if we did not mention it just yet. But when the time comes, you may say that you expressed yourself with great eloquence and did everything just as you ought, but that I was persuaded we should not suit."

"There's the ticket," said Frederick, relieved that the ordeal was to be postponed, "but ten to one I shan't remember a word of it."

"I'll remind you," said Georgiana firmly.

"You're a good sort of girl, Cousin Georgiana," said Freddy admiringly. "Shan't forget it!"

Georgiana, who had read a great many novels, wondered if

there had ever been a heroine with so many men going to such lengths *not* to marry her. It was a dreadfully lowering thought but not without its humorous aspects. Sir Oliver could fend for himself, but she was determined to shield this kind innocent from the wrath of his mother and Miss Ponsonby. She wondered if she might find a way to assist him in achieving his other more lofty ambition, and she decided to speak to the rector as soon as she returned to Yorkshire. Her own fortune could easily support his living, if need be.

They had now been some time absent, and the unmistakable signs of impending rain had moved closer overhead. "Do you not think, Cousin Freddy, that we should make a push to find out where Burdick has gone? I fear it will rain soon, and your mama and Cousin Amabel will be wanting to return as soon as may be."

"Have to look for him," remarked Freddy succinctly.

"Could you not call him?"

Freddy was scornful of such open ignorance of the ways of cats. He shook his head. "Wouldn't come."

Georgiana sighed. "Well, then perhaps we should begin to search at once. I think I might have felt the first drop, and it would be quite unconscionable to keep your mother and aunt waiting should there be a storm. Where do you think we should start?"

Freddy looked about him with surmise. "Crypt," he said finally.

Georgiana could not but deplore such a low-minded preference for the Gothic and preferred not to imagine what Burdick might find there to amuse him. She shuddered a little.

"You need not come, if you don't want to. Find him myself," offered Freddy kindly.

She lifted her skirts with determination. "Lead on," she said firmly.

The entrance to the crypt was through a side door, barred by a heavy gate. The upper entrance had long ago fallen in, and the precaution Lord Eddington's father had taken of erecting a barrier to casual trespassers suggested that there was little reason for an excess of confidence regarding the stability of the remaining structure. The gate was rusted, however, and the lock had long since succumbed to the elements, so that its function was more symbolic than actual.

"Here, kitty, kitty," called Georgiana without much hope of a reply.

A distant rustle, which Georgiana found forcibly reminiscent of the passage of reptilian bodies over stone, sounded deep within, followed by the clatter of falling rock, and, distinctly, a terrified meow. At that precise moment, a flash of lightning split the skies, and the rain began to fall in buckets.

"Have to go in," said Freddy, already halfway descended into the darkness. "Sounded like Burdick!"

Georgiana, after quickly assessing the alternatives, found herself inclined to agree with this suggestion. There was no other adequate shelter, and if the animal was hurt or trapped he would have to be rescued. Miss Ponsonby's aversion to cats, however, just at the moment seemed a trifle less unreasonable.

It was quite gloomy in the crypt, which appeared to have been used as a chapel as well as a burial chamber, and the floor was littered with crumbled masonry so that they had to pick their way carefully as they proceeded. Georgiana resolutely ignored the occasional squeak and scurrying which indicated definitely that they were not the chamber's only live occupants. Of the other sort of occupant there was far too much evidence for perfect comfort, and Georgiana, who in general found above-ground cemeteries rather peaceful and not at all unpleasant, had to give herself a stern set-down for being so fainthearted.

At length they came to a section of crumbled wall which appeared to have tumbled down quite recently. In fact, Georgiana thought she could still taste the dust in the air. From behind this barrier suddenly issued a wail of such a hair-raising nature and dimension that persons of more superstitious sensibilities might have been forgiven for supposing it to issue from some outraged being on the wrong side of mortal existence.

The outrage, in any case, was quite real. Frederick peered into the dim recesses through a gap in the fallen masonry, and the howls increased exponentially. "Steady on, old chap. Soon have you out."

Burdick's reply to this was not indicative of confidence in a comfortable outcome.

Another flash of lightning, quite close, illuminated the crypt with sudden, dazzling clarity. She could see Freddy's face, strained, anxious, and streaked with dirt, outlined in stark clarity. She laid a hand on his arm. "I'm sure he hasn't been seriously injured, or he . . . he couldn't keep making that noise, surely?" she suggested. "Oughtn't we try to dig him out?"

He moved a few stones tentatively, and the pile shifted ominously. "Don't dare," said Freddy with a worried look. "Might collapse altogether."

Georgiana gave a hurried look at the roof, thought better of it, and resolutely lowered her gaze. "We'll have to get help, then. Oh, why won't it stop raining? Clarice and Amabel will be desperately worried, not to mention dreadfully uncomfortable, and I don't think they will be very pleased to learn we will require the groom's services to help dig out the cat."

Freddy, who had his arm thrust through a gap in the wall, was not attending her. "Can feel him," he said excitedly. "Mad as fire! Hair's all on end. Just hang on, there's the dandy. Ouch!"

The wall moved. "Freddy—be careful. It's—"

The ancient masonry gave way even as she spoke. The wall crumbled, collapsed, and pinned Freddy's arm beneath a mammoth pile of rubble. From the other side of the pile there was complete silence.

Chapter 10

"CAN'T MOVE MY ARM," Freddy told her after a few heartbeats of stricken silence. "Think it's broken."

"Oh, Freddy," she said, attempting without success to dislodge the large chunk of wall that had come to rest across his outstretched arm, "I can't move these bricks. Now we are in the basket!"

"Shouldn't say that," said Freddy seriously. "Lady Louisa wouldn't like it." He paused. "Don't hear Burdick."

"I did," said Georgiana mendaciously. "Just after the wall fell. I'm sure he's all right."

"Mad as fire," suggested Freddy, repeating his earlier assertion.

"Well, he has only himself to blame, leading us into this dreadful place," said Georgiana, attempting to distract him from what she knew must be the painful process of removing as much as possible of the debris around his arm. "Doubtless he was after a snake or some such delightful thing." She looked at him closely. "There, I hope you may be a little easier now. I must leave you, and go get help."

"Rain," suggested Freddy faintly.

"Oh I believe it has quite stopped by now," said Georgiana in what she hoped was a cheerful tone. "Besides, it does not signify. We must get you—and Burdick—out as soon as may be. It would be so shocking if you were to catch a cold as well as break your arm."

Frederick gave a sickly chuckle. "Knew you were a right 'un, Cousin Georgiana."

*   *   *

Despite her optimistic weather prediction to the entombed Lord Nugent, Georgiana was drenched to the skin almost from the moment she left the shelter of the crypt. She would have endured with grateful pleasure a storm worthy of *The Tempest* in exchange for the privilege of quitting what had rapidly become a thoroughly loathsome place, but the driving rain pelting her face and the sodden state of her riding habit made it difficult to see and generally hampered her progress. She tore her skirt rather audibly on the gate, but she did not pause to inspect the damage. Her best hope was in retracing the most direct route back to where they had left Clarice, Amabel, and the carriage, and she concentrated all her attention on recognizing the landmarks they had passed.

At length, chilled and exhausted, she came out into the clearing where she had last seen the rest of her party. She stopped and looked around her in confusion.

The clearing was empty.

At first she thought she must have mistaken her way, and the suggestion drove her quite wild with frustration and anxiety. But no; there was the road, and there was the unmistakable sign that the carriage had stood there awhile. She could not believe that Mrs. Oversham and Miss Ponsonby would have left them there, however acute their degree of discomfort and inconvenience, and she began to fear some dreadful accident.

"Clarice!" she called, trying to make herself heard over the storm. "Amabel!"

A few minutes of such activity convinced her of its futility, and she tried to set aside her misery and indignation to decide how she had best proceed. She was unfamiliar with the neighborhood and did not know whether the nearest residence was one mile away or four, or in what direction. The road they had traveled from Pemberton had been sparsely populated, and she did not remember a house much closer than Pemberton itself. On the other hand, she could not say what might lie ahead on the road, of help or hindrance. She was peering anxiously in both directions, trying to decide whether to stand her ground and wait for the inevitable return of the carriage, go back to the crypt with Freddy, or take her chances on the road, when she saw, or thought she saw, someone riding hard down the road toward her.

She dashed the water from her eyes and stepped out into the roadway, waving her arms.

Evidently he had not seen her. The horse shied, and the rider uttered a strangled oath, reining in the animal expertly until it regained its footing and came to a halt. Then he dismounted and stepped over to where she stood. "Good God, you little fool! Whatever possessed you to do a thing like that? You could have been killed!"

Georgiana, however, heard none of these accusations. She burst into tears, and unthinkingly threw herself into his arms. "Oh, C-Cousin Oliver!"

He let her sob for a few moments, patting her shoulder and gently calming her as one might a frightened child or an animal. She came to herself at last, disengaged herself with some embarrassment, and said damply: "I beg your pardon! I did no mean—it is only—"

"Yes, yes, my child; I can see that you have had a rather difficult time of it. I have brought an umbrella, but I rather think it is too late to spare either your person or your attire from a most pernicious wetting. You look even more discreditable than you did when you dragged in out of that snowstorm at Litchfield's hunting box."

She gave a watery chuckle. "I don't doubt it. I am so sorry to have startled your horse but—"

"You were in urgent need of assistance, I collect," he finished for her. "Where, by the by, is the redoubtable Frederick?"

"Trapped in the crypt. Cousin Oliver, you must come at once! A section of the wall collapsed on him and I'm afraid he has broken his arm."

"In the *crypt*?"

Even over the noise of the storm she could hear the note of amusement beneath his inquiry. "It sounds ridiculous, I know," she said, "but he was trying to rescue Burdick, because the wall had already collapsed on *him*, and I'm very much afraid he may be dead!"

"Good God! Freddy?"

"No! I mean, I fear it is Burdick who has been killed, and Freddy will be so upset!"

"Georgiana, am I to understand that there is—was—a third person in the crypt with you?"

"Not a person, no! Burdick! Freddy's cat!"

"Ah, now I perceive why the name is not unfamiliar. I must say that I am looking forward to hearing the complete version of this tale at another time, when there is more leisure to enjoy it. I really must go and liberate poor Freddy. Would you care to wait in the shelter of that tree until I return?"

"No, I would not," retorted Georgiana. "I am coming with you!"

"Clarice and Amabel promised to send out a search party as soon as they reached Pemberton," he suggested. "You will not have long to wait."

"How can you think I would leave Freddy there like that? You might need my help."

He looked at her intently, and, she thought, with surprise. "As you wish. I'll take you up on Jupiter as far as the gate, and we will go the rest of the way on foot."

When she had mounted in front of him, she had leisure to ask him the questions she had been burning to know the answers to since she had encountered him on the road. "Cousin Oliver, how came you to be here? I thought you were visiting your own estates! And where are Clarice and Amabel?"

"I arrived back at Pemberton to discover that you had all set out on a picnic," said his voice in her ear. "I did not think to follow you then, but when I was stabling Jupiter, the groom told me you had chosen Loki to ride. In general he is quite an unexceptionable sort of horse, if you care for that sort of plodding animal, but he is quite petrified of thunder. I daresay the groom forgot to tell you since it didn't look to storm."

Georgiana closed her lips on the statement that it was not she who had selected her mount. "Did you come to warn us then? That was kind."

"Soon after I set out the storm broke, and I feared you would have trouble. A mile or so down the road I met Loki racing madly cross country back to Pemberton, with Frederick's Traveler in close pursuit. Shortly thereafter I encountered Clarice and Amabel in the carriage, and they told me where to look for you."

"Did *their* horses bolt, too?" she could not forbear asking.

"When the storm broke, they returned to the clearing and found your horses gone," he said smoothly. "They thought you had returned to Pemberton, and their own team was anxious and restive as well. They thought it best to return home at once with the carriage and Amabel's mount and discover what had become of you."

Something in his tone told Georgiana he expected her to act as if she believed this story, so she murmured "of course," and remained silent until they reached the gate. But her mind was in turmoil, and she could not account for Clarice and Amabel's having so easily left them in the midst of a raging storm without making more of a push to discover their whereabouts. By the time they had returned to Pemberton and discovered that she and Freddy were still missing, the two of them would have been alone for hours in what was obviously a most uncomfortable storm. Georgiana was caught up short by the sudden suspicion that perhaps Clarice had *wanted* her to remain out alone with Freddy. It would be foolish to think that such an unfortunate accident would compromise her reputation enough to force him to marry her, but Georgiana knew that Freddy was susceptible to his mother's persuasions and not necessarily strong-minded enough to override her representations of his duty. Besides, she had lived in the small circle of neighborhood for long enough to realize how easy it would be in such circumstances to set tongues to wagging, and she began to think she had better be more wary of Clarice's plans to trap her into marriage with Freddy than she had realized.

The rain was letting up by the time they reached the entrance to the crypt again, but it still looked sodden and dark and distinctly uninviting.

Sir Oliver turned to her with a bemused smile. "Did you go in there?" he inquired. "I salute you."

Georgiana was surprised to realize that the prospect of entering the structure with Sir Oliver was far less terrifying than it had been the first time with Freddy. "Be careful," she told him as he prepared to step in ahead of her. "I fear it is not very stable."

He put a hand on her arm, momentarily barring her way. "Are you sure you will not wait outside?" he asked in a low, serious voice.

"Quite sure," she said firmly, lifting her chin with determination.

He gave her another of his strange, assessing looks, and entered the darkened chamber. It was very dim and silent. "Freddy?" she called softly.

Freddy was lying as she had left him, his face shadowed and strained with pain and anxiety. "Glad you've come," he told them in a faint voice. "Heard him move. Sure he's alive."

Sir Oliver, who was busy stripping off his damp coat, did not reply to this. He wrung it out and then rolled it up and placed it under Freddy's head. "Sorry, Freddy," he said at length, examining the pile of masonry on his arm. "I'm afraid this will hurt a bit. Wish I'd thought to bring some brandy."

"Burdick," began Freddy anxiously.

"All in good time, old fellow," said Sir Oliver soothingly, beginning to remove the heavy bricks and building material from atop Freddy's arm and shoulder, while Georgiana hovered beside him, eager to render whatever assistance she could. Freddy offered no complaint, but when Sir Oliver hefted the last formidable chunk and attempted to help him rise from the floor, he fainted.

"It's just as well," he said cheerfully, loosening Freddy's neckcloth, and, with the addition of his own, fashioning a makeshift sling into which he eased the victim's arm. "It looks to be just a small break, though I'm no doctor, but it will be better for him if he does not come to himself for a while. Can you manage to help me with him a little?"

"Y-yes, but—"

"But?" he inquired politely, lifting an imperial eyebrow.

"The cat . . ." Georgiana suggested helplessly.

Sir Oliver lifted a finger to his lips and shook his head at the pile of crumbled wall meaningfully.

"We can't just leave it there," whispered Georgiana urgently. "It would break Freddy's heart."

"You seem to have become rather well acquainted with Cousin Frederick in a short space of time," said Sir Oliver. "You saw what has already happened to the wall, and frankly I am a bit nervous about undertaking further excavations. In fact, I believe—"

A piteous moan, unearthly in its tone but unmistakable in its message, sounded from the other side of the rubble pile. "Oh, he *is* alive!" cried Georgiana joyfully.

Sir Oliver sighed. "Very well," he conceded. "But it is of the utmost importance that we remove Freddy from this—I trust you will admit—rather disagreeable place first, so that he does not sustain further injury. Try if you can help me to get him to stand."

Freddy came round again as they supported him on his feet. "Thanks, but needn't fuss," he said with an attempt at bravery. "Perfectly able to walk myself. Don't wish to be a nuisance."

"Remind me to ask you what you wish, if I should sometime wish to know," replied Sir Oliver. "Oblige me by leaning on Cousin Georgiana's arm while I assist you out of this accursed crypt."

Freddy grinned feebly. "Much obliged to you both."

Freddy's extraction from the crypt, though deliberate and undoubtedly painful, was accomplished in due course. The rain, fortunately, had stopped, and they were able to make him as comfortable as possible by propping him up against the trunk of a rather large oak tree. When he took note of his surroundings, Freddy was not in a jubilant mood. "Burdick's dead," he said morosely.

"No, no, he is not!" Georgiana assured him urgently, hoping it was true. "Cousin Oliver and I heard him cry while you were passed out."

Freddy's expression brightened momentarily and then faded into despair again. "Never get him out."

Georgiana glanced at Sir Oliver in mute appeal. "Nonsense," said Sir Oliver, resigned to his fate. "I was just going back to get him."

He was rewarded by the look of gratitude in two upturned faces. "I'll come with you," suggested Georgiana warmly.

"No, you most emphatically will not," said Sir Oliver

firmly. "If . . . an accident should occur, someone whole-bod-
ied must be left to advise Lady Louisa's carriage of our whereabouts."

Georgiana felt a pang of conscience. "Perhaps you should
not go in alone," she said worriedly.

He smiled at her and lifted her hand to his lips in a way that
made her heart pound in her ears. Then he went back into the
crypt.

The minutes seemed to lengthen interminably for the two
watchers beneath the oak, and Georgiana tried to distract
Freddy from the pain of his injury and his anxiety about his
cat with stories about her own childhood pets, to which she
was fairly sure he attended not at all. At length, when she
could barely stop herself from running back inside to have a
look, they heard a rumble, and the unmistakable clatter of
falling stones. Georgiana gave a sharp cry, leapt to her feet,
and ran toward the entrance, just as Sir Oliver, masonry dust
clinging to his face and shoulders, emerged. He cradled a limp
burden in his rolled-up coat. "Do you know," he said with a
shaky laugh, "I rather think that a career of unremitting benevolence is a great deal more exhausting than I thought it would
be."

"Oh, I am so sorry I asked you to go in there," said Georgiana with feeling. "Are you all right?"

"Yes, but I am inclined to believe it would be most unwise
to enter the crypt again. The entire ceiling very nearly fell in
on me. We must inform his lordship at once."

Georgiana looked down at the burden in his arms. "And it
was all for nothing, then!"

"Oh no! The large gray gentleman is very much alive. A bit
concussed, I think. He favored me with a baleful glance and a
hiss when I rescued him. Now I think he is merely sleeping it
off."

The cat, as if in answer, stirred a little within the coat, and
began to purr loudly. "You, sir, are a toadeater, which I particularly despise above all things," Sir Oliver said severely. "Besides, you are entirely lacking in insight. Left alone I should
doubtless have abandoned you without a backward glance.
You owe your salvation to another, I do assure you."

Burdick appeared to accept such remonstrances with equanimity and redoubled his efforts at expressing his approval of the status quo in audible terms. "Shameless," concluded Sir Oliver sadly.

Georgiana, with a choke, ran over to assure Freddy that his pet would survive. Sir Oliver laid his burden down gently beside its master and then led Georgiana a little ways apart.

"Will you be all right here by yourself for a while while I try and find the Pemberton carriage?" he asked her seriously. "It will be dark soon, but I am afraid Freddy might faint again if I attempt to lead him on a horse, and then he might do himself greater injury. It is turning cold, and you are still wet, so I do not like to leave you, but I can think of no other course of action to follow."

"Of course you must go at once," Georgiana hastened to assure him. "I am not quite . . . comfortable, but it is not so cold as all that. And I am sure we must get Freddy home as soon as possible."

"Good girl," he said approvingly. For the second time that day he lifted her hand and kissed it. "Do you know," he said, looking down at her with a smile, "that I had quite forgotten since this adventure started that you are not *really* my cousin Georgiana at all? I wonder how that may be?"

Georgiana, in some confusion, could not answer him. There was a whole universe of things to say, or nothing. She dropped her eyes and her hand trembled a bit in his.

He looked at her searchingly for some moments and then let her hand fall abruptly. "I will be back as soon as I can," he said in a matter-of-fact voice which effectively disclaimed the dangerous shoals of his earlier warmth. "There is, I believe, a back road, by which we may bring the carriage much nearer. I should hope to be back within the hour. Take care the cat does not escape again!"

Then he turned and strode off rapidly, leaving her feeling confused, and chilled, and very much alone.

Chapter 11

CLARICE AND AMABEL'S assurances that they had no choice but to abandon Cousin Georgiana and Frederick to their soggy fate having been seconded by Sir Oliver, the household had little option but to accept them, and Lady Louisa went so far as to suggest that it was the truants who had been so inconsiderate as to cause everyone to fly into a pelter and keep her horses standing in a storm. After Sir Oliver's gentleness with Freddy and the cat, Georgiana was inclined to alter her opinion a little and admit that there were aspects of his character more favorable than she had hitherto supposed. She had hoped, after his treatment of her, that a new degree of understanding might have sprung up between them, but on the contrary, she saw even less of him than before. When she came down to breakfast it was to find that he had just quit the table; when she entered the drawing room he was always just leaving it. She could only presume that he was eager to make it plain to his great-aunt and, perhaps, to Miss Ponsonby as well that he had no interest in attempting to secure her affections. She was surprised that that realization should cause her a pang and put it down, with a self-deprecating laugh, to wounded vanity. If he wished to put the matter unalterably behind them, he had only to propose to her, and then present her grandmother with the fact of her refusal. That he had not yet done so she attributed to a wish not to disturb the emotional balance of the household before they went up to London or not to cause his great-aunt undue distress.

In fact, Sir Oliver was somewhat puzzled by his own reactions. His initial confusion as to Miss Bucklebury's—strange,

he could not easily think of her by that name—respectability
had caused him to make—he must admit it—a damned fool of
himself, so that he could scarcely have been more eager than
she to end the acquaintance altogether. When the terms of that
ridiculous bet, so carelessly agreed to, had forced him to offer
her the chance to enter his life on a footing of uncomfortable
and almost unthinkable intimacy, he had not for a moment really expected her to accept. He knew he was guilty of dazzling
her with the prospect of a glittering life far beyond what she
might ever achieve on her own in order to induce her to do so,
but that she did accept, whatever her financial deprivations,
must forever diminish her in his eyes. Sir Oliver, with the
complacency of the very rich, felt quite certain that if she were
the girl of upright background and delicate principles she had
represented herself to be, no social inducements or material
persuasion could have enticed her to yield to his plan. He was
inclined, therefore, to disparage her character as a mercenary
one, and to be on his guard to prevent her taking advantage of
Lady Louisa and the others, however much they might deserve
it.

Georgiana, however, had confounded all such expectations.
She had not only entered into a needless battle of wills with
Lady Louisa, but she showed no inclination to ingratiate herself with the others at all. For a while, Sir Oliver had thought
she might be making a bid for Freddy out of a mistakenly optimistic view of his fortune and position, but the incident in the
crypt convinced him that her feelings for him were composed
chiefly of a disinterested compassion. Contrary to what he had
expected, Georgiana had shown herself to be kind, consider-
ate, and full of spirit, and he found himself liking her in spite
of himself.

Though she was undeniably a Beauty, he could not feel
himself in any danger. Georgiana displayed all too readily a
lamentable tendency to cross swords with *him*, and besides, he
had resisted the lures of eligible females for years and was
perfectly resigned to his bachelorhood. An upstart governess
posed no threat to his well-ordered life, and when he had elevated her to the social heights she apparently craved he need
have no compunction about abandoning her to an uncertain fu-

ture. Still, a friendship between them would only increase the awkwardness of their parting, and while he had no doubt he would ultimately be only too thankful to see her go, for the present he had no wish to wound her feelings. A little distance, though not so great as to seem cold, might be salutary.

Georgiana could no longer feel quite comfortable, in light of the events at the picnic, in the company of Clarice and Amabel. That Frederick's mother would stop at nothing short of ruthless means to wed him to a fortune bespoke a desperation that Georgiana pitied but must be wary of. Amabel, with less excuse, had mounted her on a horse known to be both skittish in storms and an uncomfortable ride, and the result might have been a bad fall or worse. She could understand that Miss Ponsonby might resent her presence and her fortune, but such naked hostility was beyond her experience. She was well aware that Amabel nursed a *tendre* for Sir Oliver, but since Sir Oliver, with the exception of that one afternoon at the crypt, appeared to dislike her intensely, she could not feel that jealousy was a motive for Miss Ponsonby's treatment of her. In the few days that remained before the family went up to London, she felt the best strategy might be to absent herself as much as possible from the household, and thus she unconsciously followed Sir Oliver's example and began putting some distance between herself and the other members of the family.

Georgiana had long been accustomed to early morning rides at Holcombe Hall, and now she revived a custom that both refreshed her and indulged her need for solitude. The discreet presence of a groom chafed her at first, but he, like herself, was a Yorkshireman, but lately employed at the Pemberton stables, and they soon arrived at a modus vivendi whereby he remained within hailing distance but out of sight.

The spring countryside in the early morning was a tonic to her drooping spirits, and she soon ranged farther and farther afield. She often crossed into the wooded areas of their neighbor's estates, but Kimball, the groom, reported that despite their political differences Pemberton stood on such terms with its neighbors as to render this acceptable, and in any case she never met anyone on her rides.

Lady Louisa, noting that her granddaughter was away from the house a great deal and seemed a trifle silent, suspected that Georgiana might be pining for Yorkshire and proceeded to regale her with tales of the triumphs that would soon be hers in London.

"There's not a chance in the world you won't take," said the old lady bracingly. "You ain't a homely Joan, and with my backing and Oliver's I shouldn't be surprised to see you the toast of the town within two weeks. Then there will be all manner of parties and foolishness, and never an idle moment. I shouldn't wonder it's been a trifle dull for you here, with just the family."

Georgiana, touched by this unexpected concern for her state of mind, hastened to assure her grandmother that she had not found her stay dull in the least. "For I'm used to a very quiet life, you know, Grandmama, at Holcombe Hall."

Lady Louisa frowned at this reminder of her granddaughter's previous existence. She had hoped that by now Oliver might have made a push to secure the girl's regard, so she need have no thought of every returning to That Place again. But Oliver was showing himself stubbornly resistant, and the girl was pining away over something, though she couldn't guess what. Neither of them were in the same room together for more than an hour a day, and when they were, they scarcely spoke above the commonplace. Lady Louisa could not fathom the youthful mind, which resisted so strongly what was so plainly in its own best interest. "Freddy is not pestering you, is he?" she inquired with sudden suspicion. "Or Clarice pushing him on to you?"

Georgiana shook her head. "Freddy is a perfect gentleman," she said truthfully, omitting the second part of the question in her response. She wondered if this might not be an appropriate moment to broach the Problem of Freddy with her grandmother. "Grandmama, could you not help Freddy find a position in the church? It is what he most particularly wishes, but he feels you are all against it."

Lady Louisa's jaw dropped open. "In the *church*? Take Communion from that . . . that bird-witted nodcock? We should all find ourselves drinking water from the flower vases, can tell you. Whatever put a cork-brained scheme like that into your head?"

Georgiana said seriously, "Well, it was the cat, actually."

Lady Louisa's expression, never terribly benign, practically glowed with ire. "That vermin!"

"As a matter of fact," said Georgiana carefully, "Freddy reminds me a little of St. Francis, and I'd like to help him get what he wants."

Her grandmother laughed mirthlessly. "St. Francis! You're short a sheet, girl! I suppose you expect me to give him a living! Well, you're far out there, I can tell you. I'll put bread in his mouth as long as Clarice is my dependent, but I'll do no more than that. I'd sooner waste money on a—a cockfight than a goosecap like Frederick."

Georgiana, seeing that her grandmother would not budge, determined that as soon as her fortune was in her own hands she would do something for the unfortunate Freddy.

One morning, when she had awakened particularly early (her body still kept country hours, whatever the Pemberton fashion might be), she took a new and longer ride which skirted a stream along the edge of her grandmother's property and led her eventually to the top of a small hill, which offered a prospect of their neighbor's house and garden below. She had never seen the house before, a fine Jacobean mansion with landscaping by Brown, and she was in the midst of admiring the excellent view it presented when she suddenly discovered she was not alone.

"Oh, I beg your pardon!" cried Georgiana to a stout, middle-aged woman who stood regarding her steadily with bright blue eyes. "I hope I do not trespass! I was out for a ride and stopped to admire the lovely prospect."

"It is beautiful, is it not?" said the woman in a heavily accented voice. "But I, like you, am a guest. The house belongs to my good friend, Sir James Winterhaven." She strode forward, and Georgiana was able to see that she presented a rather extraordinary figure. Her blue velvet riding habit was ornamented with silver spangles, and her fair hair hung in masses beside her throat like a lion's mane. Her cheeks were painted a startling red, but there was nothing about her to suggest the courtesan. Her manner was determined, and her eyes, which looked out from beneath rather formidable black brows, sparkled with intelligence.

Georgiana sketched a curtsy. "How do you do? I am Georgiana Oversham. My grandmother is a neighbor of Sir James."

She waited for the other woman to introduce herself but she did not. The blue eyes surveyed her with interest. "You ride out alone?"

Georgiana waved a hand in the direction of the copse where she had left her groom. "My groom is there," she said, "but . . ."

"Ah! You prefer freedom and solitude, like me!"

"Oh dear!" cried Georgiana. "I *have* intruded. I am so very sorry. Do, pray, excuse me."

The woman's plump hand closed gently over Georgiana's wrist. "You are a very pretty-behaved girl," she said with a smile, "and you are not intruding. Will you not sit for a while? There is a bench over this way."

It was quite civilly requested, but something in the tone suggested that the speaker was used to getting her way, rather like Lady Louisa.

The bench had clearly been constructed with persons of less prodigious girth in mind, so that Georgiana had to squeeze in beside her hostess in order to take a seat. "So," inquired her benchmate when she had finished disposing her voluminous skirts, "why does a beautiful young lady like yourself prefer the solitude of an early morning ride? It must be love, I think!"

Startled, Georgiana assured her it was no such thing and murmured some platitude about the salutary effects of country air.

"You think my comment impertinent," said the other wisely, "though you are too well-bred to say so. Naturally you are quite right. But I have found through very painful experience that it is usually a man who is at the root of a young girl's unhappiness, and I can see at a glance that *you* are unhappy. You are not married?"

"No."

"If you were, then I would know where to look for the

:ause. The only person more likely than a lover to cause mis-
ry is a husband. I know it was so with me."

Georgiana thought this was one of the oddest conversations
she had ever experienced in her life, but she could not help
being intrigued. "Are you a widow, ma'am?" she inquired po-
itely.

She was not prepared for her companion's gusty laugh.
'Alas, no! My husband no longer loves me and we are . . . estranged. He had banished me to Europe, but from time to time I
return, as I have now, to visit friends. I do not tell him, for it in-
furiates him even to be in the same country with me."

"I'm sorry!" cried Georgiana, appalled.

The blue eyes twinkled. "Do not pity me. There are com-
pensations, I assure you. I am not what I seem."

I am not what I seem either, thought Georgiana, or rather, I
do not wish to be what I seem and am. Oh, it is all too confus-
ing. "I shall never marry," she said, startling herself.

The woman smiled. "You are either very wise or very foolish. Why not?"

"Because," said Georgiana, surprised to find herself confessing her deepest fear to a total stranger, and a rather eccentric one at that, "I will never know if a man values me for
myself or for my fortune, and how could I marry if I could not
be sure of *that*?"

"Are you so very rich?" asked her new friend sympathetically.

"Very," confessed Georgiana with a sigh. "Forgive me; I
know it ill becomes me to complain—"

"Nonsense. I too am so accursed. Besides, I feel that you
have no one to confide in, and since we are unlikely to meet
again there can be no harm in your honesty. Believe me, I am
very discreet at need!"

"You are very kind," said Georgiana. "I do not mean to pry,
but I should like to know . . . well, what is one to do, ma'am?
Did your husband . . . ?" she stopped, feeling she had perhaps
gone too far.

"Did he marry me for my money?" said the woman with
booming frankness. She smiled. "In a manner of speaking. For
my position, in any case. Certainly not for the fairness of my

body, which . . ." She broke off abruptly, seeing Georgiana's innocent gaze of inquiry trained on her. "I am not sure I can advise you. The obvious solution would be to declare oneself penniless, but few, I fear, would have the courage to face the aftermath such a declaration would bring."

Georgiana looked at her feet. "I have done so," she said in a small voice.

"Have you? That is courage indeed."

Georgiana shook her head. "Not courage, but pique. And now I have cause to regret it."

Her companion chuckled. "My child, you must humor a stranger's curiosity and tell me how this comes about. I was quite resigned to a dull morning, and now you have come along to enliven my day. Come! I shall keep your confidence, I promise you!"

Georgiana, thus encouraged, found herself pouring out the tale of Miss Bucklebury and the Mail-coach, Miss Leroux and the snowstorm, and the perfidious behavior of Sir Oliver and his companions. When she got to the part about Sir Oliver's bet with Mr. Utterby and Lord Litchfield her companion had to retreat behind her handkerchief, and by the time she had finished recounting, with rather more detail than she had intended, the tale of the family's reception of her, Clarice's clumsy attempts to throw her into Freddy's arms, and the dramatic loss and recovery of Burdick in the crypt, her listener was openly wiping her eyes.

"I am so s-sorry, my dear, but it does quite undermine one's gravity," she said after a moment.

Georgiana smiled. "I grant that it is rather diverting, but the problem is I don't quite see how I am to extricate myself."

"Nor do I, to be truthful. But comfort yourself with the thought that this Sir Oliver richly deserves any discomfort your disclosure may heap upon him, and I cannot see that you have materially deceived anyone else. I wish I might be there to see it! How long will you stay up in London?"

"We go up day after tomorrow, and my grandmother is planning my come-out within the fortnight. After that I should very much like to go home to Yorkshire," she confessed.

"My dear, will you indulge an old woman's whim and in-

vite me to your come-out? It has been a long time since I attended a London party!"

Georgiana hesitated. Her grandmother would not like it if
the woman were the wife of a cit, or in some way not respectable.

Her companion read her thoughts with a smile. "I am perfectly respectable, I assure you. I think you will even find that
I am known to your grandmother. Indeed, I am received in
every house in the country save one, and that one is my husband's. You need not fear to invite me."

"Of course not, ma'am," replied Georgiana, embarrassed.
"But to whom should I direct the invitation?"

The woman gave her an amused look and said, "Forgive
me! My manners are at fault. If you would direct the invitation
to Lady Brunswick, in care of Sir James, I shall be sure to receive it." She rose, which caused the bench to wobble a bit. "I
cannot say when I have enjoyed a chance conversation more,"
she assured Georgiana. "For the present only, will you not
mention to your grandmother or anyone else that you have met
me here? I would not wish you to lie, of course, but merely
omit to mention the fact of our meeting. It could cause a bit of
unpleasantness if my husband were to hear of my visit here,
you see, and I do not wish to bring trouble upon the head of
my kind host."

"Is your husband so very angry, then?" asked Georgiana,
rather astonished that someone would go to such lengths to interfere with his estranged wife's enjoyment or vent his wrath
on her hapless friends.

"Quite angry and rather powerful," the woman conceded.

"Is he likely to resent *anyone* who invites you somewhere?"

Her companion laughed. "Oh no, you are quite safe! It is
merely that Sir James is rather a . . . special case."

Georgiana assured her that she might count on her discretion.

"I knew I might. You are too good. I wish you luck, my
dear, and wish I may be there to see how it all turns out. Good
day!"

She turned and walked down the hill, and at the bottom a groom appeared as if by magic, leading a splendid horse. He helped her to mount, and then they rode off, leaving Georgiana to wonder whatever had possessed her to confess so much to a perfect stranger.

Chapter 12

THE REMOVAL OF the family to London was accomplished in due course, and when the carriage rolled into the alley that led through the Pemberton woods, Georgiana had her last glimpse of the house. Already it was hard to remember that she had only seen it for the first time a few weeks before, and now she found herself wondering if she would ever see it again. Because it had been her father's boyhood home, her attachment to it was surprisingly strong, despite the dubious welcome she had received there, and she told herself that in happier circumstances she would be glad of the chance to return. But no; when Lady Louisa died Pemberton would go to Sir Oliver, and after she had made a fool of him in London, she would be the last person he would ever invite to his home.

Georgiana was amazed to see the transformation a few weeks' time had wrought in London. The streets were full of carriages, the shops of patrons, and the tray in the front hall was already, upon their arrival, piled high with invitations. As Clarice and Amabel were scarcely more hardened to this prospect than Georgiana herself, the three of them spent an enjoyable hour after tea in pleasurable contemplation of the activities to come. Georgiana's name was on not a few of these (although she had no acquaintance in town outside the family with the exception of Lord Litchfield and Mr. Utterby), an inclusion which she assumed she owed to the good offices of Sir Oliver already working on her behalf. Rumors of the Non-pareil's exceedingly wealthy and quite beautiful cousin caused a flutter in the heart of more than one mama of a hopeful and expensive son, as well as awakening trepidation in the breasts of those with worthy daughters. Georgiana, in happy ignorance of the probable effects of such rumors, thought that the stories she had heard about the unfriendliness of Londoners were mistaken, and she was glad to find that fashionable people were not, after all, so predisposed to shun one as a provincial as she had been led to believe. Clarice could have enlightened her, but she, finding herself the recipient of invitations and attentions from some persons who had not previously included her in their most exclusive parties, was too elated to quibble. Miss Ponsonby contented herself with frequent reminders to "Cousin Georgiana" about the undesirability of offending any of the Patronesses of Almack's or transgressing any of the other rules of London life, but even she was remarked to be in a mood of unusual amiability.

Their first callers were Lord Litchfield and Mr. Utterby. Georgiana had known she must face this ordeal sooner or later, and Mr. Utterby had in a manner of speaking thrown down the gauntlet at their last meeting, but she had not expected him to turn up on their doorstep scarcely a day after their arrival. It was clear from the outset that Mr. Utterby, at least, meant to make mischief. Though his hints and threats of disclosure were not as disturbing to Georgiana as he had reason to suppose, he did have the power to complicate the situation rather uncomfortably, and she could not rid herself of the notion that he really ought to play fair. He insisted, for example, upon bringing up topics about which he assumed she would know nothing, in order to embarrass her. Thus:

"I am persuaded, Miss Oversham, that your home at Holcombe Hall must be one of the loveliest in Yorkshire. It was extensively renovated by your father, I believe."

Georgiana, who thought with amazement that he must have been studying the guidebooks in order to trip her up on some detail or other, could only murmur her acknowledgement.

"And the gardens? Are they in the Italian style? Or the English?"

"Both," countered Georgiana with a smile.

"Will you not tell us more about your home?" he persisted. "I am quite interested in classical houses, and I believe yours is one of the finest in the county."

"You are, Robert?" inquired Lord Litchfield in astonishment. "Since when?"

"My dear Lionel, I fear there are a great many things you do not know about me. And I do assure you, I have a particular interest in Miss Oversham's house. Will you not describe it for us in detail, Miss Oversham?"

Mr. Utterby had reckoned without Miss Ponsonby's dislike of hearing anything of Georgiana's praised. "Perhaps, since you are so interested, Cousin Georgiana could draw you a picture of the house," she said in a colorless tone.

"I am afraid that I am but an indifferent artist, Mr. Utterby, and though I have lived in the house all my life, I fear that I lack the eye and training to supply the details in which you have such an interest. However, I believe there are some excellent guides to Yorkshire houses, and you may find the description you require in one of those."

"Good suggestion," interjected his lordship. "Do you find London to your taste, Miss Oversham?"

"Oh yes, it is quite delightful."

Miss Ponsonby, who had warned Georgiana that excessive enjoyment was the sure mark of a gapeseed, said repressively, "We find it a shocking squeeze, of course, but it is always so diverting to meet new people as well as one's old friends."

"But it is all so very new for you, Miss Oversham, is it not?" said Mr. Utterby with something only a trifle less obvious than a leer. "That is to say, compared to what you are used to."

Even Clarice could hardly miss the import of that remark. Her back stiffened a little. "Oh, when one is used to moving in the first circles, I expect it is much the same everywhere. And Cousin Georgiana is being made most welcome, you know. Will you take some refreshment?"

"I thank you, no. We must take our leave of you, but may we hope to see you all at the Marchioness's tomorrow evening? The Miltons always open the Season with the deadliest party, but no one who is anyone will miss it. I'm quite sure Oliver would want you to attend, Miss Oversham. In fact, I see that he has just arrived, doubtless to tell you so himself, so I will say my farewells. Mrs. Oversham, Miss Ponsonby,

Miss Oversham, until tomorrow, I hope! My regards to Lady Louisa. Oliver, your servant! I was just taking my leave."

"I must say," said Clarice when the door had closed on them, "that I cannot quite like Mr. Utterby's manner. I am not sure why he was on at Georgiana about her house and how different from London her previous life was—as if we do not do just the same at Pemberton—but I found it rather impertinent. Such a contrast to Lord Litchfield, who is a perfect gentleman. Did you find your house in order, my dear? We had so much to do here, and poor Lady Louisa was sadly out of frame."

"Perfectly," responded Sir Oliver, whose domestic staff was the envy of all his acquaintance. "Where is Aunt Louisa?"

"In her bedroom, and I should not advise you to disturb her," said Clarice frankly. "One of the maids has already been dismissed for bringing her chocolate a half hour early, and I had to go down to the servants' quarters to persuade her that Lady Louisa would never remember the incident at all by this time tomorrow. The girl had the insolence to suggest that Lady Louisa tried to hit her with her hairbrush, which I told her could not be possible. But I do not know where we would find another maid on such short notice at the beginning of the Season, so we must keep her on, I suppose!"

"I can see that you have had a most trying day, Clarice," responded Sir Oliver with what to Georgiana sounded like a notable lack of sympathy. "Perhaps you should lie down as well. Amabel, Cousin Georgiana, I have come to solicit the favor of your hands for a dance at the Marquess of Milton's party tomorrow night."

"Yes, Mr. Utterby said it was quite de rigueur to attend," said Georgiana dryly.

"What he said was that Sir Oliver would particularly *wish* you attend," corrected Miss Ponsonby, "though I am at a loss as to why he should phrase it in that manner. Naturally, I shall be happy to stand up with you, Oliver."

"Thank you. You must not mind Robert; he sometimes finds the world too amusing for his own good. Miss Oversham, will you do me the honor? The Marquess is too high a stickler to permit the waltz, so you need not fear," he added wickedly.

Georgiana gave a little choke. "On the contrary, it is you who need not fear. Your dancing slippers will be quite safe. And your credit will not suffer!"

"That *does* relieve my mind!" he said with a laugh.

"I suppose it might," said Georgiana, imbued with an odd spirit of recklessness after her escape from Mr. Utterby's exhausting presence, "except that I believe you care a great deal less for your credit than you would like everyone to suppose. Nor profoundly for anything else, I should think."

"That is most unjust of you, Cousin Georgiana," remonstrated Miss Ponsonby.

"On the contrary, it is right on the mark," said Sir Oliver, although he was momentarily taken aback by the observation. "But it is rather uncivil of you to point it out just when I am sparing no pains to establish *yours*," he added with a smile.

She saw at once that he had checked her, because she could not, under the circumstances, retort that by establishing her credit, he stood to be the gainer. "Did I offend you?" she asked, acknowledging his hit with a laugh. "I trust not."

"One should never be offended by the truth," he said with a wry smile. "It is perfectly true that I do not care a great deal for anyone or anything. I find it quite restful, on the whole."

"Well I should find it sadly flat," replied Georgiana with decision. "While I can see that it might be not entirely satisfactory to spend one's life in alt or cast down by dejection, to be perfectly comfortable at all times would bore me to distraction!"

"Well I, on the other hand, am inclined to agree with Sir Oliver that excessive displays of emotion are rather vulgar," commented Miss Ponsonby with a touch of acid which left no doubt as to her meaning. This did not have the hoped-for effect, for it caused Sir Oliver, in a display of that breeding so much esteemed by herself, to lead his cousin quietly but firmly from the room.

"Is Utterby teasing you?" he asked Georgiana when he had led her into the library.

She felt a great deal of constraint in answering him, because she did not wish to lay open her suspicions about Mr. Utterby's true character and abuse him to his friends. "A little," she said cautiously. "He—he means to win the bet you know, and he thinks to expose me by asking me a number of questions—about the—*her*—house and so on—which he hopes I may not be able to answer."

"And *were* you able to answer them, Miss Bucklebury?" he asked in surprise.

"Well, yes, a little," she said diffidently, strangely disturbed that he should still refer to her by her governess name in private. "The house is rather well known in our part of the country, and one hears stories . . . and by the by, *Cousin* Oliver, did we not agree that you would call me 'Cousin Georgiana' even in private? If you keep switching back and forth like this someone is bound to hear us!"

"You appear to be quite a practiced deceiver, *cousin*," he said smoothly. "I see that I need not have troubled to worry about you, though I will have a word with Utterby nonetheless. I do not want him making hints and accusations that might upset Aunt Louisa, for I wish she may never know the full extent to which we have deceived her!" he added bitterly.

"Do you repent of your deception, then?" asked Georgiana hesitantly.

He regarded her with a dark, impenetrable stare. "Yes, Miss Bucklebury, I am afraid that I do!"

Georgiana dressed for her first London party in a state of mingled excitement and dread. She was quite becomingly attired in a robe of jonquil over a white satin underdress, ornamented only with her pearls and a delicate spray of tiny yellow roses artfully disposed to set off to advantage her dusky curls. At three-and-twenty she did not have to dress with the simplicity of a girl just out of the schoolroom, but she had not brought her own diamonds, and she did not wish to put herself under obligation to Clarice by accepting her offer to loan her a set of her own. The admiration of Clarice's personal maid, whom she had sent to assist her, as well as her reflection in the mirror, assured her that she was nevertheless in her best looks, and the glittering prospect of a London social life, however brief its duration, could not be entirely dimmed by the certain knowledge that Mr. Utterby would do his best to ruin it for her, and that Sir Oliver found her presence wearisome.

By ten o'clock the Marchioness's drawing rooms were filled to overflowing, and Sir Oliver was nowhere in evidence. Georgiana had all the satisfaction of being very kindly received by a number of people to whom she was introduced, and she soon gave over any attempt to remember names or titles, existing merely in a happy cloud. Her reputation as a considerable heiress had clearly proceeded her, for one or two gazetted fortune hunters, whom Amabel felt it her duty to point out, hastened to make her acquaintance in a manner that reanimated all her disgust at such insincerity and calculation. Still, she began to find her feet, and felt much more confident of her ability to hold her own among even the most punctilious members of the ton.

Last of all the guests to arrive were Mr. Utterby and Sir Oliver, who came unhurriedly up the stairs to greet their hostess with languid charm. The former, catching sight of Georgiana already surrounded by admirers, said ruefully: "Your little governess appears to have succeeded on the ton without your help, Oliver. She is quite the most dazzling creature in the room, and with all the rumors of a magnificent fortune I should be quite astonished if she did not have London at her feet within the week, particularly if you are determined to let it be known that *you* are paying court to her as well."

"Giving up, Robert?" suggested Sir Oliver with a grin.

"Oh dear me, no. Merely wondering what I could do to thrust a spoke in her wheel."

"You must, of course, try, if you are so determined. But leave the girl herself alone, and keep my family out of it," said Sir Oliver.

"How very stern you are all of a sudden! I shall keep to the rules, you may be assured. But do not build a stable for my chestnuts yet, dear boy. It wouldn't do to underestimate me, you know."

"I never do, Robert. You do it so consistently yourself."

*   *   *

In a few moments, Georgiana, enjoying the admiration and attentions of several young tulips of fashion, was gratified to see Sir Oliver making his way toward her across the room. This was by no means a rapid process, as her cousin had many friends and acquaintance who commanded his notice and greetings. She had not previously realized what the true effects of his social position would be, but seeing him now in a crowd, she saw that he was both esteemed and, perhaps, a little feared. The merest touch on a man's shoulder was enough to clear a passage for him, and even the slightest raising of his quizzing glass sufficed to depress pretension. It was said of him that one's elevation or ruin could be accomplished in the lift of his eyebrow, and Georgiana, though she loathed the idea altogether, could no longer doubt its truth.

There could be no one in the room who doubted that he intended to elevate *her*. He reached her side, smiling, and lifted her hand gently to his lips. "How do you do, Cousin Georgiana?" he said with a warmth which, had she not known it to be insincere, would have quite melted her heart. "It appears that London likes you very well indeed."

His proprietary manner and his presence had the effect of causing all her other admirers to melt away, which she found irrationally irritating. "Coming it much too strong, Cousin Oliver! There is no one left to hear!"

Sir Oliver, elegantly attired in a black coat and knee breeches, a white waistcoat, and a perfectly arranged neckcloth that was the despair of every young gentleman in the room, raised his glass to look at her. "Do you have some objection to compliments, cousin? I had formed the opinion that you were just now receiving any number of them, and you did not appear to be visibly distressed."

She laughed at that. "Perhaps, but it was all nonsense, and I did not believe a word that was said. We both know *why* I am likely to receive such attention, and I hope I may not be such a goose as to be taken in! But I must say, I did not expect *you* to be amusing yourself at my expense."

One of Sir Oliver's famous eyebrows lifted now. "Cousin Georgiana, your case is nowhere near so desperate as that! I must hasten to assure you that it is perfectly possible for someone to pay you a sincere compliment."

"I wish you would stop making me laugh!" she said shakily. "You know quite well I only meant that it is the *rich* Miss Oversham whom the gentlemen make the object of their gallantry, cousin to the Nonpareil, the Social Arbiter of London, the notable Corinthian—"

"That will do, ma'am. Now who is being amused at whose expense?" He gave her a level, speculative gaze. "Do you know, Cousin Georgiana, you give a very fair imitation of one who does not wish to see her feet placed securely on the ladder of fashion. Or is it only *my* assistance you do not wish for?"

"On the contrary, you are most obliging," said Georgiana lightly. "But you should not, you know, expect to cast me into a state of exquisite confusion or some such thing when we both know we are playing a game whose ultimate goal is to put Mr. Utterby's chestnuts into your stable."

His lips twitched. "Can you not think of any other reason to play this game, as you call it?"

"Oh yes," she said frankly. "I think that in some ways you despise the set you lead, and you would derive a great deal of enjoyment from elevating a provincial governess to the heights of Society!"

After a stunned moment, laughter welled up in him. "You are very astute, cousin."

"Have you thought what the probable reaction of Society will be when it is discovered that you have foisted off an impostress upon it?"

"Certainly I have."

"Then should we not, in mercy, bring the game to a close?" she said seriously.

"What?" he asked her, surprised. "Do you wish to withdraw? To forfeit the considerable material advantages that could still be yours?"

She opened her lips and then closed them again, so that he wondered what she had very nearly said. "They no longer weigh with me."

"Enlighten me, cousin, if you will: why did you agree to

take part in this rather discreditable enterprise? I thought I knew, but it appears I was wrong."

"I am afraid my reasons reflect to the credit of neither of us," she said sincerely, "and if you please I would rather not discuss them. You must have guessed that my life was rather . . . restricted, and you seemed to offer a way out, however temporary. But I am heartily sorry I ever agreed!" she said bitterly, reflecting that she had told him no less than the perfect truth.

He was just enough to acknowledge a twinge of guilt, in itself a rather unusual sensation. "I daresay we both regret our impulsiveness," he began, "but for the present there is nothing to be done. I require you to continue in the role of my cousin awhile longer."

"Yes, I have not yet made it plain to Lady Louisa that we should not suit," she said, a little stung by his ready agreement.

"I was going to say," he said smoothly, "that my great-aunt has taken a liking to you, and I should not wish you to go until that can be accomplished without arousing her suspicions. I do not want to distress her!"

"Nor do I," agreed Georgiana.

"Then we are agreed that you will stay on, at least for a while?"

"Until the party Lady Louisa and Clarice are planning," said Georgiana. "But after that, I must go back to Yorkshire, whatever may happen!"

Chapter 13

WHILE SIR OLIVER was occasioning comment by the assiduous attention he was observed to pay to his beautiful cousin, inspiring in the breasts of his devoted copyists an ardent desire to follow his example, Mr. Utterby was no less dedicated in his efforts to bring about Georgiana's downfall. Mr. Utterby's debts were daily becoming more pressing, and he had long harbored an envy of his friend's easy fortune and social success which he had been at some pains to hide. Now he found it surprisingly easy to contemplate the prospect of undermining Sir Oliver through Georgiana, and he could not afford to indulge in any pangs of conscience as to what might become of her after he had unmasked her deceit. She had entered into the bargain open-eyed and out of what Mr. Utterby could only believe were the basest mercenary motives, so that she deserved whatever fate might befall her. He was highly suspicious of the mantle of virtue she had assumed at Litchfield's hunting box and in Lady Louisa's drawing room in London; he knew she was lying about something, and thought that if necessary he could always ferret out what it was. But he did not anticipate having to go to so much effort. The means to undermine her were closer at hand, and more subtle, and if he did not achieve an immediate success he had a fallback plan which would almost certainly accomplish his goal.

Within hours of the moment when the last carriage pulled away from the door of the Marquess and Marchioness's mansion, the news that Sir Oliver Townsend appeared to like his rich and beautiful cousin very well indeed was all over town. Such intelligence was not greeted with universal approbation, particularly among the mothers of penniless sons. Lady Millicent Twilbank, for example, was heard to chasten her son and heir as a "clothhead" for not making more of a push to secure the pleasure of Miss Oversham's hand in a dance. When her much esteemed spouse ventured to suggest that it could scarcely matter, since no parent, however doting, could cherish the hope that his or her offspring might not be cut out by the likes of Oliver Townsend, she declared that it would give her the greatest of pleasure to be able to drive the point of the diamond stickpin he wore into a strategic point of his most excellent physique. Maria Wexwood, whose daughter had been Sir Oliver's flirt for one brief, giddy Season before he had withdrawn his attentions and caused her to go into a decline from which she was rescued only recently by her marriage to Lord Resthaven, thought that it would serve him right if the heiress led him a merry dance, though she feared there was little chance of it. More likely the girl would get *her* heart broken instead, and someone ought, in kindness, to warn the child to have nothing to do with him.

More astute observers of the social scene found Sir Oliver's behavior perplexing, if not cause for condemnation. Lady Sefton and Lady Jersey were inclined to approve Georgiana's frank manners and excellent style, although their fellow Patroness of Almack's, Princess Esterhazy, dismissed her as "provincial." "You know I particularly abominate Yorkshire," she said with a sneer, "although I will say, in her favor, that she does not have the slightest trace of an *accent*."

Sally Jersey shuddered visibly at the thought. "Of course she does not; Lady Louisa Oversham would scarcely foist her off on the ton if she did, and it is my understanding that she is quite pleased with the girl. And Oliver's approval must surely indicate that she is out of the common."

Princess Esterhazy, who gave weight to no one's approval but her own, gave a little shrug.

"Still," said Lady Sefton rather unexpectedly, "it is rather strange . . ."

"What is?" inquired Lady Jersey sharply.

"Only that Sir Oliver appeared very taken with the girl, and she is not at all in his usual style."

"Provincial," muttered the Princess again.

"Well, what is that to anything?" protested Lady Jersey. "They are saying that her fortune is more than eighty thousand pounds!"

"So I have heard," commented Lady Sefton, unwilling to be seen to be behindhand in any respect, "but since Sir Oliver is rich as a nabob himself, I hardly see how that can signify. In all truthfulness, I had rather begun to doubt that he is capable of harboring serious intentions toward anyone, as he has been the most hardened flirt in London these many years. And if he ever does marry, you may rest assured it will not be for a fortune, I promise you."

"Perhaps it is Lady Louisa who is promoting a match," said Lady Jersey shrewdly.

"And that," said Lady Sefton with an air of triumph, "is precisely what has me puzzled. Sir Oliver's actions last night will very likely make his cousin the most sought-after female in London."

"Only with our approval," Princess Esterhazy reminded her with a little yawn.

Lady Sefton, whose disposition was generally rather kind, ignored her.

"My dear," said Lady Jersey silkily, "I do not precisely understand what you are getting at."

Lady Sefton smiled. "Only this: that if Oliver were bent on fixing his interest with his cousin, would he not be more cautious? Would he not take pains to shield her from comment— to do nothing that would make her the topic of malicious *on-dits*? As it is, his behavior is such as must plainly advertise to the world that he found the girl charming, and by morning a dozen suitors will have entered the lists against him."

"Perhaps," suggested Lady Jersey, "he has reason to be certain of his ability to attach Miss Oversham should he wish to. He would certainly cast any would-be suitor into the shade."

"More likely he is only amusing himself," said the Princess in a languid voice. "He may find the girl a bit *farouche*, and seeks only to appease his great-aunt."

"One can never tell with Oliver," said Lady Jersey. "It is quite odiously provoking. Shall we send vouchers or not?"

"My dear—Lady Louisa!" exclaimed Lady Sefton in a shocked tone.

"I suppose we must," Princess Esterhazy conceded reluctantly. "But if I find her at all presuming, I shall not hesitate to administer a snub."

Mr. Utterby found it quite easy and decidedly advantageous to insinuate himself into this rather precarious Eden with all the cunning and charm of his colubrine predecessor. His manner, when he chose, was affable in the extreme, and his sardonic wit made him the favorite of those whom he had never made its target. The implicit assumption of shared superiority, though humbly expressed, particularly endeared him to Mrs. Drummond-Burrell and Princess Esterhazy, and he was careful to cultivate their social patronage by performing trifling acts of indispensable service and by lending an amused ear to their set-downs and condescensions. He was far too wise to stoop to obvious flattery, so that each was perfectly convinced of his sincere appreciation for her wit and judgment.

The opportunity for mischief presented itself without delay when Mr. Utterby, hoping to stir up trouble within the Oversham domain, fortuitously found Miss Ponsonby alone and at liberty to receive him in the blue saloon. No mean judge of human nature, he had been quick to recognize that Miss Oversham's superior face, apparent fortune, and liveliness would quickly overshadow any claims Miss Ponsonby might have to notice, with the result that might be expected of any but a more saintly disposition than Miss Ponsonby's. He contrived to ruffle the waters still further by artlessly praising Georgiana's style and appearance at the Milton's party, and executed the coup de grace by remarking ingenuously that it was clear that Miss Oversham would shortly become the toast of London.

He was not disappointed with the results of his efforts. Miss Ponsonby stiffened visibly, and remarked with a little smile, "Naturally, the ton is always ready to take up the latest novelty."

Mr. Utterby, satisfied, helped himself to a pinch of snuff from an exquisite Sèvres snuffbox. He experienced a fleeting sensation of regret that he would almost certainly have to sell it soon. "Yes, a *novelty* to be sure. One so rarely encounters an air of true fashion in one who is—shall we say?—country bred. But I believe a delightful air of amazed naïveté to be quite popular—for a time."

Miss Ponsonby, scenting an ally, relaxed her rigid posture a trifle. "It is as you say," she agreed generously. "Though I believe a rustic charm may soon pall, unless of course, it is backed by a substantial fortune."

"It is my contention," said Mr. Utterby, "—and we are speaking theoretically of course—"

"Of course."

"That fortune is much less important than the indefinable air of breeding—the inherent sense of propriety, if you will—that distinguishes a *true* gentlewoman."

Miss Ponsonby, acutely sensible of all the force of such a compliment to herself, blushed furiously, but she did not miss the emphasis he had given his words.

"And then of course," began Mr. Utterby carefully, "it is always possible that one might be mistaken as to the size of the fortune, or even as to the situation as it has been represented."

This was a trifle bald, even for Miss Ponsonby. "Mr. Utterby! What are you suggesting?"

"You will forgive me, I hope. I do not wish to cause you any alarm. I am almost certainly being overly cautious. It is only my great regard for Lady Louisa and for . . . all of you, which compels me to speak."

Miss Ponsonby clasped her hands sedately in her chaste lap. "I think perhaps you ought to tell me what is troubling you," she said softly.

"'Troubling' is too harsh a word, my dear Miss Ponsonby. It is only because of my faith in your scrupulous sense of justice and acute powers of discernment that I mention the matter at all. But a moment ago I spoke of the qualities of a true gentlewoman. Have you noticed anything unusual in Miss Oversham's air, or dress, or deportment which might suggest that perhaps she is not quite what she seems?"

"Well, she is frank to a fault, of course, and does not regard as she ought the restrictions Society places on a lady of birth and breeding," suggested Miss Ponsonby.

"Precisely," agreed Mr. Utterby.

"Good God!" cried Miss Ponsonby with feeling. "You don't mean to suggest that she could be some kind of impostor!"

"Oh no!" cried Mr. Utterby, delighted that she had taken his point so quickly. "It is merely that—forgive me—to my eyes she lacks those qualities that distinguish your sister and yourself, and it would seem that if she had been reared as strictly and in a mansion of such awe-inspiring gentility as Lady Louisa believes, such would not be the case. Perhaps she has—inadvertently of course, and not by design!—exaggerated the extent of her fortune somewhat."

Miss Ponsonby, who was, to do her justice, rather punctilious about sticking to the exact truth, shook her head. "Naturally, we are aware that her family, on the maternal side, is unfortunately vulgar, but she has never to my knowledge mentioned her fortune at all."

"Ah," said Mr. Utterby enigmatically. "Well then, I don't suppose she could have purchased such an ample quantity of fashionable clothes without a substantial sum at her disposal, so I must be mistaken after all. I am glad to be so; you relieve my mind."

"Oh, but it is Lady Louisa who buys—" She stopped, as if struck by a sudden thought.

"Yes?" inquired Mr. Utterby encouragingly.

"Mr. Utterby, what you suggest must be absurd. Sir Oliver vouches for her."

"My dear, any man may be taken in by a pretty face and naïve ways, before he comes to his senses in the end. However, I see that it must be as you say, and I will trouble you no more with my foolish fancies. Tell me, what do you have planned for this evening? Have I any hope of meeting you somewhere?"

"We go to Almack's," she told him, her mind, now much engaged, only half attending his words.

"Excellent," he replied with evident satisfaction.

Mr. Utterby, highly pleased with the results of this interview, now proceeded to plant seeds of doubt in the shell-like ear of Princess Esterhazy as well. "What do you think of Sir Oliver's latest project?" he inquired lightly after a long and rather arduous interlude designed to put her at her ease, rendered so by the all-too-apparent fact that Her Highness was not in a good mood.

"Project?" inquired the Princess in a bored tone. "I do not know what you mean."

"Come, ma'am, you are hoaxing me, are you not? I made sure Oliver would never try such a thing without your complicity, and I must say it is an excellent joke."

"Mr. Utterby, I assure you that I rarely joke, and I do not know to what you are referring."

"I beg your pardon, ma'am," he said penitently. "I refer to my friend's attempt to elevate an unknown provincial to the highest ranks of the ton. He has boasted of it everywhere, you know, and I assumed you approved. Even Oliver must bow to your superiority on social matters."

Princess Esterhazy raised one expressive eyebrow. "I presume that you are referring to Miss Oversham. While I cannot deny that she is provincial, she is scarcely unknown. Lady Louisa is her grandmother."

Mr. Utterby bowed. "Certainly. And one could never tell that she is only a merchant's granddaughter on her mother's side, so regal is her manner. She gave me a set-down the old Queen might have envied for what she called my 'condescension.' "

"You do not like the girl," the Princess concluded.

"I do not like to see Society mocked," said Mr. Utterby shamelessly. "And it does not become a chit with vulgar connections to presume to aspire so high. And even her own family—no, I say too much!"

"I think it would be as well if you were to confess the whole," said the Princess soberly.

"I am reluctant to—but no, I see that you must know best. Suffice it to say that a member of Miss Oversham's family confided to me quite recently that there is some concern that she may not be quite what she seems. Her fortune, for example, or the respectability of her maternal connections . . ."

"But this is *incroyable*," cried the Princess. "Why would the family encourage such pretensions? And why should Sir Oliver seek to foist such a person off upon us?"

"The family, I fear, hopes that they may dispose of Lord Nugent by wedding him to Miss Oversham," said Mr. Utterby with a trace of disappointment over the follies of human nature animating his voice.

The Princess, who was acquainted with Freddy, nodded sagely. "That I can understand. But—"

"As for Oliver, I believe his besetting sin is a tendency toward levity," he said sadly. "I am quite sure he does not mean any harm by it, and no doubt he views bringing his cousin to social prominence as an irresistible challenge."

"You do not think, then, that he had conceived a *tendre* for this girl?"

"Good God, no!" replied Mr. Utterby.

"Then I must depress these pretensions at once," said the Princess with determination. "It is too late to withdraw the vouchers which, out of courtesy to her ladyship, I do not think I could have refused in any case. But I shall not hesitate to do all in my power to prove to Sir Oliver that at Almack's, even he does not reign supreme!"

Chapter 14

GEORGIANA REMAINED IN happy ignorance of the fate in store for her. She was looking forward to her first view of the most important social club in London, the door which opened all other doors in Society to those permitted admission. Her white crepe ball dress with velvet ribbons had just been made for her, and even the most exacting critic must have conceded that her taste was unimpeachable. There was nothing at all of the provincial about the à la mode Miss Oversham, and Georgiana's eyes sparkled with the excitement and confidence that came from knowing she was in particularly good looks. Even Freddy, whom Clarice had coerced into escorting them—"One never knows when or if Oliver will show up, my dear, and I am persuaded Georgiana will feel much more at ease in familiar company"—despite the fact that his arm was still in a sling, was moved to remark upon her appearance. "Look all the crack, Georgie!" he said, much to his fond mama's dismay.

"My love, I am quite sure Cousin Georgiana would not like to be known by such a name, when her own is so lovely," suggested Clarice.

"I, too, am of the opinion that epithets in general are a trifle vulgar," seconded Miss Ponsonby.

"Well, I quite like it," said Georgiana firmly, tucking her hand under Lord Nugent's good arm. "You shall call me Georgie if you like, Freddy!"

Entering Almack's on Freddy's arm, Georgiana was obliged to admit that it was difficult to discern what all the fuss was about. The rooms, while spacious and by no stretch of the imagination shabby, were neither splendid nor particularly ele-

gant, and the refreshments appeared to consist of a rather
sparse quantity of tea and lemonade, cakes, bread, and butter.
It was fashionable in some circles to complain that an evening
spent at Almack's was sadly flat, but no one in the fashionable
world was thereby compelled to stay away. The magnetic
power exerted by exclusivity filled the rooms every Wednes-
day night during the Season, and the line of carriages waiting
to make their way to the door often forced the occupants into a
long delay before they could be handed out.

Lady Sefton, Lady Jersey, Countess Lieven, and Princess
Esterhazy were all present when the Oversham party mounted
the stairs. Lady Sefton, always the kindest of the Patronesses,
came forward to greet them. She favored Clarice and Amabel
with a handshake and bestowed a civil nod upon Georgiana.
Princess Esterhazy, scarcely a year—if that—older than Georgiana, gave her a look so expressive that Georgiana drew
back, her fingers tightening on Freddy's arm. She did not hear
the amused comment the Princess made to her unidentified
companion, but the import was clear to everyone in the room.
Society did not approve of Miss Oversham.

Lady Sefton rather bravely presented Georgiana to a number of persons, one of whom, a redoubtable old widower of
impeccable lineage and doubtful hearing, offered to lead her
down to dance. The angry lump in her throat made it difficult
to answer him, but she accepted with a gratitude undoubtedly
somewhat removed from his usual experience. Georgiana had
a moment's glimpse of Clarice's stricken countenance and
Amabel's rather triumphant one before she stepped out on the
floor. She could not imagine what had caused the Princess to
so take against her, or to express her disapproval in such a
public fashion, but it reinforced all her notions of the injustice
and unworthiness of a life in Society. The determination not to
give way to her most urgent inclination—which was to burst
into a flood of angry tears—gripped her so fiercely that she
gave her partner a glittering smile which almost threw him
into a panic. He was not used to exercising such an effect on
beautiful young ladies, and promised himself to reward his
apothecary for the tonic mixture he had but lately had made
up.

When her elderly partner had escaped her rather alarming presence after the set was ended on the pretext of procuring for her a glass of lemonade, Georgiana was left to the company of her own party. "My dear," whispered Clarice in a tone more suited for the undertaker's than the ballroom, "whatever can have happened? No one will speak to you!"

It was quite true. The Princess had not administered anything so drastic as the cut direct, and Lady Sefton's lukewarm patronage had a mitigating influence, but a great number of persons who believed they had previously admired Miss Oversham excessively, now discovered that their opinion all along had been that she was countrified and presuming.

"I-I cannot say," answered Georgiana with an attempt at bravery.

"The rules of Almack's are very severe," suggested Miss Ponsonby, by way of explanation.

"Well Cousin Georgiana cannot have transgressed them, because we have only just arrived," retorted Clarice with unexpected firmness. "Perhaps we ought to go at once. It is not quite the thing, I know, but—"

"Glad to take you home, Georgie," offered Lord Nugent.

Georgiana, who more than anything wished herself back home in her own room in Holcombe Hall, put up her chin. "Thank you, Freddy," she said, patting his arm, "but I should like to stay for a while if you don't mind."

"Don't mind at all," he said in response to a look from his mother. "Thought you might!"

"No, but I am a little hot," replied Georgiana, who thought it not impossible that she might faint. "Do you think I might have some tea?"

"Should you like to sit down, Cousin Georgiana?" inquired Miss Ponsonby with solicitude. "There is a chair over by the wall that is unoccupied."

"No, I am quite all right," replied Georgiana, bestowing upon her another of the glittering smiles that had so unnerved her elderly partner.

"Oh, if only some one of our particular acquaintance were here to dance with you," said Clarice, almost with a moan. "It is quite *fatal* to be seen to be without a partner for the entire evening. Are you quite sure you would not like Freddy to take you home?"

"Quite sure," replied Georgiana through gritted teeth.

The waltz, though still derided by those of the most exacting rectitude as somewhat fast, had some time before found its way into the sacred precincts of Almack's, and was struck up now. Even without the tutelage she had received from Miss Ponsonby, Georgiana knew that it was the inviolable rule of the establishment that no lady might be induced to take her place on the dance floor without the express approval of one of the Patronesses.

It was all too apparent that no such approval would be forthcoming, even if a would-be partner had been brave enough to solicit her hand. Georgiana stood fanning herself and trying to look as if she did not mind that even Amabel was whirling round the floor, while Clarice added substantially to her discomfort by her frequent exclamations of pity and distress and Freddy kept plying her with glasses of lemonade and tea. The superior glances of more favored young ladies, who had viewed the arrival of the rich and beautiful Miss Oversham on the social scene with evident dissatisfaction, did nothing to subdue the rising sentiments of anger and frustration within her breast.

Into this scene of drama and misery walked Sir Oliver, in the company of Lord Litchfield. Sir Oliver and his lordship had spent the evening dining and playing cards with a rather elevated assembly of friends and acquaintances, and both were generally of the opinion that the assemblies at Almack's were the flattest thing in town, but Sir Oliver wanted to keep an eye on the progress of his protégée.

Sir Oliver, who had not held his position for several years without being able to determine the social climate of a room with a single, assessing glance, realized at once that Georgiana was in trouble. It would be too extreme to say that the candles dimmed or the music stopped, but the room, when he entered it, was suddenly infused with an undercurrent of drama.

Sensing the tension, he deliberately slowed his steps and made a languid obeisance to Lady Sefton, who had the good grace to flush and lower her eyes. The Princess, deep in con-

ersation, appeared not to see him. He shrugged, and made his
way over to Georgiana with the hapless Lord Litchfield in
ow. "Clarice, you are in particularly good looks this evening,
f I may say so." He raised both of Georgiana's hands to his
ips in a gesture no one could miss. His eyes glinted a little.
"Cousin Georgiana, I hope you will not think it impertinent in
ne to ask why you are looking so particularly angry when I
ave brought Litchfield here on purpose to see you."

She smiled. "I am very happy to see his lordship again," she
aid. "But I must warn you both that it is not the fashion to be
een talking to me this evening."

Lord Leighton looked instantly troubled. "Oh no, ma'am,
urely not. I heard London fell at your feet after the Miltons'
all."

"I assure you," said Georgiana, trying to speak lightly but
with a trace of the bitterness she was feeling showing through
onetheless.

One of Sir Oliver's dark brows went up. "On whose author-
y, if I may ask?"

Georgiana looked very steadily at him. "I-I am not sure. I
eem to have offended somehow, and no one will speak to
ne."

"Princess Esterhazy looked at her so very c-coldly, Oliver,"
ffered Clarice in a scared voice. "I am sure I do not know
what is to be done."

"Go home," offered Freddy hopefully. "That's the thing."

"Perhaps that's best," agreed Lord Litchfield, mistrusting
ne rather dangerous look that had begun to animate his
iend's countenance. "No doubt it is a misunderstanding
which can all be smoothed over in time."

"Unworthy, Lionel," said Sir Oliver with a rather grim
mile. "Cousin Georgiana, I have not yet had the pleasure of
waltzing with you," he said. "Will you stand up with me for
his dance?"

"Oliver—" protested his lordship with a little choke.

"Oliver, you are mad," said Clarice in a furious whisper.
"You dare not do it. You will be ruined."

"Nonsense. The Princess is not the only person to lead Soci-
y, as even she will agree."

"Yes, but even if your credit is good enough to withstand such a direct affront to Her Highness, Miss Oversham's is not. Only think, Oliver," said his lordship in a rather urgent tone, "it will almost certainly mean her undoing."

"I am willing," interrupted Georgiana, startling them all.

Sir Oliver looked at her speculatively. "You are, aren' you?"

"I have made up my mind that I wish for neither the ac quaintance nor the goodwill of the people in this room," she said firmly.

"Georgiana!" moaned Clarice softly.

Sir Oliver gave her a real smile, the one he reserved for the small circle of friends who truly knew him, and which few in Almack's had ever seen. "Brava, little cousin. I admire you courage. But I am afraid that for once Litchfield here has a valid point. Let us try the effect of diplomacy first. Even the Iron Duke would not scorn such a strategy as that!"

Princess Esterhazy had enjoyed a light flirtation with Si Oliver since her husband, the Austrian ambassador to the cour of St. James, had brought her to live in London. She was gen erally acknowledged to be a sophisticate and a wit despite he rather tender years for such a calling, and Sir Oliver's reputed infatuation with his little nobody of a cousin had done much t reconcile her conscience to the snub she had dealt to Geor giana. The thought that a girl with vulgar connections and o such a doubtful sense of propriety as to misrepresent hersel not only to her own family but to the ton as well could succeed in touching the heart of the (she had believed) heartless Si Oliver she found provoking in the extreme, and seeing the warm manner in which he treated the chit only redoubled he determination to exclude the girl from Society.

It was in this rather dangerous mood that Sir Oliver found her when he crossed the floor of Almack's to offer his greet ings and solicit her permission to dance the waltz with hi cousin. She raised one delicate black brow at him and said a imperiously as she could manage, "I am not to be trifled wit this evening, Oliver. I have the headache."

"Yes," he agreed, giving her a level glance, "I noticed you ere not in your best looks."

She gave a little choke of rage. "Your taste runs to milk-aids and country misses these days, I hear."

"My taste in company is something you of all people have ad but little cause to reprimand," he said evenly.

"Perhaps, but tastes change, *évidemment*."

"Apparently," he agreed, infuriating her still more.

"When may I wish you joy, Oliver?" she asked him scorn-ally.

"Oh, you need not trouble yourself so far as that," he told er. "I merely wish you to present me to my cousin Miss versham as an eligible partner for the waltz."

She shook her head. "That I will not do."

A flicker of something in his eyes gave her pause, but he aid with perfect good humor, "May I ask why?"

"I need not answer to anyone, not even to you, Oliver. But I ill tell you, it does not amuse me for country nobodies to put emselves forward in such a fashion as your cousin, and I ill *not* assist you in making sport of Society by advancing a irtual impostress to its highest rungs!"

"Ah," said Sir Oliver enigmatically. "May I ask how you ame by the notion that my attentions to Miss Oversham are itended to 'make sport of Society,' as you put it? Or that she not what she seems?"

"No, you may not. But I must assure you that my source is ery reliable, and I for one do not see how you could do such a ing to those you profess to hold in friendship."

"It is, I collect, a greater act of friendship to withhold per-iission for Miss Oversham to waltz? Never mind; do not an-wer me. My dear Princess, would it do the least bit of good or me to assure *you* that I have no such dishonorable inten-ons as you ascribe to me? My cousin is undoubtedly a lady, vhatever else she may be, and she has treated the members of iy family with a great deal more kindness than they deserve. f she wishes to succeed on the ton, naturally I will assist her i any way I can."

She watched him shrewdly. "Oliver, have you by any hance conceived a *tendre* for this chit?"

He smiled. "Have you seen Robert Utterby this evening? find that I have urgent business to discuss with him."

She waved a hand dismissively, angry that he would no discuss it with her. If he had confessed his folly, she migh have softened and given the girl permission to dance, but now she would never do so. "You will say it is not my business, suppose."

"Certainly not. I am never rude. You do not, I perceive mean to give your permission."

"*Impossible*."

"And if I lead her on to the floor without it?"

"You do not dare. I should ruin her thoroughly. You do no rule *here*, Oliver. There is no one superior to a Patroness!"

"I beg to differ with you, ma'am. You will excuse me, know, but I shall return shortly with a guest."

"It is a mere ten minutes until the doors are closed agains latecomers," she said with a ruthless magnificence. "And n one, *no one* is admitted without a voucher, ever!"

"We shall see," returned Sir Oliver affably.

Miss Oversham bore the news that she was not to be imme diately rescued from social purgatory by waltzing with Si Oliver with a great deal more fortitude than Clarice. Thoug she could not say so, Clarice was afraid that the stigma appar ently—if mysteriously—attaching itself to Georgiana migh just as easily enlarge to encompass herself and Freddy an Amabel as well. Clarice had never abandoned the hope tha she might one day rule over another establishment, but he chances of contracting matrimony with a suitable parti de pended upon staying on the right side of Society, and Societ was Almack's.

"Should we not depart then, Oliver?" she asked worriedl "I do not think I can bear the supercilious glances that odiou Lady Sophronia is giving me, merely because the Princess ad ministered a snub. It makes me quite ready to sink! And I'r quite certain Freddy's arm is paining him, isn't it, my love?"

Freddy, ever oblivious to hints, said blightingly, "Not a b of it, Mama. Coming along very well."

"Well, and Amabel has the headache, I shouldn't wonder

rom all that whirling about the floor. May we not go home, Oliver?"

Sir Oliver directed his inquiry at Georgiana. "Do you think you might hang on here for just a bit longer? It is difficult, I know, but Princess Esterhazy has thrown down the gauntlet and I fear we may be vanquished if we do not pick it up." A hint of humor lit his eyes. "I believe we may come about again, but if so I must depart at once. I will be back as soon as I can. Will you be all right?"

Georgiana, to her own surprise, found herself smiling. "Yes, I will. But I began to think you are enjoying this."

He smiled at her in return. "I am not. But I suspect I may! Be brave!"

"How odiously provoking," said Clarice crossly when he had left the room. "To leave us stranded here when Amabel particularly told him she had the headache. And now he will be shut out, and we shall have to make our way home alone."

"No, Mama," Freddy corrected her. "Told him yourself Aunt Amabel had the headache. You said—"

"Be quiet, Freddy," she told her beloved son impatiently. "I cannot think how we are to manage a quiet exit if you are forever talking to me."

Some twenty minutes later, when the doors had relentlessly shut against latecomers, a commotion was heard on the stairs. Clarice, who knew how strictly this inviolable rule was enforced, said with alarm, "Whatever can that be? Not—not *riots* or anything of that nature. Oh dear, I fear I shall faint if we are trapped here!"

"Riots?" inquired Georgiana with interest.

"My dear—the vulgar mob. Oh, I shall have a spasm!"

"I shouldn't think it was anything like that," offered Amabel placidly. "Perhaps it is only an . . . inebriated gentleman from one of the clubs who is trying to gain admittance. The porters will soon take care of it."

"Foxed!" contributed Lord Nugent gleefully.

"Freddy, how vulgar," said Clarice, who had begun to wonder what further tortures the evening could hold.

A murmuring in the crowd swept toward them in a great wave. The musicians, who had been in the midst of a waltz, broke off suddenly. Georgiana, who was standing beside Freddy, found that she could not see the door. "What is it?" she asked, standing on tiptoe.

"Can't tell," said Freddy, who had the best view. "Fellow has his back to me. Fat gentleman, with a taste for fancy dress."

"Freddy what *are* you talking about?" demanded Clarice with ill-disguised impatience. "You know very well the Patronesses will admit no one now."

"Can't say about that, Mama, but fellow's doing the pretty to the Princess. Say! Have a notion I've seen him somewhere before."

Clarice, by dint of much ladylike maneuvering, had managed to place herself so that she had a much-obstructed view of the entrance. She looked, and then rounded on her son with frustrated indignation. "Of course you have seen him, Frederick! It is Sir Oliver!"

Freddy remained obdurate in light of this information. "Too fat," he insisted. "Wears a scarlet coat. Oliver would never—"

Clarice silenced him with a gasp. "Oh it *is* Oliver," she exclaimed thankfully. "And he's brought the *Prince*!"

Chapter 15

PRINCE GEORGE, Regent of England since his father's permanent incapacity in 1811, was the leader of a rather more profligate and irregular set than the ton who frequented Almack's, and his eccentric taste in architecture (as exemplified by the Chinese Gothic monstrosity at Brighton), his bizarre relationship with his estranged wife, Caroline of Brunswick, and his many indiscreet affairs, often rendered him ludicrous in the eyes of Society. His quarrel with Beau Brummel (the Beau, having asked his dinner companion "Who is your fat friend?", was chided by the Prince as having had too much to drink, whereupon Mr. Brummel was reputed to have demanded that the Prince ring the bell for his carriage) some years before had exacerbated these difficulties, as had his having had the poet Leigh Hunt sent to jail for two years for calling him a "fat Adonis of fifty." Nevertheless, he was, in the right circumstances, possessed of an all-conquering charm, a graceful wit, and an ability to single out—with a particularly gracious bow or a degree of special attention—that could win over the most hardened and cynical courtier. Coupled with the immense prestige of the monarchy—owing in no small part to the rectitude and propriety with which his parents had conducted themselves—these qualities caused him to be received with an enthusiasm which might not be supposed from the remarks that were made outside of his hearing.

Though he was not in general disposed to enter the lists on one side or the other of social disputes, Sir Oliver's story had tickled his fancy. Sir Oliver was not a member of the Prince's set, but the Overshams were Tories in good standing and Sir Oliver had that very evening proven himself a lively and entertaining dinner guest, without the tone of bored amusement with which some in Society attempted to demonstrate their superiority to their future sovereign. The Prince always appeared to remain in ignorance of this condescension, but in reality he stored up such incidents and was not above occasionally paying them back in a manner not inconsistent with the dignity of the monarchy. Princess Esterhazy had attempted to elbow aside his own favorite, Lady Jersey, for supremacy at Almack's, and her husband, the Austrian ambassador, was far too conscious of the prestige of the immensely wealthy and ancient empire he represented. Prince George was not disinclined to help poor Sir Oliver's country cousin and at the same time depress the pretensions of the Esterhazys in a very gratifying manner.

Dressed in a rich scarlet uniform, a magnificent star on his chest, His Royal Highness cut an imposing figure as he strode through the doors of Almack's. The Princess blenched, and her mouth fell open, an indelicacy she immediately rectified by falling into a deep curtsy. "Sir! It is an honor! We had not—that is, we did not expect—"

"Yes, yes!" replied the Prince with just the tiniest air of impatience. "The honor is all mine, ma'am. I hope you will forgive my coming so late, but it is a long time since I have looked in at Almack's, and naturally I would not like to be backward in any little attention."

"Thank you, sir," said the Princess faintly.

"I have brought Sir Oliver Townsend with me," said the Prince. "He tells me he is in your black books, but I am sure you will forgive him, eh? I've come tonight on purpose to meet that dashing young cousin of his. Will you be so kind as to ask the musicians to strike up the waltz?"

The Princess, thus coopted, could only assent. Her fury was not assuaged by the look of amusement in Sir Oliver's dark eyes. "You do not play fair, my friend," she hissed at him when the Prince had moved on to greet the other Patronesses.

"On the contrary, Princess," he said with a smile that did nothing to reduce her desire to skewer him with something very long and very sharp, "it is you who issued the challenge. You are too just to fault me for taking it up. Come, Princess,

let us be friends again. I assure you the girl is quite innocent of
the scheming you attribute to her. It is my great-aunt who
wishes to introduce her into Society."

"It is a royal command," said the Princess coldly. "How can
one go against that?"

Georgiana confronted the prospect of impending royalty
with a full heart. The evening's humiliations and the seem-
ingly endless time between Sir Oliver's departure and his triumphant return had worn her down, and now the prospect of
meeting the Prince Regent, who was, apparently, bearing
down on her with the evident purpose of singling her out for
notice, was almost enough to overset the tight lid she had
placed on her emotions. Beside her, Amabel, who had already
been presented at court and had met the Prince once or twice
at Pemberton as well, was whispering instructions, which she
only half attended. She went down in a deep curtsy, and rose
to find His Royal Highness executing a surreptitious peek
down her bosom. She caught Sir Oliver's amused eye on her
and smiled. "Mrs. Oversham, Miss Ponsonby, how delightful
it is to see you again." It was not the least part of the Prince's
charm that he had an excellent memory for names. "And you
must be Miss Oversham," he said in a booming voice. "I have
been most eager to make your acquaintance. I wonder if I
might entreat you to waltz with me. It is seldom that I come to
Almack's, and you would do me the greatest honor."

Georgiana experienced the very agreeable sensation of feeling the envious eyes of everyone in the room upon her as she
walked out onto the floor on the Prince's arm. He was an excellent dancer, despite his prodigious girth, and spoke to her
so naturally that she soon forgot her nervousness and was able
to respond to his questions about the ruins at Fountains Abbey,
for which he expressed the greatest admiration and which she
had, fortunately, often had the pleasure of visiting. In this
happy vein she surrendered to the enjoyment of the moment,
and when he had escorted her back to Clarice and taken his
leave, having, as he said with a wink, a rather important card
game awaiting his return, she almost began to wonder if she
had dreamed it.

The aftereffects of royal approval were immediately obvi-

ous, and she was beset by gentlemen soliciting her hand for
the remaining dances. She found, however, that whatever taste
she had had for such amusements had evaporated. She cast an
appealing glance at Sir Oliver, who had been dancing with
Miss Ponsonby while she danced with the Prince, and he, understanding, appeared at her side at once. "I am afraid my
cousin is promised to me for the next dance," he said, raising
his quizzing glass at young Lord Skeffington, whose persistent
efforts to gain possession of Miss Oversham's hand had
caused her to almost wrench it from his grasp. She felt a little
shy of him after what he had just done and was not sure she
wanted to utter her thanks in the middle of a crowded dance
floor. "May we not go home now?" she asked him in a quiet
voice.

The smile died out of his eyes. "This is no time to lose your
courage, cousin."

She tucked her hand into his arm. "It is not that," she said
seriously. "But I have a great deal to say to you, and I do not
think I can wait much longer to do so."

He looked down at her, putting his arm about her waist and
leading her expertly with the guiding pressure of his hand.
"You need not thank me, you know."

"You cannot prevent me," she said warmly.

"I have no wish to prevent you," he said with a twisted
smile. "I merely wish to remind you that I persuaded the
Prince to return with me in large part to infuriate the Princess.
I never thought when I entered into this absurd bet," he said
meditatively, "that it would prove to be so amusing."

She gave an involuntary chuckle. "Do you know, Cousin
Oliver, you are frequently quite abominable."

"Naturally I do! You have more than once said so, and I
have no reason to question your judgment."

"I wish you would be serious for just a moment! I would
like to express to you my deep sense of obligation for—"

"I do not scruple to interrupt you," he said, looking down at
her with a glint in his eye, "because it is apparent that you
have nothing of importance to say. Besides, should you not be
minding the steps?"

"Oh dear!" cried Georgiana in apparent dismay, "have I

scuffed your polish again?"

"You know perfectly well that you have not. Can it be only a few weeks ago that it was far otherwise?" There was a hint of mockery in the smile that hovered about his mouth. "I am, I take it, supposed to attribute this sudden acquisition of ballroom skills to Frederick's masterful teaching. It is as well he succeeded, for it is not at all the thing to tread on the Prince Regent's toes!"

Georgiana choked. "I may have deceived you—a little," she admitted shakily. "But you were most odiously provoking, and I could not resist!"

"I cannot tell you what a relief it is to hear you admit it," he said meekly. "My valet was in despair lest you try to prove your point on my boot tops, which are his most special care!"

"How detestable you are! I should have known better than to cross swords with you, but I have an overmastering desire to do so almost every time we converse. The worst of it is, you make me quite detestable, too, when what I intended was to express my gratitude for your saving me from the most embarrassing of snubs."

"I don't think I could do that, even if I wished to."

"Save me from a snub?" she asked puzzled. "But I thought—"

"That is not what I meant," he said dispassionately, leaving her in some doubt as to his meaning.

Georgiana found that her heart was pounding and she was a little breathless from the dance. An overwhelming desire to tell him the truth swept over her, and only the difficulty of confiding such a matter on the dance floor prevented her from confessing then and there. "C-cousin Oliver, may we not end this game?" she said, stammering a little.

"The Prince's favor will restore your position, you know," he said levelly. "No one will dare to cut you now."

"I know, that is, I do not know, but I do not care! If it is truly so, can you not claim to have won the bet? I find I have lost my taste for deception," she said sincerely.

His eyes searched her face. "And you would go back to . . . where?"

She lowered her eyes. "Back to where I came from," she said with perfect truth.

"I would advise you not to throw away your chances for the sake of your belated scruples," he said in a harsh tone. "I am persuaded that you will not like the life of a governess, and I mean to assist you if I can. But you must stay until the party my great-aunt means to give for you in any case. I thought we had agreed on that."

Georgiana assented unhappily, and for the rest of the dance they talked of commonplaces, until the music stopped.

The carriage ride home afforded the three ladies none of the usual pleasures of mulling over, in relative privacy and comfort, the evening's triumphs and tragedies. Clarice was quite worn out with the emotional vicissitudes of rejection and salvation and could scarcely even exert herself to remonstrate with Freddy, whose cryptic utterances she found more than usually exasperating. Amabel, for reasons best known to herself, was in a decidedly ill humor. The remaining occupant was engaged in a tumultuous inner struggle which so absorbed her that she scarcely attended to Miss Ponsonby's desultory observations on the frailties of the ton on the one hand, or Clarice's piteous sighs and exclamations on the other.

Georgiana had very nearly told Sir Oliver the truth about herself at Almack's, and she was very much of the opinion that she must do so without further delay. She had long since relinquished the wish to humiliate him in some public and painful fashion, and she was rather ashamed of herself for undertaking the bet in the first place. There was no doubt that Sir Oliver had behaved in a high-handed manner toward her, but her outraged pride had led her into complicity in a scheme which she had very soon begun to regret. She sensed that Sir Oliver also regretted the deception, as he saw it, and might reasonably be expected to welcome the opportunity to extricate himself from a situation that had become uncomfortable to them both. That he had shown no urgent inclination to do so she attributed to an unwillingness to upset Lady Louisa, and, perhaps, to be vanquished by Mr. Utterby's traps.

The reason for her own reluctance was not far to seek. The

dread of seeing his expression turn from warmth—for there *had* been warmth there, she was sure of it—to dislike when he learned of the trick she had served him made her hesitate. What he had done for her—involving the Prince in her social reclamation when he believed her to be a penniless governess—had involved substantial risk to his own standing, and she was not eager to requite such generosity with the unpleasant truth. Besides, no little awkwardness would inevitably attend their meeting after her revelation, and she foresaw endless complications and censure within the family.

There was, moreover, a further reason for her reluctance, which she was scarcely willing to admit even to herself. She could only contemplate with some misery the revelation she had received, in a rather blinding fashion, when Sir Oliver had taken her in his arms on the dance floor. Every warning she had ever received from Clarice or Amabel or even his own friends recalled the danger of trusting him too far, and while her heart told her she might confide in him, her brain, and her experience, revolted at the prospect of almost certain exposure and rejection.

She awoke from her reverie to find herself contemplated in a rather frank and malevolent fashion by Miss Ponsonby, while Clarice dozed against the pillows, snoring slightly. Georgiana wondered if her thoughts, and her unhappiness, were visible to the other girl, and determined that nothing would make her so careless as to open her mind to Amabel. It had for some time been apparent to her that Miss Ponsonby wanted Sir Oliver for herself, though Georgiana doubted very much whether she really had a heart to lose to him, and she could only imagine the disastrous consequences if she were to somehow perceive that Georgiana herself was hopelessly, miserably, and irrevocably in love with him as well.

Chapter 16

LADY LOUISA WAS moved to unexpected good humor by the news that none other than the Prince Regent himself had rescued her granddaughter from social ruin at the hands of a Foreigner. However much she might sneer at the ton, she was well aware of what a life excluded from its precincts could really mean, and she could only admire Sir Oliver's adroit handling of the situation, and speculate upon the gratifying reasons that he should so exert himself on his cousin's behalf. Lady Louisa was too selfish herself to condemn or even recognize the vice in others, but she was very well able to perceive that it was seldom indeed that her great-nephew was disposed to take any trouble over anyone but himself.

Her mood, as she sat down to breakfast the morning after the incident at Almack's, was therefore benign, though she did not go to such extremes as to communicate this to the servants, or to any of the assembled members of her family. "I take it, miss, that you have succeeded in setting London about its ears," she said to Georgiana with a cackle, biting into her toast. "Hmmph! Waltzing with Prince George! Not that I hold with the waltz, mind you. I daresay I could give you another name for it!"

"Oh, Lady Louisa!" cried Clarice. "It is not at all improper! No one could be more punctilious than Mrs. Drummond-Burrell, and you know she sanctioned it some time ago."

"I know indecency when I see it," insisted her ladyship with relish. "But I wish I might have been there to see every eye in the room on my granddaughter and His Royal Highness!"

"Yes, it is unfortunate that there will be so much gossip and speculation, when that is most particularly what one wishes to avoid," said Miss Ponsonby sourly. "And I fear Princess Esterhazy was quite seriously displeased."

"Pooh! Do her good! There are too many namby-pamby girls without enough spirit to keep from toadeating the Patronesses as it is."

"Well I am afraid *I* might have toadeaten her," confessed Georgiana with a smile, "but she did not give me the chance. She snubbed me as we came in the door, and I am still not sure what I might have done to offend her."

"It's quite true," offered Clarice. "My nerves were completely shattered. If Oliver had not appeared, I do not know what we should have done. It was intolerable, I can tell you. No one would speak to poor Cousin Georgiana!"

"I take it that great nodcock you gave birth to was as useless as ever," said Lady Louisa acidly.

Freddy looked up from his sausages with a mildly puzzled expression. "Ma'am?"

"You are unjust, Grandmama," said Georgiana swiftly, before her grandmother could utter a blistering retort. "Freddy offered to take me home, and perhaps if I had been sensible I would have accepted his very kind offer. I assure you there was nothing anyone could do." She frowned. "I fear that Amabel is right. We have made an enemy of Princess Esterhazy, and I am quite sure that all the idle talk is only beginning. Perhaps it would be more comfortable for everyone if we were to cancel my come-out," she said calmly.

"Nonsense!" cried Lady Louisa scornfully. "What do I care for a lot of useless tattle? Besides, if the Prince stands your friend, you need not fear Princess Esterhazy. Hoity-toity! I wish I might see her taken down a peg. As a matter of fact I thought I might invite His Royal Highness to the party, and I have every expectation that he will be gracious enough to stop in."

"Do you think he might wish to?" inquired Georgiana, thinking that such an entertainment might prove a little tame in view of what Prince George was reputed to prefer.

"He came to *my* come-out," offered Miss Ponsonby.

"Oh yes; he was a particular friend of your grandfather's,

Cousin Georgiana, and he has been kind enough to notice us—
Amabel and Freddy and me—as well," offered Clarice.

"Spoke to me twice about his horses," said Freddy, who
sometimes disconcerted his relatives by attending to what they
said.

The magnificence of this condescension caused a moment
of silence to descend upon the table.

Lady Louisa was the first to break it. "Widgeon!" she
hissed. "I shall have to ask Oliver to attend to it." She sum-
moned the butler with a wave of her hand. "Dukeworth, do
you send round a note to Sir Oliver asking him to wait upon
me this afternoon if it is quite convenient. Say that I will require his good offices on behalf of Miss Oversham."

Georgiana, who, in light of the previous evening's revela-
tions, could not view such a visit without a flutter of confusion
within her breast, immediately resolved to be out of the house
when Sir Oliver came calling.

Sir Oliver, owing to a lengthy and rather annoying appointment with his tailor in Old Bond Street, was somewhat late in
receiving Lady Louisa's summons, and in consequence feared
he might arrive upon her doorstep after she had already retired
for her afternoon nap. The prospect did not really trouble him,
because her note, though written in a tone Wellington himself
would have hesitated to use with a subordinate, was not particularly indicative of urgency. Besides, if she was asleep, he
might hope to speak with Georgiana alone.

Sir Oliver found himself pitchforked into a state of indecision and difficulty. His own feelings for the girl he had persuaded to call herself his cousin under rather regrettable
circumstances had dragged him into a state of nagging uncertainty. He found himself strongly attracted to her, in a way that
was not at all typical of his usual flirtations. He liked her composure, her compassion and kindness toward Lord Nugent,
and her courage in the face of social opprobrium. The devil of
it was that the more he saw of her the stronger these feelings
became, and he found himself thinking about her rather more
often than was comfortable to his peace of mind.

Thanks to his having introduced her to his family and the

world as Miss Oversham, he could not envision any possible way of continuing a relationship with her as the governess— what in the deuce was her name? Amelia Georgiana, that was it. He thought of her now as Georgiana Oversham, without hesitation or scruple. He knew that he had wronged her by putting her in a position that would make her scorned in the eyes of the ton when the truth came out, but he was too world-lywise to believe for a moment that their fragile friendship could withstand such buffeting or such censure. He ought, in mercy, to send her away before the inevitable unmasking, but he was reluctant to hasten what must be their final parting. If he had thought she returned his feelings he might have risked everything, but he was not even sure she had overcome her obvious initial dislike (so well deserved!) of him. As it was, since he could not see into her heart, he must be careful of not beginning something he would be unable to finish with honor.

Thus embroiled in such unsatisfactory visions of his own future, he was surprised to find himself almost colliding with Mr. Utterby on his great-aunt's doorstep. The meeting did not improve his affability, for he was quite certain he had his friend to thank for the previous evening's near disaster. "How very fortunate, Robert. We have some business to discuss, I believe!"

At that moment the footman opened the door to them, and greeted them with the intelligence that her ladyship had retired to her bedroom to rest, and that Mrs. Oversham and Miss Ponsonby had gone out shopping.

"And *Miss* Oversham?" prompted Mr. Utterby.

"Miss has gone out for a walk in the park with some friends, sir."

"Well, I'll not stay then," said Mr. Utterby, beginning to turn away.

Sir Oliver's hand on his arm arrested him. "Stay, Robert, for just a few minutes. Jason, might we use the yellow saloon?"

"Oliver—" began Mr. Utterby.

"Be at ease, Robert. I'll not detain you long."

Mr. Utterby, bowing to the inevitable, followed him into the house with a sigh.

When Dukeworth had brought refreshments and left them

alone, Mr. Utterby raised an inquiring eyebrow. "Your move, I think."

"You have a vast deal of explaining to do," suggested Sir Oliver calmly.

Mr. Utterby smiled. "I presume from that remark that I have succeeded in thrusting a spoke in your wheel after all."

"Not at all. But your innuendo in the ear of the Princess resulted in a rather uncomfortable evening for Clarice and my cousin until—"

"Your *cousin*?" asked Mr. Utterby in a mocking tone.

"For the purposes of this conversation, yes," replied Sir Oliver. "I was going to add that she was both embarrassed and humiliated by the Princess's snubbing her in front of half of the members of the ton. That is unworthy of you, Robert."

"I warned you, did I not?" asked Mr. Utterby softly, and saw Sir Oliver's hand clench involuntarily.

"I take it this is about something more than whether you are required to part with your chestnuts."

Mr. Utterby smiled. "You were always very astute, Oliver."

"Would it be useless to offer you my assistance?"

"Quite useless. I could not take it from you, though I should like to very much. I have just that shred of conscience left, but do not tempt me too far. Pray satisfy my curiosity: did I succeed in ruining Miss Oversham?"

"You did not."

"Ah. How very . . . disappointing. I was quite persuaded that I would, though I did have a contingency plan, I will admit. Am I permitted to know what went wrong?"

"I persuaded the Prince Regent to attend Almack's for the express purpose of asking my cousin to dance."

"You unman me. I am lost in admiration. I should not have thought of that."

"Since I have satisfied your curiosity, perhaps you will satisfy mine," said Sir Oliver.

"Anything, dear boy. We shall not meet frequently after this, I daresay."

"Most likely not. What are you doing here?"

"Ah. The contingency plan. I came to ask Clarice and Amabel and of course Miss Oversham to the theater. There is a

ovely new actress I am persuaded they would wish to see. I
might even include Lord Nugent, just to observe his reaction."

"Miss Cecelia Leroux, I take it, is the actress you speak of?"

"Most certainly."

"And you would contrive to have her recognize Cousin
Georgiana and point that out to Clarice and Amabel."

"Did I not say you were astute?"

"You will not issue such an invitation, Robert," said Sir
Oliver in a quiet tone.

"Very likely not," agreed Mr. Utterby.

"I take it that you are not so lost to a sense of what is sporting as to inform my great-aunt or any other member of my
family directly that Cousin Georgiana is not, in fact, Cousin
Georgiana?"

Mr. Utterby looked genuinely taken aback. "I find it deeply
insulting that you could even suggest such a thing."

"My apologies. I would like to be certain that there will be
no . . . incidents at least until after my great-aunt's party."

"You may be certain of nothing except that I shall come
about again."

"If you injure the girl, the consequences to yourself will almost certainly be unpleasant," suggested Sir Oliver in an even
tone of voice which nevertheless made his listener shrink back
a little against the cushions.

"You astound me, Oliver. I'd no idea you had conceived a
tendre for the chit. You should take care you do not fall into
the parson's mousetrap!"

"I will," promised Sir Oliver.

"More to the point, it is high time you disposed of Clarice
and Amabel honorably. You could hardly wish to take possession of Pemberton with the two of them in residence, particularly if you mean to install your wife there."

"Robert, this conversation is beginning to bore me."

"Only think," persisted Mr. Utterby, "what life would be
like with Miss Ponsonby casting die-away glances at you at
any hour of the night or day, while lecturing your bride upon
the *bearing* required of one who has ascended to the
Townsend-Oversham dignity."

"Robert, I fail to see—"

"Only this. You will, I believe, admit that the situation will shortly become intolerable. I am willing to rid you of your burden—to take her off your hands."

At this unfortunate moment, Georgiana, who had just returned from her walk in the park, walked past the yellow saloon. Mr. Utterby's comment arrested her progress, and without meaning to eavesdrop she paused in frozen attention beside the door.

Sir Oliver sounded scornful. "You would marry her?"

"I would. For a price."

"I see."

"I thought you would. It would save you the trouble of producing some respectable widower in search of a mama for his passel of brats and willing, I might add, to overlook a certain lack of fortune."

Georgiana, her hand over her mouth, ran soundlessly up the stairs. She could not bring herself to hear what Sir Oliver might say to his friend's proposal. She had heard enough to know that it was the death knell to any hope she might have of his ever returning her regard, but she would not stay to break her heart. She had heard the scorn in his voice, and the manner in which Mr. Utterby had referred to her as his "burden."

She was glad now that she had placed a guard on her sensibilities. It was too late to prevent the wounding of her feelings, but at least she had the consolation of knowing that she had never given him reason to believe he had a place in her heart. It was of the utmost importance that he never learn what a fool she had been. "The situation will shortly become intolerable," Mr. Utterby had said. She could only vow that she would never reveal by so much as the flicker of an eyelid how nearly he had hit the mark.

If she could have, she would have run home to Yorkshire that afternoon, but she would not give him the satisfaction of driving her away. She could not bear to give rise to the sort of speculation *that* would evoke. Let them wonder, she vowed bravely, and burst into tears.

Sir Oliver, meanwhile, was entirely innocent of the devastating effect Mr. Utterby's remarks had had on Miss Over-

ham. He was rather more occupied with the effect they were
aving on himself. "You cannot possibly be serious."

"I admit I have none of the husbandly virtues, but I doubt
vhether Miss Ponsonby would care about that. I am at *point
on plus,* my friend. I am in deadly earnest."

"And so am I. I should do everything in my power to induce
Miss Ponsonby not to accept, were you to make her such an
ffer."

Mr. Utterby shrugged. "Oh you need not go so far as that, if
ou don't wish to oblige me. All that would be necessary is to
efuse to make a settlement upon her, and the issue would be-
ome moot, I assure you."

Sir Oliver raised an eyebrow at him. "The only thing that
as ever made you tolerable, Robert, was your impudence.
Iowever, in this instance you have gone too far. Let us con-
ider the matter unsaid, for I cannot but feel that it might be
nhealthy were the subject to arise again."

Mr. Utterby, rising, sketched him a mocking bow. "As you
rish, Oliver. But you leave me no choice. Be warned—I am a
esperate man, and desperate men can be dangerous!"

Chapter 17

HAVING ENJOYED a bout of weeping which left her exhausted and not a little inclined to believe that the hour of her birth had been a singularly unfortunate one, Georgiana sternly took herself to task for having been such a fool as to think the redoubtable Sir Oliver Townsend might ever succumb to the charms of a girl he believed to be a penniless nobody. She was deeply mortified that he apparently regarded her as a burden to be shed in some expeditious manner as soon as he had won the bet, but she was forced to remind herself that other than a certain warmth in his eyes when he had spoken to her and a willingness to enter into an agreeable banter, he had never given her any reason to believe that his affections might be engaged. *Fool,* she told herself again, *he warned you.* If only she had listened to her head instead of her heart!

She was determined not to betray her unhappiness to the rest of the family by giving way to melancholia or listlessness, and she succeeded so well in plunging into the preparations for her party with a kind of a glittering restlessness that Miss Ponsonby kindly reminded her that a rest in the afternoon might do much to restore her color, and that judicious applications of Gowland's lotion were said to eliminate both freckles and circles under the eyes.

Clarice was demonstrating an unexpected efficiency in arranging what must be considered Georgiana's debut. The refreshments, the awnings, the champagne, and the red carpet had all been ordered, and the flowers would consist of sprays of yellow roses, which all except Miss Ponsonby agreed would set off Georgiana's coloring to perfection. The cards of invitation reminded Georgiana of an incident she had almost forgotten, her meeting with the rather eccentric Lady Brunswick, who had asked to be invited to her party. Georgiana was of half a mind not even to bring the matter up, but the stranger had asked particularly to be included and Georgiana had given her word. The woman, who apparently spent most of her time on the Continent, would very likely never receive the invitation in any case, so there could be very little harm in sending her a card.

"Yes, dear," replied Clarice absently to her inquiry as to the propriety of including a total stranger among their number, "I am quite sure there could be no objection to any friend of Sir James Winterhaven's. He is very good ton, even if he is a Whig." Clarice was preoccupied with the issue of whether Frederick's irksome arm would be out of its sling by the evening of the party, so that he could lead his cousin out onto the dance floor. She was quite pleased by the friendship that had grown up between her son and Miss Oversham, but she looked in vain for signs that it might be developing into anything more than that. She knew she could not count on Freddy to make a push to secure Georgiana's affections, but she intended to use every means at her disposal to induce him to make a declaration on the night of the debut. It was probably his last chance, and if only he were not such a nodcock as to muff it they might all be so comfortable.

"I think it is very unlikely she would turn out to be vulgar, or with a family in trade, or anything like that," she told Georgiana, turning over a cream-colored envelope in her hands and admiring the excellent penmanship with which she had addressed it, "but of course you must check with your grandmama first. Lady Louisa is very correct and would like to be consulted on such things. And I am wondering, my dear, do you think I should wear my sea-foam gown? I did think to have a new one made up, but Sir Barnaby Philpot was kind enough to say it made him think of the ocean's wild depths or some such thing when I wore it, and you know he has ten thousand pounds a year!"

Lady Louisa, who had been watching the developing relationship between Georgiana and Sir Oliver with possessive interest, was certain that the Oversham fortune would soon be back in the hands of the family, where it belonged. She had no illusion of directing Sir Oliver or his affairs, but if she might see him married to Georgiana and settled as the acknowledged heir to Pemberton, with all that entailed, she might die, if not happy, at least with satisfaction. She had known Sir Oliver since he was in leading strings, and if he had not gone top over tail over her granddaughter she was very much mistaken. He had certainly never given her any hint of his intentions, but when she had heard the eminently satisfying tale of Prince George's rescue of her granddaughter, she was sure she could not be wrong. Her great-nephew had many virtues, but not the most doting of his admirers had ever accused him of exerting himself to such extremes to effect the comfort of anyone else. Since her ladyship's character was not notably generous, she found little to censure in this attitude, but as she was able to put the most agreeable construction on his present behavior, she had no objection to his having altered it.

Since she had little expectation of Sir Oliver's confiding his success with his cousin, she thought she might discover from her granddaughter whether he had come up to scratch. She began to imagine the triumph of announcing the betrothal at the forthcoming party, where the presence of royalty would set seal on their social cachet forever. She even nourished the hope that Georgiana's fortune, once safely wed to Oliver, might dower Clarice and Amabel, and take them off her hands as well.

Thus it was in a mood of satisfaction that she received Georgiana in her sitting room one morning shortly before the party. If she had been less selfish, or more interested, she might have noticed that Georgiana seemed unnaturally pale and not at all inclined to cross her. If she had discerned these alarming signs, she would doubtless have attributed them to lovesickness, or some such foolishness, but she did not notice. In fact, Georgiana was finding it rather exhausting to pretend to be in spirits when her heart was sore, and she did not sleep well at night.

"I have brought up the list of invitations for the party," she told Lady Louisa. "Clarice says you have already approved most of the names, but perhaps you would like to see if they are correct."

"Yes, of course. If you would get me the tablets beside my table, and a pencil. . . . Yes, yes . . . One must include Sir Geoffrey Morehouse, I suppose . . . The Miltons, of course . . . Clarice has such execrable handwriting it quite strains my eyes! Hmmph!" She gave a little chuckle. "Will Prince and Princess Esterhazy attend, I wonder?"

Georgiana forced a smile. "I cannot say, ma'am."

"Ha! Sly boots! Still, you will not wish to have such a one as that for an enemy, when you are married. I daresay Oliver can bring her round without too much difficulty, however!"

There was no mistaking the import of this. "Ma'am, I—"

Lady Louisa had returned to her list. She gave a crack of laughter. "Ha! Sir Barnaby Philpot! That man milliner! Clarice's doing, no doubt. He is as great a looby as Frederick. I wish he may never set foot across *my* threshold!"

Alarmed, Georgiana ventured to inquire in some trepidation whether his name should be stricken from the list.

"No such thing," barked her ladyship. "If he must dangle after Clarice, perhaps he may be brought up to scratch and take her off my hands."

Georgiana, rather shocked by this unfeeling and somewhat mercenary statement, could find nothing to say. It was, perhaps, less surprising, though no less painful, that Sir Oliver should share his great-aunt's sentiments on such matters.

Lady Louisa regarded her shrewdly. "You do not care for such pound-dealing, I see. Well, it does not signify. I always speak my words with no bark upon them. Clarice and I deal well enough together, but there is no affection lost between us. She led my son a merry dance. And she had not been here a twelvemonth when she invited her sister to Pemberton as well. Mealy-mouthed miss! The pair of 'em think I haven't noticed Amabel has set her cap for Oliver!"

She returned to her scrutiny of the paper in her hand. Her ladyship had always been rather vain about her vision and would not admit to the need for glasses. The words on the page, as she regarded them, seemed to twist and writhe.

She thrust the list away impatiently. "This will do! Clarice has included everyone I wished to invite."

"There is one person, ma'am—"

"It will serve!" her ladyship snapped. "I have read the names, and I approve. Did you know, miss, that the Prince himself has agreed to look in on us?"

"It is an honor, ma'am. Clarice says he goes to very few private parties these days that he does not host himself."

"That is true, I believe," agreed her ladyship, preening. "Of course we are not on intimate terms with him, nor would we wish to be. His set is very fast, you know. Even Oliver does not approve." She frowned. "I lay it all at the feet of *that woman*."

"That woman?" inquired Georgiana.

"Princess Caroline," responded her grandmother impatiently. "Had he not married someone so unsuitable, or for whom he had not conceived such antipathy, he might have found a steadying influence and settled down. I know the Queen has always thought so." She shrugged. "There is always the possibility that he may be detained, or prevented. But if he should so much as set foot within doors, your acceptance is everywhere assured, I promise you!"

Georgiana found herself incapable of saying that such acceptance no longer mattered to her, and that she longed for the party to be over so that she might go home.

"Do you know what would make me happiest of all?" asked Lady Louisa, almost playfully.

"What is that, ma'am?"

"To be able to announce your betrothal on the night of the party."

Aghast, Georgiana struggled for words. "Oh, Grandmama, there can be no question of that—"

"Humdudgeon! Are you going to tell me you haven't had any offers?"

A number of gentlemen of varying degrees of eligibility had in fact proposed to her, but she shook her head. "No one I could acquit of having designs on my fortune."

"Then let me speak without any roundaboutation," pursued

Lady Louisa. "Have you succeeded where Miss Ponsonby could not?"

Georgiana stared at her.

"Come, girl, stop gaping. You cannot be ignorant of my meaning. Has Oliver proposed to you or not?"

Georgiana struggled to keep her voice firm and light. "Of course not, ma'am."

Her grandmother sounded annoyed. "What's holding him up? You need not scruple to consult me first, you know. You have my blessing."

Georgiana drew in a breath. "Oh, indeed, it is not that. There can be no question of such a relationship between us."

"Missish! You will lose him, you know, if you assume such airs."

"Ma'am, I beg you will attend to me when I tell you neither of us has ever entertained such a notion about each other. I hope we are . . . friends, but it can never be more than that between us."

Lady Louisa put her hand over her heart in an ominous gesture. "Nonsense! What can you be saying! I have seen with my own eyes what there is between you. There must be some misunderstanding."

Georgiana was nearly desperate to extricate herself from this uncomfortable conversation, but she wanted to make it clear to her grandmother that there was no possibility of a relationship between them. She was more than capable of taxing Sir Oliver with it otherwise, and Georgiana did not think her fortitude was sufficient for that. "Grandmama, I beg you will not distress yourself. I do not wish to cause you any unhappiness, but I feel I must insist that you are quite mistaken if you think you have perceived any feelings between Sir Oliver and myself other than civility and friendship. I am persuaded we should not suit, and any other assumption on your part can only cause your great-nephew a degree of embarrassment I am sure you would not wish to excite."

Lady Louisa lowered her brows thoughtfully. "I see what it is. He has not made his feelings plain, and your own are wounded."

"On the contrary, he has made them exceedingly plain," insisted Georgiana with a trace of melancholy.

"Idiot!" muttered Lady Louisa darkly.

Miss Ponsonby had not been idle in the time since she had been forced to watch Georgiana whirl around the floor of Almack's in the arms of, first, her future sovereign, and second an apparently admiring Sir Oliver. That he could be so deceived by someone who, Mr. Utterby had all but confessed had misrepresented herself substantially to her relatives was wormwood to Miss Ponsonby's soul. She could not sit idly by while Lady Louisa and Clarice and Frederick and Oliver exerted themselves on behalf of one who was unworthy of such devotion. That *he* could have persuaded the Prince Regent to save Miss Oversham from toils of her own making must mean he was blinded by partiality, for Miss Ponsonby, like Lady Louisa, had rarely seen him take so much trouble on anyone's behalf. She could not doubt that when he learned of the deception perpetrated against him he would cast off the offender at once, and then he would need someone to help assuage his wounded pride. Miss Ponsonby did not doubt that it was her duty to save him, and all of them, from Georgiana's encroaching ways.

Unfortunately, she was not precisely informed as to the nature of Miss Oversham's imposture, and her careful scrutiny was scarcely more revealing. She knew that Miss Oversham had arrived without the clothes, abigail, or other appurtenances of an heiress of apparently staggering wealth, but she had explained that in a rather bizarre and convoluted tale of snowstorms and lost luggage. Miss Ponsonby would have been inclined to dismiss this story out of hand, in light of Mr Utterby's hints, except that Sir Oliver himself vouched for at least a part of it. A quick search of Georgiana's room revealed no more satisfactory results, and the servants, discreetly questioned, could produce no incriminating evidence.

Still, ever since her enlightening conversation with Mr. Utterby, Miss Ponsonby had been studying Georgiana carefully and she was convinced she was hiding something. There was something unnatural in her reticence to talk about a home and lifestyle, which, had they belonged to Miss Ponsonby, would have afforded a rich subject matter with which to edify and impress. Moreover, of late Miss Oversham had been out of spirits and rather melancholy, despite an obvious determination not to appear so, and Miss Ponsonby could not but be certain that this was owing to the working of a guilty conscience.

There was nothing to be done but consult Mr. Utterby. Miss Ponsonby was somewhat loath to do so, for she was no fool and perceived that he had his own ends to serve, though she could not yet discern what they were. Nevertheless, she found his company rather agreeable, and if it was necessary to bend her principles a little and admit an outsider to the distasteful task of uncovering the family's dirty linen, she felt that Mr. Utterby would be a worthy ally.

She sent round a note to his lodgings asking him to wait upon her at a time when she knew the others would be out. Mr. Utterby received this communication without the surprise its sender had supposed, although he was inclined to view Miss Ponsonby's potential participation in his schemes as an unnecessary complication at best, and at worst a hazardous risk. Still, Mr. Utterby was in many respects a fair man, and he had to admit that he had brought it on himself. He had needed someone within the family to assist in undermining "Georgiana's" credibility, and Miss Ponsonby was the obvious candidate. He might still make use of her, but Sir Oliver had effectively circumvented his stratagems, and now he intended to move on to more desperate measures. Mr. Utterby sighed and resigned himself to a rather tedious afternoon.

Miss Ponsonby had arranged herself decorously on the sofa, her pale lilac dress in unfortunate contrast to its yellow hue. She offered Mr. Utterby her hand with a grave air, in a manner befitting one whose mission is unpleasant but obligatory.

"It is good of you to come," she told him, settling her skirts again. "I daresay you will have forgotten the conversation we had earlier about Miss Oversham, but—"

"I have not forgotten," Mr. Utterby assured her.

"I am afraid you will not like to become embroiled in our family affairs, but I must consult you on a matter of some delicacy, and of course I speak to you in the strictest confidence."

Mr. Utterby hastened to reassure her that she might rely upon his discretion, and added that he hoped she knew he would always endeavor to be of service in any matter touching herself or any member of the family.

Miss Ponsonby flushed with gratitude. "You are very kind sir. I hope I do not ask you to break a confidence when I ask you how you came by the information that Miss Oversham may not be . . . is not . . ."

"What she seems? I am afraid, my dear Miss Ponsonby, that I am not at liberty to disclose my source."

"Oh," said Miss Ponsonby, disappointed.

Mr. Utterby waited patiently for what he knew must come next.

"I will not press you, of course," said Miss Ponsonby after a moment. "It is only that I fear Sir Oliver may have been taken in, and since you are such a particular friend of his, I thought . . ."

"I fear you may be right," agreed Mr. Utterby most unsatisfactorily.

"You believe, then, that he has conceived a *tendre* for this girl," suggested Miss Ponsonby heavily.

"I believe he has some partiality for her which may have caused him to overlook certain questionable aspects of her character which are obvious to you and me."

"Forgive me, Mr. Utterby; you must speak plainly. What are these questionable aspects? I have scrutinized Miss Oversham's behavior rather carefully and I believe her to be hiding something, but I do not know what it is. But if it is a serious matter, is it not our duty to save Sir Oliver and Lady Louisa?"

Mr. Utterby suppressed a smile. "Indeed, ma'am, you are very right. You will regard it as a confidence, I know, if I tell you there is some reason to believe that Miss Oversham is not Miss Oversham at all. I hinted that such might be the case before; now I have even more compelling evidence."

Miss Ponsonby experienced a sensation somewhere between horror and glee. "You shock me, sir."

"I cannot yet be certain," warned Mr. Utterby, "but I believe I have uncovered a person who has encountered Miss Oversham under another name."

"Infamous!" cried Miss Ponsonby.

"That is just what I thought."

Miss Ponsonby rose majestically from her couch. "You will excuse me, I know. I must go to Lady Louisa without further delay!"

Mr. Utterby had to sit on his hands to keep himself from reaching out to restrain her forcibly. "Oh no, no!" he cried in a tone that made her look at him curiously.

"You would permit this dreadful deception to continue?" she inquired in an outraged tone.

"No indeed, ma'am. I am in accord with your thinking in every particular. Only one must proceed with the greatest caution. Think what a fuss and scandal there will be!"

"I do not think that a scandal may be averted in any event," said Miss Ponsonby with a certain relish.

"Doubtless you are correct, but in that case it is even more important to be certain of our witness. Besides," he said slyly, "I know that it cannot but be repugnant to one of your delicate scruples to be the bearer of such tidings to her ladyship and Sir Oliver."

This aspect of the situation—the undesirability of being the agent of unmasking Sir Oliver's favorite—had not occurred to her. She resumed her seat on the sofa. "I shall be guided by you," she said primly.

"Excellent!" exclaimed Mr. Utterby, with feeling. "Now if you will permit me, here is what I would suggest. . . ."

Chapter 18

SIR OLIVER, having conceived an overmastering desire to shield the girl masquerading as his cousin from every adverse wind, was somewhat at a loss as to how to extricate her from the embarrassing situation he had created without a scandal. He had always meant to let Society know the joke he had played on it, but now he foresaw that to do so would bring unwelcome notoriety on Georgiana's head. His mind whirled with a number of schemes for achieving her removal from Lady Louisa's household without such an undesirable result, but the only thing he could come up with was to have Georgiana continue as Miss Oversham forever, something he feared neither she nor the real heiress in Yorkshire would countenance. He could quite possibly come up with a plausible reason why she must remove herself from the London scene, but no reasonable scenario for keeping her by him.

Sir Oliver, in fact, had fallen deeply in love, and he was undergoing the hitherto entirely novel experience of not knowing whether or not his beloved returned his regard. He had thought she had forgiven him for the unfortunate circumstances of their meeting, and for the high-handed treatment he had subsequently accorded her; her manner toward him had grown warmer, and once or twice he had had reason to believe she might not be completely indifferent to him. However, since shortly after the incident at Almack's her behavior had been punctiliously correct, and decidedly distant. He, too, had noted the hollow eyes and pallor that betokened sleepless nights and a troubled mind, and he could not think of any explanation that was flattering to his hopes. He made every effort to see her alone, but she seemed to be avoiding him. Whenever he entered a room she had just quitted it, and whenever he called she was not at home.

On the morning of her interview with Lady Louisa, he chanced upon her alone at last, in the same saloon where Mr. Utterby had so recently held colloquy with Miss Ponsonby. Her eyes, when she raised them to his, had a dazed and rather stricken look which filled him with foreboding.

Georgiana, realizing that her grandmother would in all probability tax him with having failed to attach her, screwed up her courage to acquaint him with the outcome of the interview. Not for anything in the world would she let him see her wounded feelings, or that she did not willingly concur in the agreement that they should not suit. She strove for a light tone and said firmly: "I am very happy to see you, sir, because there is a matter on which I can set your mind at rest."

"Really?" he asked with a smile. "And what is that?"

Georgiana took the bit between her teeth. "I have made it clear to Lady Louisa that she must not expect any sort of romantic attachment between us."

The smile died out of his eyes. "Indeed?"

Georgiana studied the bracelet on her wrist with avid attention. "Yes. I should like to have consulted you about the proper timing, but the subject came up quite naturally, and I thought it best to make it plain once and for all."

"I see."

"As you can see, I have kept my bargain with you," she said brightly.

He brushed a speck of snuff off of his coat sleeve. "Most admirably."

Georgiana, her heart heavy as lead, went merrily on. "I do not think Lady Louisa was seriously disturbed. She was out of reason cross, of course, but in time she will come round to the notion. She is very fond of you, you know."

"Tell me," said Sir Oliver in a dry voice, "did you express your own wishes on the subject or merely what you believe to be mine?"

"Oh, my own as well, naturally," said Georgiana, the words twisting like a knife in her heart. "I did not want there to be any confusion about the matter whatsoever."

"No, naturally you did not. I am . . . indebted to you, Cousin Georgiana. How strange that I should always call you so!"

"It is my name," she reminded him.

He shot her a startled glance.

"One of them."

"I had quite forgotten. I know so very little about you after all, it seems. Tell me, have you decided what you will do after my great-aunt's party?"

"I shall leave at once," she said firmly.

"And do what? Accept one of the offers of marriage you have received? Fade into obscurity as governess to someone's brats? Will that satisfy you?"

She attempted to smile. "How can you be sure I *have* received any offers?"

"I hope I am not unduly immodest if I say that very little goes on in Society which does not come to my ears."

"Then you will know that they were all gazetted fortune hunters, so that does not signify." Her eyes met his. "In any case, I will have been the toast of London, however briefly, and that counts for a great deal."

"But not with you, dear cousin. I am not so unobservant of your character as to believe you care a fig for any of that."

"I do not believe any one of us really knows the other," said Georgiana with an attempt at cheerfulness. "Did you not just say so? In any event, I am not quite sure what I shall do, but eventually, if it is quite acceptable to you, I should like coach fare to Yorkshire."

"Mail-coach?" he asked with a bitter laugh.

"Post chaise, I think," she said with an answering smile.

"I should prefer to send you wherever you like in my traveling carriage," he said in a low voice. "And I should like to make some settlement on you to recompense you for—for the disruption of your life! There is, of course, a considerable sum of money at stake should we win the bet—which I feel certain we shall do. Robert's team will fetch a handsome price, and some of the clubs have laid on bets as well. I should like to give you half, for you have very properly earned it!"

"I cannot accept either," she said calmly. "Sometime . . . sometime soon, you will understand why. I hope, when you have had time to reflect, that you will be able to forgive me for the part I have played in all of this."

He almost snatched up her hand and kissed it, but her distant manner held him off. "I suspect it is I who should ask your forgiveness," he said.

She looked at him with a full heart, remembered his conversation with Mr. Utterby, to which she had been an unwitting eavesdropper, and found herself incapable of telling him the rest of the truth. "We have both of us behaved rather badly," she said lightly. "Perhaps we should just leave it at that."

"Perhaps we should," agreed Sir Oliver grimly, rising from his seat.

Georgiana held out her hand to him. "We will not meet again until Lady Louisa's party, I think. On that night I shall tell her that I have received an urgent summons from my aunt and uncle at Holcombe Hall and must go home at once. I would like to say good-bye now, if I may."

He took her hand gravely and raised it to his lips. She drew back involuntarily, and he dropped it at once. "Forgive me! I presume too much," he said coolly. "Speak to my secretary before you go; he will make whatever financial arrangements you desire." He executed a formal bow. "Good-bye, then! And good luck!"

Chapter 19

NOT ALL THE extremely trying events of the past few days could entirely eradicate Georgiana's pleasure in the dress she was to wear to Lady Louisa's party. It had been shockingly expensive, but Madame's representations of the importance of à la modality at a gathering at which His Royal Highness was to be present had overborne her arguments and her inherent reluctance to go even further into her grandmother's debt. She wished she might have had her uncle set up an account for her in London, but she had not thought of it in time. She was determined to send her ladyship a sum equal to her expenditure for clothing as soon as she got back to Holcombe Hall; in the meantime the dress *was* beautiful. The slim three-quarter dress of sarcenet, all in ivory, and worn over a shimmering underdress of ivory satin was adorned only with a wreath of yellow roses in her hair and a necklace of Lady Louisa's diamonds round her neck. She did not look like a girl just out of the schoolroom, in the first bloom of youth, but her air of style and assurance gave her beauty a depth one did not find in a child of seventeen.

Quite a number of floral tributes had been sent up to her room, but Georgiana had elected to carry the one sent by Lord Nugent. Georgiana had no doubt that Clarice had set him on to it, but it was nearing the end of her visit, and she meant to show him whatever kindness she could.

"You see, my love," said Clarice when the family had sat down to dinner before the ball, "Georgiana is carrying your posies." Her look of satisfaction and Freddy's of blank incomprehension confirmed Georgiana's suspicions, and she hid her smile behind her napkin.

"Thank you, Freddy," she said at length. "They are quite lovely. And they match my dress so perfectly."

"Can't quite remember—" began his lordship with disconcerting honesty.

"Of course you do, my love," said his distracted parent hurriedly. "You asked me what flowers Cousin Georgiana would particularly like, and what sort of dress she would be wearing."

"If you say so, Mama," said Freddy with a shrug. "Glad you like 'em, Georgie!"

With this his much afflicted mama had to be content, and she directed her next remark to Lady Louisa. "I am surprised that Oliver does not dine with us today."

"I invited him," said her ladyship with a withering look at Georgiana, "but he said he had other plans."

"Does he mean to come to the party?" inquired Miss Ponsonby with an edge to her voice.

"Of course he means to come," snapped her ladyship. "Disown him if he didn't!"

Miss Ponsonby, who was rather becomingly arrayed in lavender crepe, smiled into her plate and then directed a brief, assessing look at Georgiana. It was the friendliest emotion Georgiana had seen her display since the evening at Almack's, and she wondered what it betokened. Amabel had taken to glaring at her with outright hostility and to uttering veiled remarks whose import there was no mistaking. Georgiana did not believe that such antipathy could have arisen merely from the brief attention bestowed on her by the Prince Regent and wondered what she had done to inspire such intense feelings. She was aware of Amabel's proprietary interest in Sir Oliver, but it would take a far more fanciful imagination than Miss Ponsonby's to be jealous of his relationship to Georgiana. His pointed avoidance of dinner only underscored his feelings in that regard. Georgiana sighed, and pushed her food around her plate with her fork.

The ball, which began at ten o'clock, was held in the room set aside for the purpose in the back of the house. The light of a hundred candles, suspended in a great crystal chandelier, cast a warm glow over the masses of flowers arranged at each end. An excellent orchestra had been engaged and no expense spared on the refreshments or the supper to follow. Clarice, resplendent in the sea-foam dress so admired by Sir Barnaby Philpot, stood next to Lady Louisa at the head of the stairs and reflected with satisfaction that while it might be an exaggeration to say that the cream of the Upper Ten Thousand would be present in her mother-in-law's ballroom, there were enough distinguished guests present to create a quite satisfying crush.

Earliest among the guests to arrive were Lord Litchfield and his sister Lady Lonsdale. Georgiana had not seen Jeannette since her kindness to her following her arrival at Lord Litchfield's hunting box, and she greeted her with a warmth that set Miss Ponsonby, watching Georgiana's every move closely, to gnashing her teeth. This unfortunate expression was noticed by Lord Nugent, who asked her innocently if she was feeling quite the thing. Since Lady Lonsdale, who had been a friend of the Oversham family since she was in the cradle, was still standing by her, she merely gritted her teeth and told Freddy that he had trod on her toe. Mr. Utterby had told her he would arrive late in the evening, but she could not help watching the door for him anxiously. She watched Georgiana talking to their guests with every appearance of a granddaughter of the house, and longed for the moment that would unmask such insolence.

Sir Oliver arrived in due course, his excellent figure shown to advantage in black satin knee breeches, a white waistcoat, and a waisted, long-tailed coat. The younger members of the household had by this time been released from their posts on the stairs to mingle with the guests, and Sir Oliver was able to claim the first set, a country dance, with Miss Ponsonby. Georgiana, who had been led into the same set by Freddy, could see that despite the supposed attractions of dancing with Sir Oliver, Miss Ponsonby's eyes were riveted on the door. She could only suppose her to be waiting for the Prince, who had not yet put in an appearance. From Sir Oliver's face and person Georgiana kept her eyes firmly averted.

"Georgie!" said Freddy suddenly, startling her.

"Yes, Freddy?" she inquired, bringing her attention with some difficulty back to her partner.

"You *don't* want to marry me, do you?" he asked her anxiously. "Mama said I should ask you. Told her you'd already said no, but she said you might have changed your mind. Haven't, have you?"

"No, indeed," she said soothingly, trying not to laugh at the relieved expression on his face.

"Thought you wouldn't. Wouldn't if I were you," he confessed ingenuously. "Thing is, have to marry money. Mama says you have pots of it. Do you?"

"Pots," agreed Georgiana gravely.

Freddy sighed. "Knew it. Aunt Amabel said you might not, but Mama told her she was a goose to listen to rumors." He shook his head mournfully. "Don't need much myself; never have. But Mama sets a lot of store by it."

Georgiana smiled. "Indeed she does." She glanced over at Clarice, who was dancing with Sir Barnaby. "Perhaps your mama will marry money herself, so you won't have to."

"Do you think so?" asked Freddy hopefully.

"I am sure there is every chance of it," said Georgiana. "Freddy," she said seriously, "I—I may have to go away very soon. Would you like to come visit me in Yorkshire? It would not only be to visit me. I have a friend who is a rector, and I feel very sure he would like to meet you."

Freddy's face brightened and then fell. "Don't like to leave Burdick. Lady Louisa might get rid of him."

"Naturally Burdick would be welcome as well," she told him. "Though I do not think he will enjoy such a long journey in his basket!"

"Brandy," disclosed Lord Nugent confidently. "Loves the stuff! Foxed in no time! Sleep right through it!"

Georgiana's next partner was Lord Litchfield, who led her expertly in the waltz and complimented her on her exquisite taste in ball gowns. "I should not have recognized you, Miss— Miss Oversham!" he said with a charming smile. "You are all the crack, you know! Even my sister is envious!" In a lower voice he said in her ear, "When is the bet to be paid off?"

Georgiana stiffened a little. "I gather that this evening is the final 'test.' After this, you must settle it among yourselves as you see fit. Sir Oliver has not confided in me what arrangements he has made."

Lord Litchfield did not notice the coolness of her tone. "Lord, Utterby will be in a taking! There won't be a party in London to excel this one in magnificence or distinction. You can't fail. Oliver told me His Royal Highness is expected to attend."

"Yes, but he has not yet appeared. Perhaps he will not come after all."

"Oh no, he is always late," said Lord Litchfield knowledgeably. "Sometimes comes when the musicians are packing up, so that they have to start all over again. Always manages to snabble all the oysters at supper though," he said meditatively.

Georgiana laughed. "Well, there are *lots* of oysters, so I do not suppose we will run out. I hope he does come, though, because my gr—Lady Louisa seems to set great store by his presence."

"All of 'em do," agreed Lord Litchfield. "Man's an intolerable dresser, though. Wait till you see the cut of his coat!"

Georgiana hastened to assure him that she was sure that her future sovereign could not but present a pale reflection of her present partner's sartorial magnificence, which seemed to content him. He ventured upon a new topic. "Don't suppose you know what's amiss with Oliver? Almost came to blows with Utterby last night at the club. Been dipping deep, too. Not at all like him."

Georgiana replied in the most frigid accents that she could manage that she rather fancied Sir Oliver and Mr. Utterby had fallen out over the conduct of the bet, although it was in no way any concern of hers.

Lord Litchfield looked at her strangely. "Just as you say, ma'am. Robert is well enough, in his way, but his envy of Oliver leads him into some queer starts. Still, shouldn't think that was all of it. If I didn't know it was Oliver, I should say it was woman trouble."

"Indeed?" inquired Georgiana.

"Yes," replied Lord Litchfield, happily unaware of the dangerous ground he was treading. "There is no end to his flirtations, and I am convinced he hasn't a heart to lose!"

Georgiana wondered if this was meant as a warning, and said lightly, "I daresay. You must ask him, then. We have not seen him here very often of late."

"Shouldn't like to do *that*, ma'am," said his lordship seriously. "Devilishly private about his *amours*. I shouldn't think—" He broke off suddenly. "What did I tell you? Worst-fitting coat I ever saw in my life!"

Georgiana, somewhat puzzled by this speech, looked where he was directing her. The music stopped suddenly. Prince George might have been wearing a coat whose fit was scorned by such aspiring sprigs of fashion as Lord Litchfield, but his presence galvanized the room. He was coughing heavily, and his protuberant blue eyes were watering, but he came forth graciously to greet Lady Louisa, who had risen from her rout chair, her bosom swelling with pride. The Prince appeared to be bursting out of his tightly stretched corset, but he was in an affable mood and inquired enthusiastically after the refreshments.

Georgiana, upon being presented to him, was called a "taking little puss," and he made broad references to his "flirtation" with her at Almack's. Those who were frequently in his company were conditioned to such flummery, and even Miss Ponsonby managed a smile when he opined, in a rather loud voice, that Sir Oliver Townsend was quite a dog for keeping such a string of beauties all to himself. He circulated around the room for a while, greeting friends and accepting the homage of the assembled guests, and then he removed to the card room with some of his intimates for a rubber of whist.

Lady Louisa sat back down again at once, her store of civility exhausted. "Oliver," she called, beckoning him to her side, "you will see that he has what he wants, won't you? I've given orders, but Dukeworth is getting senile and one can't be sure he'll know what to do. Caught the fellow with his mouth open like a gapeseed last time Prince George came. Thought I'd have to turn him off!"

This description of the monumentally rigid Dukeworth threatened to give Georgiana a fit of the giggles, but Sir Oliver promised soberly to make sure their illustrious guest's needs were met.

"Where in the world is Clarice?" inquired her ladyship irritably. "Someone needs to make sure the supper will be out in time. His Royal Highness won't like to be kept waiting."

Georgiana volunteered her services, but her grandmother said, "No, no, stay here and enjoy yourself. I don't want the young men to be angry at me for cheating them of a partner," which earned Georgiana a scowl from Miss Ponsonby.

Freddy, whose gaze and attention had been wandering, said suddenly, "There's Mama. Looks to be in a taking."

Clarice, coming up on the arm of Sir Barnaby, was indeed flushed, whether in triumph or happiness one could not say. There was no mistaking Sir Barnaby's feelings, however. He clasped Clarice's small hand in his large one, and beamed at them in such a fatuous manner that even Freddy had cause to stare.

Sir Barnaby was by no means a willowy man, but his girth had been tamed by every means permitted to one who fancied himself a member of the dandy set. He was tightly laced in at the waist, and his shoulders were extravagantly padded, and the fobs and seals that hung from him seemed, to Georgiana's discerning ear, to clatter a little when he walked. Happily, his disposition as well as his fortune was amiable, and he was impervious to insult, which was fortunate, since more than one quizzing glass had been raised to observe his progress across a room. Georgiana glanced with some trepidation at Sir Oliver, but she could detect nothing worse in his expression than a touch of amusement.

"Oh, Amabel, Freddy, Lady Louisa! And dear Oliver and Cousin Georgiana, I am so very happy. You must wish me joy!"

"Yes, ma'am," said Sir Barnaby, his faulty instincts leading him to address Lady Louisa in a jocular tone, "I have brought Mrs. Oversham bang up to the mark at last! She had agreed to hang up the ladle as soon as may be."

"I congratulate you," said Sir Oliver, attempting to divert his great-aunt from her prey.

"It is good of you to say so," said Sir Barnaby with an acknowledging bow. "I don't mind telling *you* it wasn't easy. Took a deal of address, if I do say so myself."

"Looby!" croaked Lady Louisa like some malignant frog. "Nobcock!"

"Beg pardon, ma'am?" asked Sir Barnaby, confused.

"Did you want me, ma'am?" asked Freddy, his attention roused by her ladyship's apparent summons.

"Chaw-bacon!" concluded her ladyship.

"Your mama is going to marry Sir Barnaby," explained Georgiana kindly.

"Thought we'd never turn her off," muttered Lady Louisa darkly.

Sir Barnaby was beginning to perceive that his love's mother-in-law was not in spirits. "My sweet life," he began doubtfully, "do you not think—"

He was interrupted by Lord Nugent. "Are you rich?" he inquired.

Sir Barnaby, unused to such directness, sputtered a bit. "Naturally, it is most proper of you—that is to say, of course you will be concerned about settlements, and so forth. I can only assure you that I can offer your dearest mama—you will not, I hope, object to my referring to her in so personal a manner?—the elegancies of life, and I shall be happy to have my man of business wait upon yours as soon as it may be convenient. I hope, when all is settled to your satisfaction, that you will be able to wish us joy without reservation."

"But are you rich?" asked Freddy as if he had not heard a word of this speech.

Georgiana, who knew the import of this question, laid a restraining hand on Lord Nugent's arm.

"I am," replied Sir Barnaby helplessly.

"Oh, Freddy," entreated his mother.

Lord Nugent was not to be diverted from his course. "I say! Now I won't have to marry Cousin Georgiana!"

"Freddy!" cried his appalled parent.

"Jinglebrains!" contributed Lady Louisa.

"Of course you will not, Freddy," said Georgiana kindly, patting his arm.

"I am afraid I don't quite see—" began Sir Barnaby.

"Oh la! It is all a hum, my love!" cried Clarice in an anguished tone. "Cousin Georgiana and my Frederick are such good friends they will have their little jokes. I declare, it has grown quite hot! Do you think you might procure me a glass of champagne, my love? My throat is quite parched."

Georgiana, happening to catch Sir Oliver's eye just at that moment, had to bite her quivering lip and turn her head away to maintain her gravity.

"There was never the least question of it," said Lady Louisa in a tone which brooked no argument.

"No," interjected Miss Ponsonby with unexpected heat.

Chapter 20

MR. UTTERBY had laid his plans with the greatest care. His arrival must be timed as late as possible, after all the other guests were assembled. Mr. Utterby wanted maximum exposure of his unmasking of "Miss Oversham's" deceit. On the other hand, in the event of a Royal Presence, it was imperative to wait until His Royal Highness had retired to the card room, as he invariably did. Mr. Utterby did not want a Scene which the denizen of Carlton House could not but find distasteful. In that case, it might be Mr. Utterby who would find himself excluded from Society instead of Sir Oliver and the girl.

There was also the matter of keeping his accomplice, Miss Leroux, in the dark as to his intentions. Cecilia was in many respects an extremely biddable girl, and generally compliant in fulfilling his demands, but he feared that she would balk at serving the governess an ill turn. She was shrewd enough to guess that her traveling companion was involved in some deep doings, but she did not begrudge another girl her opportunities, and besides, it was the governess who had rescued her from the storm. If she now wanted to call herself Miss Oversham and masquerade as a lady of Quality, Mr. Utterby suspected that Cecilia would raise no objection. It was therefore imperative that she play her part unwittingly, because he did not want her spiking his guns.

He had told Cecilia he would be taking her to a ton party, and advised her to wear a costume which emphasized her profession, since actresses were all the crack. She was not quite naive enough to swallow this without question, but he was so eloquent at representing to her the triumphs that would be hers if she were to cut a swath among the swells that he at length overbore any qualms she might have regarding the correctness of his advice.

He was highly pleased with the results. While Miss Leroux's gown of watered silk was not precisely transparent, it was of the most daring cut imaginable, and left no onlooker in doubt as to the nature of its wearer's attributes. It would not, he reflected with satisfaction, leave any doubt as to her respectability either, and this was exactly the effect he wanted to achieve. Mr. Utterby had no qualms about employing Cecilia in such a fashion to gain his own ends; the resulting rumors and tittle-tattle would have a salutary effect on her career, which would go far to excuse any temporary embarrassment she might feel.

"By the by," said Mr. Utterby when he was handing her out of the carriage in front of the Oversham house, "Sir Oliver Townsend tells me that the girl who was traveling with you when we met"—here he bestowed a warm smile upon her—"what was her name?—Miss Bucklebury, if I do not mistake!—has been invited this evening. I am very glad, for it means there will number at least one other among your acquaintance present."

"I am sure I should like to see her again," said Miss Leroux without much interest, "for she was very kind to me, you know!"

"Then by all means you must tell her so," suggested Mr. Utterby affably. "Come, let us go up."

Georgiana, innocent of Mr. Utterby's plans for her ruination, was enjoying the exquisite torment of a dance with Sir Oliver. "My dear cousin," he was saying, his eyes regarding her with amusement, "you are quite incorrigible. This is your moment of glory, and I find you laughing at the very pinkest of the pinks of the ton!"

"You know perfectly well I did no such thing," she retorted with a little choke.

"It looked to be a very near thing, I assure you. You did not see your own face."

"No, but I could see yours. How are we to maintain our gravity when he is soon to be a member of the family? I do not think it will be possible to keep him apart from Lady Louisa forever!"

If he noticed her "our," and the unconscious inclusion of herself as a member of the family, he did not say so. "Nor from Lord Nugent. Has Freddy been pestering you to marry him?"

"Oh no! It is only that Clarice has told him he needs to marry a wealthy woman, and I think she has pressed him to try to fix his interest with me. I have tried to assure him that he need not consider it, but he seems to have the liveliest fear of displeasing her."

"Poor fellow. The situation is not without its ironies."

"I beg your pardon?"

"I daresay if she knew the truth she would spare no pains to keep him away from you. He is not in such dire straits as all that. He possesses, if not a fortune, at least a competence, and the title is a rather old one."

"Oh . . . yes," she said absently, looking at his waistcoat.

"Perhaps now that Clarice is to be married she will leave him to find his own pursuits . . . it *is* a nice waistcoat, is it not, Cousin Georgiana?"

She smiled. "I'm sorry. I was distracted."

"Apparently. Tell me, are you satisfied with your success? You have all London at your feet, though I am not coxcomb enough to believe it has been entirely my doing. Are you happy, Georgiana?"

Georgiana brought her courage up to the sticking point and took a breath. Whatever he thought of her, however much he might regret ever having met her, she must tell him the truth *now*. She could not deceive him for another minute, and if her courage failed her now it might be some time before she had an opportunity to confide in him. His hand tightened over hers. "Are you happy?" he repeated.

"No," said Georgiana, expelling her breath. "I am not. Sir Oliver, there is something I must tell you—something you must know at once."

He raised an eyebrow. "Yes?"

"I am not—"

"Miss Leroux, Mr. Utterby," announced the footman in stentorian tones.

"Good God! He's brought the actress here," cried Sir Oliver. "He means to unmask you before the entire ton."

"It does not matter—" began Georgiana.

"You don't understand. They will not forgive you. Your prospects will be quite ruined. I must try to head him off!"

"Cousin Oliver, I—" Georgiana called after him, but he had already moved toward the head of the stairs.

"Robert, this is not well done of you," he said in a tone that made Mr. Utterby step back a little.

"Nonsense," said Mr. Utterby with bravado. "I warned you. You remember Miss Leroux, I take it?"

Cecilia, who was drawing startled glances from the gentlemen in the room and rather less admiring ones from the ladies, discovered at once that Mr. Utterby had misled her as to the tenor of the party. The gathering had every appearance of what she must characterize as the stuffy and respectable, and she did not believe that a stage actress would find quite the welcome there her companion had led her to believe. One person in particular, a tall, rather pinch-faced girl in lavender crepe, was regarding her with a look that almost shriveled her insides. "Robert," she began to protest, "you said—"

"Cecilia, my dear, where are your manners? Do you not remember Sir Oliver Townsend? You met him under rather unforgettable circumstances, do you not recall? And there is your particular friend, Lord Litchfield."

"How are you, sir?" said Miss Leroux politely although his lordship blushed. "Robert, you said—"

"I have said a great many things in my time, my dear," said Mr. Utterby calmly. "Pray do not remind me of them now."

"Robert," said Sir Oliver in a warning tone, "you will not make mischief in my great-aunt's house."

"I do not understand," said Lady Lonsdale, who had come up with her brother, Lord Litchfield. She was regarding the rather outrageously clad figure in the most revealing dress imaginable with a fascinated eye.

"Of course you do not!" said her brother, a bit desperate to avoid a scene on the one hand and prevent Sir Oliver from calling Mr. Utterby out on the other. "Supper! That's the thing."

This helpful suggestion went unheeded. "It is not *I* who will make mischief," Mr. Utterby told Sir Oliver, as if there were no one else in the room. "Besides, it is my duty to make public what I have discovered. You cannot be so lost to all sense of what is owing to the Overshams and the ton as to be party to a fraud."

"This self-immolation on the altar of duty is something I had not previously encountered in you," said Sir Oliver. "Besides, it did not stop you from becoming a willing participant yourself."

Lord Litchfield's hand on his arm reminded him that he was on the point of creating the scandal Mr. Utterby so obviously craved. He looked at Lady Lonsdale's puzzled, anxious face and said quietly, "I will not quarrel with you now, Robert. But do take Miss Leroux away before my great-aunt catches sight of her! She has a bad heart, and nothing will save you if any harm comes to her!"

"You wrong me, Oliver; you always did. My quarrel, as you put it, is not with her ladyship." He raised his brows. "Ah, here comes *Miss Oversham* now. No doubt she wishes to renew old acquaintance."

Miss Ponsonby, watching the drama begin to unfold from the sidelines, did not wish to put herself forward too quickly. She had no taste for the vulgarity of a public quarrel; a quiet revelation, repeated in the right ears, would serve as well. She disdained the scene Mr. Utterby had created by dressing his Incomparable in a manner that could not fail to attract attention. Miss Ponsonby had little faith in the respectability of actresses in general, and in Miss Leroux's none at all. She was naturally reluctant to become involved in what had all the earmarks of a rather distasteful imbroglio, but Georgiana was coming forward on Freddy's arm, and Miss Ponsonby did not want to miss a moment of that encounter. She moved forward with heavy steps.

Georgiana was determined to avert a scandal which would upset her grandmother and the rest of the Oversham household by the only means at her disposal—telling the truth. She had only a moment to regret that she had not already done so with Sir Oliver, and what the probable outcome of such a revelation made in such a fashion must be. Nevertheless, she had to do it. She could not let Sir Oliver call Mr. Utterby out or ruin himself by quarreling in public. She recruited Freddy to escort her and made her way calmly up to Miss Leroux, who was looking rather uncomfortable and embarrassed. Mr. Utterby, who was watching her with a sardonic smile, she ignored completely.

"Miss Leroux—Cecilia—how nice it is to see you again! I have heard that your new play is quite a sensation! May I present Lord Nugent? He is a sort of cousin of mine, and very eager to make your acquaintance."

Freddy, who, until he happened to open his mouth, was quite impressively handsome, smiled and bowed. Miss Leroux offered her hand and fluttered her eyes with pleasure.

"Miss—Bucklebury, is it not?—I do not quite recall! Robert said you would be here tonight! Are you a governess in the household?"

Miss Ponsonby, who had come stealthily up behind Georgiana and Freddy, gave a little snort.

"No," said Georgiana kindly. "I—I am afraid I am guilty of deceiving you a little when we last met. I did not wish to be known, so I assumed another name and identity. I am Miss Oversham, and Lady Louisa is my grandmother."

"Ooooh," commented Cecilia. "Where is she?"

"I believe she is preparing to lead the guests into supper with Lord Nugent's mother," offered Georgiana. "Would you care to join us?"

"Take you in myself," said Freddy, obviously impressed.

"Ooooh," said Cecilia again.

Mr. Utterby tapped her arm lightly. "Very admirable, Miss Bucklebury," he began.

"Why does he keep calling her that?" inquired Lady Lonsdale of her brother in a bewildered tone.

"Foxed," suggested Lord Litchfield desperately.

"It is no use, my child," said Sir Oliver in a quiet tone. "Do not distress yourself. Mr. Utterby is just leaving." He turned to Mr. Utterby. "You have made your point, I believe. If you like I will acknowledge defeat, but have the decency to leave my great-aunt's house at once."

"I should like to oblige you, dear boy," said Mr. Utterby with a sneer, "but if I do your resourceful governess will no doubt pass it off with some Banbury tale of hiding her identity. I am forced to admit that she is quite as accomplished an actress as Cecilia."

"No, but—" protested Georgiana.

"Be quiet," said Sir Oliver, and knocked Mr. Utterby down with a single, swift blow to his jaw.

Mr. Utterby, contrary to expectation, seemed rather amused, although he rubbed his jaw gingerly and spoke in a thickened voice. "My congratulations, Oliver. I did not think you would risk it." He picked himself up off the floor. "I have what I came for, I believe. Come, Cecilia, we shall retire from the lists for tonight, and let tongues wag as they will."

"Does that mean we are going home?" inquired Cecilia, who was rather looking forward to supper with Freddy.

"Yes, my dear, it does," replied Mr. Utterby with a shrug.

Miss Ponsonby, to whom such an ending was a very paltry revenge for the insults suffered by her acute sensibilities, forgot all her resolutions and inhibitions and stepped forward. "I must protest! It cannot end there. Every scruple of female delicacy has been violated by this—this—"

"Hush, Amabel," warned Sir Oliver.

"I will not be silenced!" declared Miss Ponsonby, quite white with anger and lost to any pleas but the promptings of her own venomous resentment. "We have nurtured a viper in our bosom—one who has dared to defile the Oversham name—"

The footman had been urgently signaling for some few moments the arrival of a very late guest, and Sir Oliver, seeing a possible diversion to what was rapidly becoming a Cheltenham Tragedy, signed to the man to make the announcement.

The footman, relieved of his charge, complied with enthusiasm. "Lady Brunswick," he said in a voice that shook the walls.

"Good God," said Sir Oliver in a strangled voice.

"Now we *are* in the basket," said Lord Litchfield in an awed tone.

Chapter 21

GEORGIANA, WHO HAD momentarily forgotten who Lady Brunswick might be, was suddenly reminded that this was *her* guest, the mysterious companion of her early morning ride, and wondered what there might be about a rather eccentric but otherwise unremarkable middle-aged woman to inspire such a reaction. She could not yet see the newcomer, but she stepped forward to greet her.

One glance was sufficient to demonstrate that whatever else she might be, Lady Brunswick was far from unremarkable. Since Georgiana had seen her last she had donned a deep black wig and tinted her eyebrows to match, which, together with her bright blue eyes, gave her a rather fierce look. Her complexion was a fiery red, owing, perhaps, to the exertion involved in getting her ample body up the stairs.

But all this was as nothing beside her attire. She had chosen a dress more fit for a girl than a matron, and the sheer spider gauze was of such a scanty quantity that her décolletage was practically scandalous. She wore a wreath of red roses in her hair, and a scarlet mantle, with a gold trimming round it, hung from her shoulders. The effect was rather like a volcano erupting in the midst of the party, and a babble of voices arose from the guests.

Georgiana, her progress momentarily arrested by her awe at this spectacle, heard Miss Ponsonby let out her breath like a goose. "How did *that woman* come to be invited to this house?" she hissed.

Georgiana turned around, surprised. "I did. Clarice said I might. Who——?"

She was startled to hear Mr. Utterby give a laugh of genuine amusement. "Perfect," he said.

If Miss Ponsonby was angry before, now her face was as scarlet as the newcomer's mantle. "My sister would not—" she began, but she was interrupted.

"Where may I find Miss Oversham?" inquired the guest in her heavily accented voice.

"Here," Georgiana said bravely, stepping out from the crowd. "How do you do, ma'am?"

"Well, I thank you," said Lady Brunswick, looking almost as amused as Mr. Utterby. "It was so kind of you to send me a card. I thought you had quite forgotten me."

"Oh no, ma'am," said Georgiana politely. "Do you know my grandmother, or shall I present you? I believe she has just gone into supper."

"Indeed I do know Lady Louisa, but she would not thank you for presenting me, I assure you," said her ladyship enigmatically.

Sir Oliver, who had given a quiet order to Dukeworth, stepped forward and, to Georgiana's surprise, executed a deep bow.

"Sir Oliver," said Lady Brunswick with a delighted smile, "how splendid to see you again."

"We have not had the honor of seeing Your Royal Highness in England for a number of years," he said in a tight voice.

"Oh, I come over now and then to see my friends. Officially, of course, I am still in Italy."

Georgiana, who had stood till then in a mist of incomprehension, felt her heart miss a beat. She understood at last what she should have seen at once—that her guest was not a mere Lady Brunswick, as she had called herself, but Caroline of Brunswick, Princess of Wales, wife to the Prince Regent. She sank into a low curtsy, and would have sunk through the floor if she could.

"We are honored, ma'am," said Sir Oliver smoothly. "I hope you will not take offense if I take the liberty of informing you that His Royal Highness is in attendance as well. At present I believe he is in the card room."

"Oh la! That will not do!" She gave an amused chuckle and

put her finger under Georgiana's chin. "My poor child! You did not guess at all! Well, I shall retire at once. It would be a poor trick to serve you if I were to cause a scandal at your debut. My husband cannot abide my presence in the same room, and I fear that if I stay there will be a scene that will not reflect so very well on the Crown!"

Not till then did Georgiana appreciate the enormity of what she had done. Prince George's loathing for his estranged spouse was reputed to be beyond rationality, and to have invited them both to the same party was a social solecism from which there would be no recovery. Georgiana could only be glad she was not living in the time of Henry the Eighth.

"Shall I summon your carriage?" suggested Sir Oliver helpfully.

"That will not be necessary. I—"

They were never to hear what alternative arrangement the Princess might have made, because at that moment her husband emerged from the card room on his way into supper and caught sight of his estranged spouse. Not all the torments of an eternity in purgatory could rival that moment's excruciating agony for Georgiana. Unfortunately, the Prince was, if not disguised, at least very well to pass, and his public manner, though in general punctilious, suffered from a loss of inhibition.

"Madam!" he said, staring at her with the horror of one who has just been confronted by a denizen of a charnel house, "is it indeed you?"

"Certainly it is I," she said, sweeping toward him in a river of scarlet silk, before whom the guests parted in stricken silence. The fall of a stickpin to the floor would have resounded from one end of the room to the other.

She dropped before him in a graceless curtsy. "You have gained weight, Husband, and your color is too high. Are you ill?"

"Naturally I am ill!" he replied. "Your presence in this house must necessitate my immediate removal from it in order to preserve my health. And besides, at least I do not *jiggle*!"

"Now that is ungenerous, sir," said the Princess, warming to

the argument, "and untruthful as well. I have it on the best au-
thority from Lady Bessborough that—"

"Enough!" he roared, the Royal Countenance overspread
with an alarming flush. "Why have you come back to torment
me?"

From her vantage point on the ballroom floor, Georgiana
could see Clarice and Lady Louisa, newly emerged from the
supper room, clutching each other in near hysteria and stony
silence respectively. She could only wonder why Fate, which,
since her departure from Yorkshire had not treated her with
anything resembling benevolence, had not seen fit to remove
her from the earth at a suitably early age instead of permitting
her to endure such an agony of humiliation and shame. She
watched, helpless, as the Royal Drama continued to unfold.

"I have not come to see you at all," retorted the Princess. "It
may perhaps surprise you to learn that I have many friends in
England who are happy to give me the rank and consequence
you deny me."

"Damned traitors, all of them! They use you, madam, to
make a fool of me!"

"No one has to use me in order to accomplish that," said the
Princess with exasperating calm.

"Take care how you expose yourself, Mistress Harpy! And
count your friends carefully. Mine is one foot that will never
cross the threshold of any household that plays host to you!"

As this number included some of the Prince's own brothers,
the threat was far less serious than it sounded, but Georgiana,
observing the ruination of the Overshams with dismay, remained in ignorance of this fact.

"I regret to find you the victim of such a stupid prejudice,"
said the Princess, "and you really are quite alarmingly red.
Such choler is very dangerous you know!"

"Indeed, madam, the cure is close at hand. Have the good-
ness to convey the news to Lady Louisa that I shall not be
staying to supper. I am seriously displeased," he added unnecessarily and strode from the room.

In the moment of stunned silence that followed his exit,
Georgiana heard a little moan. She glanced up quickly in time
to see Clarice crumple to the ground. She stepped forward and

felt Miss Ponsonby's grip on her wrist. "Leave her alone," she hissed. "Haven't you done *enough*?"

Clarice's movement, however involuntary, released the other guests from their spell. With one accord, they began moving swiftly toward the door.

Mr. Utterby, who had stayed to observe the evening's events with the utmost satisfaction, came up to Georgiana and executed a mocking bow. "My congratulations, ma'am. Had I known you meant to ruin yourself and Oliver in such a spectacular fashion I should not have exerted myself so much. I do confess to feeling a tinge of regret over the probable outcome for Lady Louisa and Clarice, who have always been kind to me, but on the whole I cannot conceive of a more satisfying dénouement. Tell Oliver I shall expect to see his grays in my stables as soon as may be. Cecilia, my dear, come! We are going."

Cecilia, wearing a rather dazed look, could only give her hand a gentle squeeze and follow in his wake.

"Lord, what a dustup," said Freddy, appearing at her side. "Fellow looked mad as fire. Seen him before somehow!"

"Yes, Freddy," replied Georgiana wearily, "that was the Prince Regent. How is your mama?"

"Taken to her bed," said his lordship. "Lady Louisa, too. Angry with you, Georgie!" he added in a perplexed tone. "Can't think why!"

"I can well imagine," she said with a little groan. "Oh, Freddy, I am in a coil!"

"Help if I can, Georgie!" he said generously.

"Pardon me, Miss Oversham," said Princess Caroline, who had completed her sweep of the near-empty ballroom and was plainly preparing to depart. "I have just learned that your grandmother is a bit unwell and has retired, so I will take my leave of you. I know you will not wish me to apologize for the appalling way in which my husband has behaved. I do not ask for your sympathy. One day I will be restored to the consequence that befits my rank, and then all who snubbed me shall be very sorry! Until then, Miss Oversham, I bid you adieu!"

Georgiana, rising from her curtsy, looked after the Princess's retreating form in astonishment. "Do you know," she said to no one in particular, "I think she may have done it *on purpose*."

"Very likely," said Sir Oliver grimly. "There has not been such a disastrous royal visit since Elizabeth bankrupted half of her courtiers on her progress through England."

"Oh, sir, I did not see you," said Georgiana, turning. "How is Lady Louisa?"

"Somewhat tired," he said curtly. "Freddy, your mama wished me to ask you if you could find her fan, which she dropped when she took ill. It is ivory and was a particular present from Sir Barnaby."

Georgiana experienced a moment of dreadful premonition. "Sir Barnaby?" she inquired.

He did not misunderstand her. "Departed, without making his excuses," he said when Freddy had gone off in search of the desired article. "He cannot cry off as easily as that, of course, so perhaps it is only momentary cowardice."

He studied her face with an absorbed expression she could not quite interpret. "Madam, may I have a few moments of private speech with you?" he asked in a tone that did not bode well for her comfort.

Without waiting for her reply, he put his hand on her arm and led her a few steps out onto the balcony, where they were out of view. He swung her around to face him, not very gently. "And now, ma'am, perhaps you will tell me how it is that you came to invite the Princess of Wales to my great-aunt's house!"

Chapter 22

"DID YOU SET OUT to cut up the peace of my family deliberately," Sir Oliver asked her, "or did you somehow stumble on the means accidentally?"

"That is most unfair," replied Georgiana, stung. "Of course I can see that it is not at all the thing to invite both of Their Royal Highnesses to the same party by intention, but I didn't *know*. She misled me, probably deliberately, and said her name was Lady Brunswick. She said she was received everywhere. She *asked* me to invite her. How could I possibly know who she really was?"

"Indeed, how could you?" he suggested in a tone that made her itch to hit him.

"You do not believe me?" she asked him.

"I do not know what to believe," he said frankly. "Miss Ponsonby will have it that you are in league with Robert Utterby to discredit us all. I had formed a different picture altogether of your character, but . . ."

"And why, pray, should I wish to discredit you all?" she asked him, her eyes blazing.

"For money," he said simply.

It was on the tip of her tongue to remind him that she had more money than she could spend in three lifetimes when she realized that he, like Mr. Utterby, had not believed her confession to Cecilia. "But—" she began.

He raised a hand to silence her. "Spare me a moment more of your attention. I wish to make the situation perfectly clear to you. You are ruined, ma'am, quite beyond repair. You are entirely without prospects. This will cause such a scandal that

no establishment where the story is known will employ you,
and you may expect no offers of marriage."

"I see," she said calmly. "And this is because I invited the
Prince's wife to a party which he attended?"

He looked at her in surprise. "No, ma'am, it is because our
deceit of Lady Louisa was unmasked before the entire world. I
hold myself as much or more to blame as you," he said bitterly.

"Generous! I should think you might!" she retorted, her
anger mounting. "I always did think it was a shabby trick to
play on her. But I have something to tell you—"

Sir Oliver gave an odd little laugh. "Did you? You must
permit me to make reparations. I have thought of a scheme
which I hope will go far toward setting all to rights, at least
that which can be mended."

"What is that?" asked Georgiana suspiciously.

"Madam, will you do me the honor of becoming my wife?"

Sir Oliver, an accomplished flirt and for many years the
biggest prize on the Matrimonial Mart, was finding his first
proposal surprisingly difficult. The mixture of emotions
seething within his breast—anger, chagrin, doubt—were at
war with his heart, which told him he might trust Georgiana
absolutely. He was badly shaken, and he was as self-conscious
and embarrassed as a bantling.

Georgiana stood as though turned to stone, the color flooding her cheeks. She put her hands up to them, and her eyes
filled with tears. "How—how d-*dare* you?"

Sir Oliver, perceiving that she thought he had been mocking
her, proceeded to make things worse. "No! That is, you mistake my intention! I never meant to—"

"No, of course you did not," said Georgiana with scathing
bitterness. "Did you not 'employ' me to convince your grandmother that you would not marry at all? Having just favored
me with your opinion of my character, you will forgive me if I
say that I know you will be relieved to hear that I reject your
suit. I forgive *you* for your part in my ruination, if that is what
it is. You need not go to such an extreme as to offer for me.
We are quits now. I release you from any sense of obligation."

"You do not understand," said Sir Oliver, horrified by the

mess he had made of things. "Society will not receive you un
less I make you my wife."

"Sir Oliver, what I wish to make plain above all things is
the contempt I feel for what you term 'Society.' Since I have
been in London I have seen nothing to make me wish to be re
ceived into any such group. I cannot but feel that I will man
age very well without it."

"You are mistaken," said Sir Oliver. "You do not know the
world."

"Perhaps not. But it is my own affair. I—"

She broke off suddenly as a hand drew back the curtain.
Miss Ponsonby stepped onto the balcony. Her face was very
pale, and her voice was tight. "Oliver, you must come at
once," she said quickly. "Clarice fears that Lady Louisa has
suffered a heart attack. She thinks you should send for the
doctor."

"Good God!" he cried. "I will go myself. Is she breathing?"

"Yes, but there is a tightness and pain across her chest, and
she cannot lie still."

"She must be made to do so!" he commanded. "I shall re
turn as quickly as possible." He left the room, and not until
much later did he remember that he had not yet told Georgiana
that he loved her.

"I must go up to her," said Georgiana without thinking
when he had gone.

Miss Ponsonby all but thrust her thin body into her path.
"You!" she cried, her bosom heaving. "You shall not go any
where near her! Haven't you done enough?"

"I must explain!" said Georgiana. "She must not be allowed
to think—"

"The servants have orders to keep you away from her," said
Miss Ponsonby. "Clarice told them herself. You can do noth
ing more than you have already done. Clarice feels that it
would be best if you were to quit the house as soon as it is
light."

"I cannot leave until I know whether my grandmother is all
right!"

"Your *grandmother*? Are you so lost to shame that you

even now persist in trying to hoax us? I will leave you, before the insults you have visited upon this household make me utter such words as do not befit a lady."

Georgiana perceived that it would be useless to try to persuade her of the truth while she was in such a state, and in any event, in the respects that mattered, Amabel was perfectly correct: it was her fault that her grandmother had had a heart attack. If she were to die, Georgiana did not see how she could live with herself.

It was several anxious hours before she could learn anything more about the state of her grandmother's health. The doors to her ladyship's room were closed against her, and Georgiana did not want to risk a scene by appearing where she was unwelcome. Her ladyship's peace and quiet must be her foremost concern. The doctor had been roused from his bed and taken up, and the very long time he had stayed with his patient did little to allay her fears. When she heard the carriage pull away from the front door at last, she sent her maid, Betty, to discover the news.

At length she heard footsteps in the hall and a tap on her door. Betty, filled with self-importance at being sent on such an errand, and with a gossip-inspired but imperfect notion of what lay behind it, entered the room with a yawn. "La, miss, it's that late I can hardly stand up," she said.

"Naturally you must be very tired," said Georgiana sympathetically. "When you have told me the news, you must go to your bed."

"Yes, and with the party, and the extra cleaning, and all the clothes to lay out"—Betty continued, bent on her grievances—"and your packing to do, miss, begging your pardon—"

"That will do, Betty," Georgiana said with exasperation. "How is her ladyship?"

"Just a minute, miss," said the maid with just a hint of disrespect. "I've scarcely any breath left to form the words."

"On the contrary, you seem possessed of a great deal of it," said Georgiana curtly. "Please tell me at once whether Lady Louisa is gravely ill."

"Oh la, miss. Sir Oliver said to tell you that you were not to worry, that the doctor said it was only mild chest pains, but that he has gone to find a—a—"

"Specialist?" prompted Georgiana.

"Yes, that's it, miss. A specialist to make sure. And after he left, Miss Ponsonby said to be sure to tell you that her ladyship needs rest and quiet more than anything else."

"I see. Thank you, Betty. You may go to bed now."

"Yes, miss." She turned, but before she had gone many steps, Georgiana called her back. "Oh, Betty, I shall go out very early tomorrow, and while I am gone I should like you to deliver a note to my grandmother, and one to Sir Oliver. I shall leave them here on the mantel. Can you remember that?"

"Certainly, miss. Sir Oliver and Lady Louisa. Good night, miss!"

Georgiana toiled at some length over these epistles, crossing out lines and ripping up sheets until she was tolerably satisfied with the results. The letter to her grandmother begged her pardon for the embarrassment of inviting Princess Caroline to her party, proclaimed her ignorance of the guest's real identity, and hastened to assure her that, despite anything she might hear to the contrary, she really was Miss Oversham of Holcombe Hall, and she hoped, when her grandmother had made a full recovery, to be allowed to come up to Pemberton to visit her again and explain matters more fully.

The letter to Sir Oliver cost her some pangs. She was still furious at him for the manner in which he had high-handedly offered to assume the *burden* of her ruination by offering to marry her, as if she were no more to him than an unwelcome obligation. Never had she been more thankful for her fortune and the home that awaited her at Holcombe Hall. If she were ruined in London, it would scarcely matter in Yorkshire. Still, she could not think of a way of telling him the truth about herself and her motive for concealing it that would not wound him further, and that she was curiously reluctant to do. Finally, she recounted the mere facts, without explaining the rest, and trusted that his relief at being free of the obligation of supporting her might make him content with such a sketchy explanation.

She briefly considered staying to face him, but after the

evening's encounter she quailed at the prospect, and she doubted very much whether there was any more to be said. They could only hurt each other now. Moreover, she was certain that her continuing presence in the household would provoke its members, and she did not want a confrontation with Amabel that would be certain to upset her grandmother. In time, when the tempest had subsided, there was every chance of restoring her relationship with her family to at least the appearance of civility, but at present that was quite impossible.

By the time she had finished writing it was almost dawn. She lay down her pen, folded the letters, addressed them, and put them on the mantelpiece. Then she picked up the portmanteau with her traveling things (the rest would be sent or would stay, whichever her grandmother wanted), took a last look around, and closed the door.

Sir Oliver's secretary having obligingly provided her with the fare for a post chaise and the wage for a maid to accompany her, her financial needs were not a problem, but nevertheless she was not looking forward to further adventures on the road. She was wondering how to get a hackney to convey her to the ticket office when, slipping out the front door of the house, she encountered Freddy slipping into it. He was clutching Burdick, who was clearly not in an affable mood.

"Cat fight," explained Freddy, pointing to a hairless patch on the animal's left shoulder. "Ran away last night. Didn't like the fuss."

"I do not blame him in the least," said Georgiana. "Freddy, I am so glad I ran into you. I am going home to Yorkshire and I wanted to say good-bye."

"Wish you wouldn't," said his lordship. "Burdick likes you!"

Georgiana thought this intelligence would be news to the cat but nodded agreeably. "Well, I like him, too. But I must go, Freddy. I cannot stay here after what happened last night."

"Tell you what," said Freddy, inspired. "Come with you!"

"But, Freddy, I am going all the way to Yorkshire. And I am taking the post chaise. It would not be proper for you to go with me."

"Meet you there, then. Take another carriage. Like to visit

Yorkshire." He looked at her inquiringly. "Thing is, won't be too pleasant around here for a bit. Like to come, if you'll have me."

"Oh, then, of course; come as soon as you like. I am sure your mama will have no objection," she said, though she had no such assurance. "But I must go now, Freddy. I must get a hackney to the ticket office."

"Get you one myself," said Freddy, setting down the cat and running off. Surprisingly, within a few minutes he appeared with the carriage.

She wrote down her address for him and the directions, but she had no real expectation that he would pursue the visit. She gave him her hand and a cousinly kiss, and said he must feel free to come to her at any time. Then, with a little backward glance of regret, she was handed into the hackney and drove off.

She had wronged Lord Nugent, however. His determination to flee what he supposed must be a very uncomfortable period (though the reasons for this were imperfectly understood) had focused his attention rather more sharply than usual, and he was emphatic in his decision to set out at once. Accordingly he packed a small valise and secured a rather larger basket and a brandy bottle from his closet. He considered and dismissed the idea of informing his valet of his departure, for he suspected, correctly, that this venerable personage would inform on him to his mama. In the end he shrugged, and trusted Georgiana to make things right with his esteemed parent, quite forgetting that Georgiana was even now on her way out of London.

Last of all he picked up the fractious cat and packed it, protesting, into the basket.

An hour or so later Betty awoke with the conviction that it could not possibly be time to arise and assume her duties, and that no Christian household would expect her to make such an exertion and sacrifice. She took advantage of the household chaos and went back to sleep for an hour that was all the more satisfying for having been stolen. By the time she remembered the notes in Miss Oversham's bedroom they had already been found by Miss Ponsonby's maid Maria, who took them to her mistress.

Miss Ponsonby was sorely tempted, but her rectitude was as much a product of self-love as of principle, and her image of herself was not of someone who read other people's mail. She suffered no pangs of conscience, however, nor a moment's indecision, about what she must do. With delicate distaste, she lifted the notes to Lady Louisa and Sir Oliver, and gently lowered them into the fire.

Chapter 23

SIR OLIVER, having engaged the services of a Harley Street specialist for Lady Louisa on the following day, retired to his own house to spend what remained of the night tossing and turning in his bed. The evening's events, replayed many times in his troubled mind's eye, were not conducive to reposeful sleep, and his attempts to banish the memory of his maladroit proposal to Georgiana were unsuccessful. He realized that he had made her think he was mocking her or reluctantly assuming an unwanted obligation, and he was impatient for the morning to arrive so that he might disabuse her of this distressing notion. Now that their deception was unmasked and she had refused his suit and his assistance, he was uncomfortably aware that he had lost the one sure hold he had on her. She must, of course, leave his great-aunt's house without delay, and Sir Oliver, in the absence of a mother or sister he could send her to, hoped to install her with Lord and Lady Lonsdale. He did not doubt his ability to persuade her of the inadvisability of attempting to seek a position when the small portion of London society who did not attend Lady Louisa's party would have the story before afternoon, and he would have given all of his riches to be able to protect her from the scorn and notoriety that would inevitably be hers. If he could with honor have called Robert Utterby out, he would have done so, on account of the pain and torment his envy had brought down on all their heads.

He was less troubled by the ostracism that would undoubtedly fall to his lot. For some time he had been unutterably weary of the life he led, and he longed to turn his attention to more constructive pursuits. Besides, Prinny's rages were intense, but they were rarely of long duration, and Sir Oliver guessed that his resentment against the Overshams would burn itself out rather quickly. He could only be glad that Sir Barnaby had come up to scratch just minutes before the devastation began; Clarice's acceptance and their public betrothal meant that he could not with any honor attempt to cry off. Still, Sir Oliver, like Freddy, foresaw a most uncomfortable period ahead, and when morning came at last he went down to breakfast blue-deviled and out of sorts.

He was engaged in moodily pushing some sausage and a bite of eggs round and round his plate with his fork when his butler brought him a thick cream-colored envelope on a tray. "Excuse me for disturbing you, sir. The man indicated it was a matter of some urgency and—" He raised his eyebrows eloquently, by which means he communicated to Sir Oliver that the sender was someone of importance.

"Thank you, Frampton," said Sir Oliver calmly. "Is he waiting for a reply?"

"No, sir. He is, I believe, preparing to set out for the Continent with his mistress."

"Ah." He turned the letter over in his hands and saw that it was closed with the seal of the Princess of Wales. "Thank you, Frampton. That will be all."

The message was scrawled hastily and spelled poorly, by which means he knew she had honored him by writing it herself. "Dear Sir Oliver," the note read, "I hope you will forgive me for inserting myself into your game, but I could not resist. By now you will have learned the truth about Miss Oversham, and no doubt you will forgive *her* as well. One thing, at least, I can set to rights: I have given it out that the party was set up expressly to humiliate *me* and that it succeeded so well in this I have fled back to Italy in chagrin. Believe me, Sir Oliver, that nothing could be more effective in restoring you and your family to my husband's good graces, and I predict that within a day or two you will be the most popular man in London, at least with the Tory set. I hope that may make amends. Your much despised and abused Princess, Caroline."

Sir Oliver, torn between amusement and surprise, sat for some moments in silent assessment of his future queen. Then he shrugged and pushed his plate away, and went to inform Frampton that he was going to pay a call at the Oversham mansion.

His mood lightened and his tiredness a thing of memory, he paused for a moment on his great-aunt's doorstep to contemplate the pleasurable prospect of assuring Lady Louisa that the Overshams would no longer be the pariahs of the previous evening, and in fact might even be considered to have rendered a service to His Royal Highness. Sir Oliver apprehended with a certain benign cynicism that this intelligence could go far toward restoring her ladyship to good health and might induce her to bear with equanimity his own and Georgiana's role in deceiving her. He would remove his beloved from the house at once, if he could, and then he would convince her of the sincerity of his attachment. For the first time in many days, he looked forward to the future with a kind of optimism.

He suffered a check, however, when Dukeworth informed him, with a discreet little cough, that the household was in turmoil. Lord Nugent had disappeared during the night without informing his valet of his intended whereabouts.

"Well, there is no reason to make deep doings of it," suggested Sir Oliver, who had little patience with the way Clarice coddled and spied on her son. "Perhaps he went to his club."

"That I cannot say, sir, though I believe Mrs. Oversham has inquired. Ahem! The, ah, young lady appears to be missing, too."

"The young lady?"

"Miss, ah, Oversham, sir."

"Good God! Since when?"

"Betty, the young person who was waiting on her, says she told her last evening she would be going out quite early this morning," Dukeworth said in a colorless tone.

"I see," said Sir Oliver grimly. "Did not Miss—Oversham leave a note to inform anyone as to her whereabouts?"

"I really couldn't say, sir," replied the butler impassively. "Mrs. Oversham and Miss Ponsonby are in the yellow saloon, if you would care to go up."

Clarice looked as if she had sustained a severe shock and

waited only until the servant had withdrawn before crying out, "Oh, Oliver, it is perfectly dreadful! Freddy has disappeared, and I am perfectly sure he has eloped with *that girl*! What are we to do? She will ruin him!"

Sir Oliver, who was looking rather pale, broke in on this to inquire in a tight voice what reason she might have to suppose Georgiana had departed in Lord Nugent's company.

"She has done it for revenge, of course, and out of desperation," continued Clarice, undeterred by his inquiry. "Amabel made it clear to her that she must depart instantly from this house, and now she has enticed Freddy to go off to Gretna Green."

"It is much more likely that they are not together at all, and Freddy has gone riding, or some such thing."

"No, because that *animal* is missing as well," insisted Clarice.

Sir Oliver's dark brows lowered into a scowl. "And how did *you* come to turn her out of my great-aunt's house, Amabel?"

Miss Ponsonby flushed. "Lady Louisa requires complete quiet and rest, Sir Oliver," she replied. "How can she recuperate knowing such a creature as that resided under her roof? Insinuating herself into the family, casting out lures for Freddy—"

"Ohhhh," moaned Clarice.

"Did she tell no one where she was going? Leave no note?"

Miss Ponsonby looked at her elegantly shod feet. "I am afraid I destroyed them."

"*What?*"

"I thought she was trying to work herself back into Lady Louisa's good graces, and I did not think she should be disturbed. I believed I was acting for the best," Miss Ponsonby said with a trace of defiance.

"You said 'them,' Amabel. Was there more than one note?"

Miss Ponsonby inclined her head.

"And to whom was the other addressed?"

She raised her eyes to his. "To you."

"I see. I collect you were protecting me as well?"

"Do you not need it? Did she not come into this house

under your protection and with your full knowledge that she was not your cousin at all?"

It was Sir Oliver's turn to look embarrassed. "Yes," he admitted.

"Oliver, you cannot mean it!" cried Clarice in a horrified tone. "Did you know all along she was not Miss Oversham?"

"There are circumstances—which I do not have time to explain. I meant no harm, but if you must blame someone, blame me. It was I who persuaded her to come here—Utterby and Litchfield and I."

"Well I do blame you!" cried Clarice. "We are ruined, Sir Barnaby may very well cry off, and Lady Louisa may be at death's door, all because you brought that girl here. And now she has taken advantage of my poor Frederick, because it is the only way she may get her hands on a competence!"

"In one respect at least I bring good news," said Sir Oliver, proceeding to enlighten them with regard to the contents of the Princess's letter.

"That is all very well," said Clarice with unusual tenacity, "but if something has happened to Freddy I will never forgive you, never!"

Sir Oliver, very white about the mouth, nodded. "I do not think I could be so mistaken in her character as to believe that she would behave in such a manner as even a drab from the stews might scorn. I must go after her at once and find out. But if I am wrong, ma'am, I will never forgive myself!"

Sir Oliver had assured Miss Ponsonby and Mrs. Oversham that he had no doubts about Georgiana's character, but nevertheless he strode off to trace her whereabouts in a mood of some uneasiness. The simultaneous disappearance of both his lordship and Georgiana alarmed and upset him more than he would have liked to admit. Sir Oliver did not like to be wrong under the best of circumstances, and the unwelcome and particularly unpalatable suspicion that he might prove to be so in this case could not be banished entirely from his brain. His face was set in rather harsh lines as he made his inquiries, and not even the intelligence that a young lady of Quality had booked passage to Grantham on a hired post chaise early that day could entirely erase them. Sir Oliver did not think that a young lady contemplating marriage over the anvil would be booking her own passage, but with Freddy one could never be sure.

He contemplated setting out at once in pursuit, but the uncertainty of his great-aunt's health and of the identity of his quarry made him postpone his departure for a day or two. When he was satisfied that the return of Lady Louisa's bad temper was an excellent indication of her imminent recovery, he set out with his team to follow the Great North Road.

After several frustrating days of wet weather and uncomfortable accommodations, he discovered that the trail had gone cold. His last intelligence, which added to the grimness of his mood, was that a young gentleman and lady had apparently met up by accident in a posting inn and continued on their journey together. Seemed very friendly, they did, and called each other "cousin," reported his source. Sir Oliver's informant could not say where they had gone, but he was adamant that the coach had left the main road. Sir Oliver at length hit upon the happy notion of inquiring after "Miss Bucklebury" instead of Miss Oversham, and was rewarded, after much discussion of the matter, with the news that a rector by the name of Bucklebury lived in the village of Havisham, not many miles distant. Perceiving that, if Georgiana/Amelia had gone to her brother's, she would not, in all probability, be eloping with Freddy, Sir Oliver felt a burden lift from his heart and shoulders, and he tore off down the lane to find the rectory.

The Bucklebury house was a rather charming one with a lovely garden and an aspect of green lawn which looked quite welcoming in the cool sunlight. He rang the bell, and the servant showed him into the rector's study, which was lined with books. He could not be still, and stood opening and closing their covers until the door opened behind him.

He turned. Miss Bucklebury's (he must begin to think of her by that name!) brother bore no resemblance to her whatsoever. His face was kindly enough, but quite plain, and the difference in their ages he must guess to be about twenty years. As he regarded him, he realized how little Georgiana—Amelia!—had ever volunteered about her home life.

The rector extended his hand warmly. "How do you do? Mary says you have just come up from London. You must be quite exhausted! May I offer you some refreshment? My wife is visiting her mother at present, but my cook makes very excellent tea cakes, I assure you!"

Sir Oliver was finding it more and more difficult to imagine his love growing up in this environment. "No, thank you," he said. "I am sorry to intrude upon you, but I have called to inquire whether your sister might be at home."

The rector seemed surprised. "My sister? Amelia? Why no! She is at present working near London as a governess."

Sir Oliver's disappointment turned bitter in his mouth. "I see. Have you no recent news of her, then?"

"She writes quite regularly. Once a week."

"Perhaps she has mentioned my name to you, then," suggested Sir Oliver, grasping at straws.

"Sir Oliver Townsend?" considered the rector. "I do not believe so. Why do you ask?" he asked gently. "Is my sister in some sort of difficulty?"

"I fear she may be!" cried Sir Oliver, slamming his fist into his knee. "And it is I who have put her there!"

"I don't quite see . . ."

"No, of course you do not," admitted Sir Oliver miserably. "I love your sister, but I am afraid I have driven her to desperation. I fear she may have eloped to the border with a young man of the household. He is rather simple, you see, and easily led, and it is I who have driven her to it!"

The rector looked at Sir Oliver's elegant figure the way one might regard a race horse who had inadvertently entered the drawing room. He made a strangled sound in his throat. "You l-love my sister? Amelia? There must be some mistake."

"Why do you say that? She is beautiful, and clever, and . . . everything a man could wish for in a wife!"

"Naturally, but I would have thought—wife? Your intentions are honorable, then?"

"Of course they are honorable!" exclaimed Sir Oliver. "If I can only find her and persuade her she is not ruined after all, that she need not throw herself upon the protection of—well, I am convinced she will think better of it. She would not do such a thing! If she will have me, I will marry her myself. I did offer, but I do not think she believed I was sincere in my regard for her. She thought I pitied her because she had been the Rage, and then she was ruined. But the Princess of Wales has made everything right again, and in any case I did not propose to her because I felt sorry for her, but because I love her with all my heart!"

During the course of this disjointed explanation, the rector had taken off his glasses and wiped them. He replaced them on his nose and regarded Sir Oliver with what could only be termed a look of amazement. "My dear boy, are you quite sure—that is, the *Rage*? *Amelia*? Are you quite certain that you are speaking of my sister, Amelia Bucklebury?"

Sir Oliver opened his mouth to reply when a movement caught his eye. A large gray cat strolled into the room, brushed past him, and installed himself comfortably in the armchair closest to the sunny window. Sir Oliver was no connoisseur of feline attributes, but he could not fail to recognize the Scourge of Pemberton and Terror of Berkeley Square. Burdick returned his gaze with a basilisk stare, and began to lick his foot.

Sir Oliver was struck by the extremely disquieting idea that he had been made a fool of. He rose and gave his host a small, cold bow. "I can see that you must be right," he said in a colorless voice. "I must be mistaken. Please convey my regards and my congratulations to your sister when you see her. I am so sorry to have troubled you!"

The rector, who was as taken aback by the frigid tone of this comment as he was by the passionate avowal of a moment before, began to think he had a lunatic on his hands. "Will you not wait until my assistant comes back?" he said in soothing tones. "He has ridden over to Holcombe Hall, but I expect him momentarily. He will be able to ride back with you, for I feel perhaps you should not be alone."

"There is not the slightest need—" Sir Oliver began, and stopped. "Holcombe Hall? Is that nearby?"

"It is not two miles distant," said the rector, wondering if he should warn the residents of what might be in store for them. "Are you acquainted with Miss Oversham?"

"No I am not," admitted Sir Oliver. "But I cannot but feel that it is high time I made her acquaintance."

Chapter 24

GEORGIANA STOOD LOOKING out the window of Holcombe Hall, absorbed in memory. Not even the view, which included a particularly fine prospect of the Italian gardens, could beguile her thoughts back to the present; they were many miles away, in London. Freddy had just left her to go back to the rectory, and his visit evoked all the painful associations she was trying, without success, to leave behind. She hoped she had done the right thing in persuading the rector to let Freddy stay on as his assistant so that he might determine whether the life suited him. When she had learned that he had not informed his mama of his intentions, she had urged him to write to Clarice at once. He had done so, but Georgiana could not help feeling that it was she whom they would blame for his defection.

She had confessed as much of her story to her aunt and uncle as she dared. They were not unnaturally a bit grieved at her having been a party to such a deception, but they could see her heart was wounded, and they left her to heal in peace. She thought it would be a long time before she began to do so.

The image of Sir Oliver—as he had looked into her eyes when he had danced with her at Almack's, when he had handed her out of the crypt during Freddy's rescue, even when he had proposed to her after the party—would not be banished from her mind. In fact it was so real that she could almost believe she saw him coming up the walk in front of the house. She shook her head to clear it. There *was* someone there, but it could not be Sir Oliver. She dared not hope that he had forgiven her so soon.

She dug her fingers into her palm and waited. She heard

Ribble's step outside the door, his fingers on the knob. The door opened. "I beg your pardon, miss, but a Sir Oliver Townsend has called. He says he is your cousin. Are you at home to him?"

The contradiction of the fear that her imagination and longing might have temporarily disordered her mind did not bring the relief it might otherwise be supposed. Georgiana bit her lip and smoothed down the skirts of her green jaconet muslin dress. She took a breath. "Yes," she replied. "Please, send him up."

Sir Oliver was impressed with the manner in which Holcombe Hall had been renovated and furnished. It was every bit as grand as Lady Louisa had led him to believe, and a great deal more tasteful. If his unknown cousin had vulgar connections, their influence was not in evidence in the arrangement of the house and gardens. In fact, he thought he had seldom seen a more delightful estate.

He was not much looking forward to the interview. He had come on a whim, and because he thought that in time the story of the impostor in London was bound to reach the real Miss Oversham's ears. He did not relish the prospect of explaining the deception to her, but he thought it would be much better coming from a member of the family than on the wings of rumor.

He realized now how Miss Bucklebury had come by her knowledge of the Hall and of the Society in which its residents moved. Her brother's rectory was one of the closest neighbors, and she must have grown up knowing a great deal about the Oversham heiress. Sir Oliver recalled with deepest embarrassment his remarks about the likelihood of Miss Oversham's vulgarity and the undesirability of such a connection, and did not wonder at Miss Bucklebury's not having informed him of the acquaintance.

He also saw that all his hopes were lost. Miss Bucklebury must have married Freddy, or her brother—a man of the cloth—would not have lied to shield her from pursuit. The presence of the cat in his house confirmed Sir Oliver's worst suspicions. There was no more to be said, though he cherished the hope that someday he might, with the greatest of pleasure, be afforded the opportunity to wring her neck.

Sir Oliver sighed and turned to the business at hand. He sent up his name and his card with the most awe-inspiring butler he had ever seen, and waited to be conducted to Miss Oversham.

The girl was standing with her back to him, facing the windows. She turned around slowly, and the polished words with which he had intended to introduce himself died on his lips. Surprise addled his wits momentarily. He thought Miss Bucklebury had taken refuge in his cousin's house, and that he was the victim of some monstrous conspiracy to humiliate and embarrass him. Perhaps, after all, she had meant to entrap Freddy all along.

"So, you have tricked me finely," he said bitterly. "Where is Lord Nugent?"

Georgiana, who believed him privy to the contents of her letter and thus acquainted with her true identity, shrank back from the mockery and contempt in his voice, though she could not but agree that these were merited. Her worst fears were confirmed, but she was a trifle puzzled that his first concern would be the whereabouts of Freddy. "Freddy is at the rectory," she said, biting her lip. "Did you not—"

"Ha!" he said with a mirthless laugh. "I knew I could not be mistaken. I recognized the cat, you see. The rector was at such pains to assure me that you were in London, but the cat came into the room and I *knew*. It is an excellent jest, is it not? I only regret that I was just then not in the mood to enjoy it!"

Georgiana grew more and more perplexed. "He said I was in London, sir? Surely you must mistake. Had you no letter?"

Sir Oliver said grimly, "The letter, I fear, was destroyed before it reached its destination."

"If it has gone astray, then he must write Clarice another at once. Perhaps you will bear it, upon your return?"

"How well you manage him already, ma'am," said Sir Oliver, with a sneer. "My congratulations. I perceive I was utterly mistaken in you. I do not see how anyone with a shred of conscience could have done such a thing to Frederick!"

Georgiana was aghast at this reaction to Freddy's becoming

the rector's assistant. "Are you mad, sir? I own I cannot quite like the way he has gone about accomplishing his goal, for it was a trifle inconsiderate to his family, but my conscience is clear. Perhaps you do not understand," she added earnestly, "that this is most particularly Freddy's wish."

"No doubt you have taught him to think so. We must agree to differ as to whether one may merely term his action 'a trifle inconsiderate' or your urging him on to it the act of a woman of character. But never mind; I see I was mistaken in much more than I realized."

The pulse beat in Georgiana's throat, and she made a strong and not entirely successful effort to control her voice. "Come, Sir Oliver, since we are speaking plainly, let us admit that this talk of Freddy is the merest diversion. What you are really angry about is that I deceived you!"

Sir Oliver sketched a mocking bow. "You are correct, ma'am. I was a bigger flat than you can imagine. Do you know that I almost instantly regretted the untenable position I had put you in? I thought I was up to every rig and row, but when I saw you—when you looked up at me—" He stopped and struggled to regain his composure. "In short, I thought I had learned to love you, ma'am. Is it possible that, clever as you are, you did not guess my proposal was sincere?"

Georgiana stood stock still, the color flooding her cheeks. She half lifted one hand in a beseeching gesture. "Then why—?"

He overbore her ruthlessly. "I will not be hoaxed again. It was a pretty revenge, was it not? I was arrogant and conceited; I needed taking down. Well, you have succeeded. I regret that you have made Freddy your victim as well, but perhaps he is too dim to perceive how he has been used. It needs only for you to present me to my cousin in order to complete my humiliation. I wonder you have not yet done so!"

Georgiana put a hand to her cheek. "Your c-cousin?"

"Miss Oversham. Your presence here must certainly indicate that she is in possession of the facts. Her own motivation for revenge is scarcely less credible than yours. Has she lent you her protection?"

Georgiana felt a trifle dizzy. "I—I do not understand. Did you not receive my letter? *I* am Miss Oversham."

"Did I not say that—" He broke off, and the color drained from his face. He appeared to experience some difficulty in finding his voice, but after a few moments' stunned silence, he said, *"You?"*

She nodded, not trusting herself to speak.

"You are my cousin Georgiana? You live here?" he persisted.

"Yes," she said quietly.

"Then why the devil did you marry Freddy?" he cried.

"M-marry Freddy?" gasped Georgiana in astonishment.

"You mean you haven't?" asked Sir Oliver, possessing himself ruthlessly of her hands.

"Of course I have not!" she said indignantly.

"Thank God!" exclaimed Sir Oliver roughly, and took her in his arms.

Georgiana, finding herself rather forcefully kissed by Sir Oliver for the second time in her life, was delighted to discover that this time the experience was an entirely agreeable one. He was holding her so tightly she was quite unable to break free, and she found herself without any desire whatsoever to do so. His actions were not those of a man who sought to rid himself of an unwanted burden, and her misgivings melted along with her resolve to hold him at a distance. This satisfactory state of affairs continued for several minutes until reason at length asserted itself. She pushed herself away a little and said faintly, "How *could* you think I would marry Freddy?"

"There is no excuse," he said, leading her over to the sofa, where he continued to keep hold lightly of her hands. "I was crazy with jealousy, or I never would have spoken as I did. Can you forgive me?"

"What did you think of me that I did not deserve?" she said seriously. "I did deceive you most shamefully. I told you so in the letters I left for you and Grandmama."

He kissed her hand. "Amabel destroyed them."

"So that is what you meant! I thought you referred to Freddy's letter to Clarice. He told her he would be staying in Yorkshire for a while to serve as the rector's assistant. I told you once that he wants to enter the Church."

"Is *that* it? No wonder the rector seemed to think"—He gave a short laugh. "What a lot of misunderstandings we have had! There is no need to quarrel for the greater share of the blame, however. It belongs to me! If I had not said all those supercilious things about my cousin Miss Oversham, you would have told me the truth about yourself before now! But, my love, how did you happen to be introduced to me as Miss Bucklebury?"

She gave him an abbreviated and somewhat garbled account of her adventures on the road, ending with their meeting at Lord Litchfield's hunting box.

He winced. "The recollection of what I said—my behavior that night—is inexpressibly painful to me."

Her hand tightened in his. "We have both done a great deal of harm. I only meant to embarrass you; I never meant to hurt Grandmama or Clarice. I thought so long as I was not deceiving *them* about who I was all would be well. But now I fear they will never forgive me."

He smiled. "On the contrary, when they know the truth they are much more likely to celebrate you as a heroine. You have quite made the family's reputation." He told her about Princess Caroline's letter and the Overshams' social rehabilitation.

She laughed. "I am glad. I did not want that on my conscience as well."

"It means," he said carefully, "that if you wish to go back to London as Miss Oversham you really will be the Rage of the Ton."

She looked down into her lap. "I would rather be your wife," she said shyly.

"Are you proposing to me?" he asked, raising her chin with his finger.

She looked into his eyes. "It is this accursed fortune. Now that you know I have it, I fear you will not propose to *me*."

"In my experience, the opposite is usually true," he said with a shaky laugh.

She smiled mistily. "In mine, too. That is why I want to marry you."

"Because I proposed to you when I thought you were poor?" he asked.

She nodded. "I do not know what you must think of me!"

"Then you must permit me to show you," he said, and took her in his arms again.